Titles By Colleen C

Minnesota Caribou:

Rochester Riot:

Reel Love:

Vegas Venom:

WHEELER

WHEELER

Vegas Venom: Book Two

Colleen Charles

This book is a work of fiction. Names, characters, places and incidents either are the product of the author's imagination or are used fictitiously, and any resemblance to actual persons, living or dead, business establishments, events, or locales is entirely coincidental. The publisher does not have any control over and does not assume any responsibility for author or third-party websites or their content.

Printed in the United States of America
First Printing, 2022

ISBN: 9798358155633

Second Wind Publishing

www.ColleenCharles.com

FOREWORD

Subscribe to my Newsletter online and receive email notices about new book releases, sales, and special promotions.

New subscribers receive an EXCLUSIVE FREE NOVEL as a special gift.

www.colleencharles.com/free

PROLOGUE

Anders

Six Years Ago...

"Dude, it's so hot out here, I swear I'm gonna sweat my balls off." My buddy and teammate, Pete Grayson, reclines on his beach chair and adjusts his sunglasses.

The majesty of Costa Rica assaults my eyeballs. After playing college hockey for four years in a state where winter means winter, I could get used to this—from the lush greenery to the vibrant flowers to the crystal blue ocean to the all-inclusive resort. Where else can you find active volcanoes, rushing rivers, and giant swings in temperature based on the topography?

We're here on spring break, enjoying one last hurrah before some of us get drafted into the NHL. I'm expected to go in the first round, so with the nerves swirling, I've been blowing off major steam.

Jeremy Jackson rolls his eyes. "Then come under the umbrella, bro. You pasty dudes from up North don't know how to handle the heat."

"Come say that to my face," Pete gripes. "You couldn't handle winter where I'm from."

Jeremy snorts. "Bro, we go to school in *Minnesota* where both mosquitoes If Marco was here and snow drifts are bigger than your head. I think I've proven myself."

"You ain't seen nothing yet," Pete warns.

Jeremy's eyebrows practically raise to his hairline. "What are you gonna do, go all *Fargo* on me?"

"You never know. I might have a wood chipper with your name on it," Pete fires back.

"Ooh, a wood chipper." Jeremy wiggles his fingers and rolls his eyes. "Please. I survived eighteen years in Atlanta. You think your redneck threats scare me? Blaze, tell this man how pathetic I find his raggedy ass. Blaze? Earth to Blaze..."

"Huh?" I shake my head and tune back into the conversation. I'm only listening with half an ear because the *real* focus of my attention is crouched in the shrubbery along the wall of the resort, holding a camera that has to weigh as much as a human infant, snapping photos of a green bird with a red belly and what looks like a fluffy mohawk.

"He's useless," Pete says with a flick of his wrist. "Every time Bird Girl's around, he gets all horned out. I bet he's got a semi inside his swim trunks."

"It's not like that," I retort.

I'm a liar. It is totally like that.

"I don't get what the big deal with her is, anyway. She's a seven at best." Pete lets his hands rest beside him as he basks in the sun. "You've hooked up with hotter chicks."

There was a time when I would have chimed in with his macho bullshit, but there's something about Bird Girl that leaves me weak in the knees. It isn't just her pretty face, or the hot body she thinks she's hiding underneath her baggy clothes. She simply seems more *real* than anyone else I've met before, more observant, more grounded. Every time my gaze lands on her, she has that cute little wrinkle between her eyebrows, the one that tells me she's intently focused on something. Usually birds. Hence the name Pete made up for her on our first day at this resort, when we spotted her trying to make friends with a toucan.

Pete has a point. Bird Girl doesn't seem to care about makeup, or how her clothes fit, or what her hair is doing. At the moment, her long, brown hair is pulled up in a messy bun, and her sweat-wicking clothes wouldn't be out of place on a safari. Usually when I'm this focused on a girl, my first thought is how to get in her panties. The trouble with Bird Girl is that I want to *talk* to her, get inside that brain of hers, and so far I can't think of a single damn thing to say—at least, not anything that would hold her attention enough to not make me seem like a stupid jock.

"You're barely a four, Pete, so why don't you stop running your mouth?" Jeremy asks. He turns to me. "As for you, get over yourself. If you don't head over there and shoot your shot in the next two minutes, I'm going to make a move."

"Don't you dare," I growl, my eyes snapping fire. "Stay away from her."

One eyebrow climbs. "I'm serious. Two more minutes of your silent pining, and I'll have officially reached my limit. It's not rocket science, Blaze. You know what she's into. Just ask about the damn bird."

Put that way, it doesn't seem so tough. I can go ten seconds without making an ass of myself. Probably.

I suck in a deep breath and launch myself out of my chair before I can talk myself out of it. I'm usually super confident around girls, but that's because I know exactly what those girls want and they know what I want. This is different and that equals scary.

Bird Girl remains intent as I approach. She just keeps adjusting her grip on the camera, inching closer to the bird in question. At first, I think she can't see me in her peripheral vision, but when I stop a few feet away from her and clear my throat, she doesn't even look up from the camera.

3

"Keep walking, buddy," she says in a flat voice. "I'm not interested in getting a drink this early."

I bite back a smile. "Of course not. You're too busy photographing resplendent quetzals."

Bird Girl pauses and slowly lowers her camera. "Oh. Are you a birder?"

"An amateur." I smile at her, trying to cover for the fact that I don't know a damn thing about birds other than what I learned on my late-night descents down the Google rabbit-hole since our arrival. Descents that may or may not have involved dates with my own hand. "And I know it's their mating season, right?"

Bird Girl grins up at me and something pings behind my ribcage. "Yeah. We're lucky to see them, especially this close to the resort."

The beauty of that smile hits me like a punch to the gut and nearly drops me. I almost feel bad for fibbing about my interest in wildlife, but I resolve then and there to make up for it by learning anything she wants to teach me.

Because I've got a few things I'd like to teach her.

I crouch down and peer at the bird she's watching so intently, trying to see whatever it is that keeps her so riveted. Wishing it was me instead. I'll admit I've spent a few nights imagining how it would feel if she caressed me like that with the intensity of her gaze. Over my biceps, down my abs and... lower. The bird shifts and shimmers in the sunlight. The feathers that I thought were purely green revealed hints of blue and black—like watching a living jewel.

I don't realize that I'm holding my breath until Bird Girl gets to her feet and stretches.

"Sorry if I was rude before. I'm Stella, by the way." She holds her hand out to me as I rise upright.

4

"Blaze," I reply.

"Well, Blaze, do you want to take your amateur birding to the next level?" Her smile's a little crooked, like she's sizing me up and isn't quite sure what to make of me yet. "There's a hiking trail that leads behind the resort. I was going to go and see what I could find out there, and you're welcome to join me."

I nod and do an internal victory dance even before she finishes the sentence. "Count me in."

"It's almost six miles through the jungle," she warns, her gaze sweeping my body again. "Some of the terrain can be a bit rough. Are you sure you're up for it?"

I point to my sneakers. "I may be an amateur, but at least I'm smart enough to wear real shoes."

She disassembles her camera and tucks it into its padded case, which she slings over one shoulder. "Then off we go."

When her back is turned, I wave back to my friends and give a thumbs-up. Both of them lift their drinks in a toast as I follow Stella toward the trailhead.

She doesn't take things slow for my benefit. Her hiking pace is more speed-walk than casual stroll, and I have to work to keep up with her.

"So," I pant as the jungle canopy closes over us. "What got you so interested in birds?"

"I want to be a wildlife photographer," she says. "I enjoy photography in general, but I *love* how, if you have a good eye, you can surprise the viewer even with familiar animals. Plus, I think if people can start to fully appreciate Earth's biodiversity, maybe they'll start to care more about the planet we share with all these wonderful creatures."

"So you're a crusader?" I ask.

Stella stops abruptly and turns to scowl at me. "What's that supposed to mean?"

5

My heart squeezes in my chest. I don't like how I feel when she looks at me like that.

I clear my throat. "That it sounds like you want to save the world."

Her eyes narrow. "And that's a bad thing?"

I hold up a palm between us. "Hell, no. It's a *badass* thing."

"Maybe this was a bad idea." Stella keeps glaring at me, as if she doesn't believe I meant my words as a compliment. "You're talking too much. You're gonna scare the animals away."

"We're not going to see any animals if we keep sprinting," I point out.

Stella humphs, but when she starts walking again, she reduces her pace.

When we head farther down the trail, we spend more time looking around, admiring the lichen-draped trees and the small glimpses of distant misty mountains whenever the canopy thins. Everything is warm and close, with the scent of the air rich in my nostrils, almost like stepping back in time. The trail provides the only hint that other humans have ever ventured here.

Stella stops abruptly and crouches down at the edge of the worn path. The ground drops away steeply in that direction, which means that we can look to our left and see the thick foliage of the trees, which on our right is a good twenty feet above our heads. She pulls her camera out of her bag, selects a lens, and lifts it to her face, all without making more than a whisper of sound.

I follow her line of sight to see what she's so focused on. A vibrant green tree frog with red eyes sits on a broad banana leaf perhaps fifteen feet from where we stand.

With my gaze so intent on the little dude, I barely register Stella leaning forward, and then further yet. Her foot reaches the edge of the trail, and the soil breaks away with a crumble. Stella doesn't even have time to cry out before I bend to catch her elbow and pull her back onto the path.

"Careful!" I exclaim.

Stella shuffles backward. "Thanks. I just get so engrossed in my work sometimes that I..."

"Lose track of where you are?" I suggest.

She wrinkles her nose as she sets about packing up her camera again. "Maybe."

Ever since we left, we haven't seen even one sign of other human life. And even without talking much, I enjoy just being near her. At first, the jungle looks like thick greenery, but if I watch her face, I can tell whenever she sees something good. After a little while, I get better at spotting things on my own.

By the time we reach a nice break in the trees, the air has grown uncomfortably hot and sticky. I wipe sweat from my forehead with the bottom of my t-shirt, when I first hear the rush of what sounds like wind. We round the corner, and the sight before us nearly knocks the breath from my lungs.

A waterfall, easily four stories tall, tumbles down the nearby cliffside into a crystal-clear pool.

"Holy crap." I blink a few times to make sure that I'm not imagining things. "I thought places like this only existed in movies and shampoo commercials."

She lifts her camera and shoots some candids. When my gaze finally shakes loose from the rushing water, I realize she's switched to taking pictures of *me*. Of my reaction.

"I heard about this back at the hotel." Once she lowers her camera, Stella giggles and takes my hand. "Come on. Let's get closer. I want to get a good angle so I can shoot it."

We pick our way down to the edge of the water, and I kneel beside it, marveling at the beauty of this little place. The path continues above us; anyone else exploring this jungle would pass by eventually.

All those people lounging around the resort are missing out.

Until today, I'd been one of them.

I stare at the waterfall, almost hypnotized by its beauty as Stella leans in to take some photos. When I look closely enough, I can see a rainbow in the mist. Whipping out my phone, I take a picture myself.

A splash in the water startles me, and I glance over to see a trim, tanned figure disappear beneath the surface. Stella's clothes lay beside her backpack in a tidy little pile and I stare at the screen of my iPhone, wondering how I missed that.

Her head appears halfway across the pool. Stella disappears below the surface of the water, the ripples skimming the surface blurring her body.

"This feels amazing," she says on a sigh of pleasure that works its way into my chest. "Care to join me, Blaze?"

She doesn't have to ask twice. The words are hardly out of her mouth before I yank my shirt over my head. When I look up again, she's gawking at my chest with wide eyes.

"You've *got* to be an athlete," she murmurs, treading water.

"Yeah?" I grin, but every single place her eyes touch burns with the heat of a thousand Costa Rican suns. "You like what you see?"

Stella brushes a lock of wet hair away from her face. "Never mind, forget I said anything. Your head's obviously big enough as it is."

"My head isn't the only big thing about me," I tease, my hands resting on the waistband of my shorts.

"Why do guys always assume that we're going to be impressed with their *size?* Having a big dick is no guarantee you know how to use it." Her tone is casual, but her eyes never leave my body.

I feel a vicious stab of envy over any man who's ever been with her, along with a pang of longing so fierce it almost floors me. "Is that a challenge?"

She bites her lip and lifts one eyebrow.

"Let's make a bet." I crouch down at the side of the lagoon. I'm trying to play it cool, but now, all bets are off. "If we were to... you know. I bet you anything you like that I can make you come before I get off."

Her laughter rings out. "Wow. Getting right to the point, aren't you?"

"Says the girl skinny-dipping in front of a near-stranger—inviting him to swim naked with her." I tilt my head. "Sure sounds like an adventurous girl who knows what she wants. Or did I misread the signs? Where I'm from, when a woman gets naked and wet in front of a guy and then eye fucks him until she has her fill, it's a pretty clear indication that she's interested in more than a nature hike and a wildlife photoshoot."

Her eyes sweep over me again, and I force myself to stay perfectly still for the inspection. The last thing I want to do is intimidate her. I'm big on full consent in every way because I never bought in to the whole predatory jock thing. Contrary to popular belief, I don't hook up with every random chick just because I can. My tastes are pretty discerning. But this particular girl has had me wound up since the moment I laid eyes on her.

If Stella is going to go all in with me, I want her to do so *enthusiastically*. I, in turn, will rise to the occasion and put her pleasure first.

Her eyes lift to my face. "Why don't you start by joining me?"

The humid air wraps around me to the point my lungs almost refuse it. "Shorts or no shorts?"

She shrugs but her twinkling eyes give her away. "If you get your clothes wet, you might get a rash when we're walking later. Better take them off. For safety's sake."

I stand upright and unbutton my shorts, then made a big show about shimmying open the zipper. Stella's eyes widen when I hook my thumbs over the waistband of my boxers and slide them down.

She sucks in a breath. "You weren't kidding."

If possible, her reaction gets me more hot and bothered. I never thought something like this would happen today. I mean, I hoped, but I would have been happy with just getting to know her better. Maybe steal a kiss or two. "I thought you weren't impressed by size?"

"I said size isn't all that matters." She swims backward, and her full breasts bob in the water. "Not that I'm immune to it."

Fuck. She's so hot, and I've spent days fantasizing about all the things I'd do to her if I could get her into my bed. All those mental images never included a waterfall, but I can tell that's about to change. Even though I'm not sure of the logistics, I'll figure it out and I'll make it work.

For both of us. Promises are important to me, and I make it a point to always deliver.

I drop my shorts with the rest of my stuff and slip into the water. To my dismay, it's a lot colder than the air around it led me to believe. I squeak in alarm and cup my junk in both hands.

Stella snorts a laugh. "I forgot how the cold affects guys. Not so big now, are ya?"

"You bring a lot of guys here?" I ask, forcing myself deeper into the water so that I can acclimate.

"No," she admits. "Only guys who recognize resplendent quetzals and follow me on crazy jungle hikes."

"That seems like a good way to weed out the weaklings," I shoot back.

The air between us is a bit heavier than it was just a second ago. "What can I say? I like a guy who can keep up with me."

"Let's say a guy wanted to keep up with you in... other areas." The water reaches my chin. Now that I'm used to it, the water is soothing and cool.

"Why, *Blaze*, are you asking me about my fantasies?" Stella's eyes sparkle, and a tingling sense of anticipation races across my skin.

"Maybe I am." I drift closer, taking my time. "Let's pretend this is all in your head. What happens next?"

"I barely know you," she says. "Why would I tell you something like that?"

"*Because* you barely know me." I lift my eyebrows. "We could do anything you want, and you won't have to look me in the eyes tomorrow. That is... unless you want to."

The smile slips off her face, and I wonder if I put my foot in my mouth. Maybe the fact that this can only be a fling is a turn-off for her. Maybe she's one of those girls who thinks sex always has to mean something.

Maybe with her, it will.

For my part, everything she does gets my blood surging, and I already want more. I fucking want it all. This chick intrigues me on a whole other level and if there's any way of turning this into something more long-term, I'll be all over it. Only a few hours with Stella is enough to convince me that she's girlfriend material. Maybe even more.

My brain fires, and I can imagine her at home in Vegas, meeting my friends. Visiting all my favorite haunts around town.

Before I can say anything crazy like, *How do you feel about long-distance relationships?*, she clears her throat.

"So you're saying that I can ask for anything, and you'll do your best to make it happen?"

"Exactly." Despite the cold water, my dick twitches and grows to an aching hardness that I already know only she can take away. And the reason I know is because I've never been this hard before. I might not be a great conversationalist when it comes to either art *or* wildlife, but if she gives me a chance, I'll trip her trigger. Whatever Stella wants from me, she can have that and more.

She offers me another of those stunning smiles and swims backward under the waterfall. I follow her eagerly, unable to play it cool a second longer as my blood strums through my veins. What is it about this girl that pulls me in like a magnet? She's *my* fantasy and it's coming true, so the only thing left to do is to enjoy it while it plays out.

Behind the waterfall is a small cave, and Stella swims inside. The water is shallow here, and the rocks are smooth. The hot and humid jungle air becomes more bearable in the mist. Even though the waterfall is huge, the noise echoes back here, blocking out the world beyond.

Stella stops inside and pushes her wet hair out of her face. She reaches for me, and I freeze as her fingers brush my skin, setting every inch of me on fire. She traces my shoulders, my pecs, my abs. Then she leans closer, her cheeks blazing, and whispers in my ear. I can barely hear her over the roar of the water.

Her sinful lips curve into an easy smile. "Do you know where the clit is located, Blaze?"

Exhaling a little laugh, I say, "You need to have more confidence in me, Stella. I love women. I love their bodies... and exploring them like we're doing to this jungle."

"I like confidence. I like it when a guy knows what he wants. More importantly, I like when a guy can read what I want. Not *rough*, but eager. I don't like pain, but..." She pulls back and her eyes flash in the light spilling through the waterfall. "I like feeling wanted—like I'm the only girl in the world. Think you can give me that?"

It's an easy question to answer. She's been irresistible from the moment I first saw her, all thick hair, heaving rack, and pert ass, and now she's inches away from me, naked, giving me not just *permission*, but *full consent*.

I wrap my arms around her, pulling her close, pressing the lean, firm lines of her body against mine. I roll my hips against her so she'll feel how hard and hot for her I already am. My dick throbs and gets so sensitive in the water, I almost groan. She gasps against my lips an instant before I cover her mouth with mine, slanting it to get deeper, teasing the tip of my tongue between her lips. One hand presses against the back of her head, tangling in the wet curls of her hair. The other swoops beneath her perfect ass and lifts her against me, so that her feet are no longer on the ground.

I crawl forward a few steps, lifting her as I go, until we reach the back of the little cave. I brace one hand against the back wall for support and lean forward until her shoulders brush the slick stone. The water only reaches my knees at that point.

"Tell me what you want," I whisper. "I need you to use your words."

"I've seen you watching me for days." Her hands slide up to her perfect tits and lift them. "You can manhandle me if you want."

Nipping at her earlobe, my hands replace hers as I massage her breasts, pinching and pulling at her nipples until she whimpers and arches into the pressure. Then I lean in and taste them, alternating between them as she thrashes when I suck deeply. Stella likes it a bit rough, and I am here for it.

"Mmm... delicious," I croon. "But your tits aren't the only thing I want to taste."

Lifting her by her waist, I shove her butt on a little shelf in the cave, which puts her sweet pussy right at face level. "I'm gonna make it so good for you, Stella. You're gonna be embarrassed you ever doubted me when you come hard all over my face."

I take her in, from the flush on her cheeks, to her heaving breaths, to her twitching muscles. Our gazes snap together, and her legs fall apart on a sigh.

My thumbs trace circles on the wet flesh of her thighs. "That's it, Stella. You're such a dirty girl. Show me how much you want me to taste you."

"Blaze..." She reaches down and holds herself open for my hungry gaze. "Let me see you first."

I hold her stare as I reach between my legs and pump my cock once. Twice. It feels like it's going to explode. Stella looks so fucking beautiful splayed out before me, touching herself with her hooded eyes and the tip of her tongue swiping her bottom lip.

After pulling her body to the lip of the rock shelf, I hook her thigh over my shoulder so I don't lose leverage. At the first swipe of my tongue on her swollen clit, she arches into my mouth. Stella shivers as I suck and lick and nip. With the water rushing around us, her screams echo off the rocks as she comes apart. I swallow every single tremor and every single sound as she rides out her peak.

Stretching my body, I capture her lips with mine and slide into her in one smooth thrust. "You need to tell me right now if I need to pull out. Otherwise, I'm gonna come inside you."

"I'm clean and I'm on the pill," she grits out. "Can I trust you, Blaze?"

I nod because words are impossible as she flexes her pelvis, driving me even deeper.

Stella gasps and tightens around me, and I groan against her shoulder. Her breasts rub against my chest with each movement, and I try to convince myself to pull away, to draw out of her and touch her more—kiss her more. *Chicks like tons of foreplay, asshole,* I chide myself, but it's too late for that. I need her too badly. After I tasted her essence and felt her pleasure as she rode my tongue, she's got me tied up in knots that I'm not sure will ever unravel.

"Blaze," she gasps, clinging to me. "Fuck me harder."

I rock my hips against her, thrusting in and out of her slick heat, wishing that this could last. I can already tell that despite my flip words and my cocky attitude, I'm too far gone to hold out for long. I start kissing her again—her throat, her collarbone, her neck, all while trying to keep my dick in check.

"Is this good for you, Stella?" I ask. "Is this how you want it?"

God, if she says no, I'm never going to recover from the shame. Not when she's everything I've ever wanted. I need this to be good for her. I need her to remember...

She whimpers and digs her fingers into my back, pushing me that much closer to my limit. "Blaze—!"

In the white noise of the waterfall and the cold water and the warmth of her body, I lose track of myself. Time stretches and warps. I alter my pace and relax, moving slow and steady, letting a small eternity lapse between each breath.

"Stella," I breathe, reaching between our bodies to strum her clit. It's hard and throbbing again as the water swirls around us. "Stay with me. I've got you, babe. You can fall and I'll be here to catch you."

Our gazes meet and hold and with a groan, she comes again, sucking my dick so deep inside her that I can't hold out one second longer either. With her sweet pussy milking me with the strength of her second release, I explode. Stella shudders and presses her forehead to mine. I've never bought into the idea of *soulmates* or spiritual connections or any of that *woo-woo* stuff, but what I feel for her in this moment is more important than pleasure, more meaningful than desire. I feel grounded.

I feel like we were destined to meet.

I feel like we might have a future.

* * *

After the most incredible experience of my life, I softly fell back to earth. And with my heart pinging in my chest and my dick hard as steel, we kissed and we connected and we explored and we fucked for two days solid. And just as suddenly, it ended without much fanfare. After a peck to my lips that ended far too soon, Stella took off to photograph sea turtles hatching into the twilight waves, and I packed to go back for my last few weeks of college before my NHL career really kicked off.

And all the loose ends remained untied.

Now I'm sitting in an airplane headed back to a grim reality without Stella and an ache behind my ribcage that I try to hide because I really can't even begin to explain to my buddies the magnitude of what happened between us.

I feel different.

Because Stella changed me.

Before this trip, I never believed in insta-love. I'm not sure I even believed in love at all. Puck bunnies are always around like a veritable buffet and we pick one up whenever we feel the need. So if I express how I'm feeling to Pete and Jeremy, they'll flip out and this flight is too damn long to be teased the entire way.

"You ditched us." Jeremy leans over and lifts up one of my earphones. "Did you at least get Bird Girl's number?"

I shake my head as I stare out the plane window, watching the brilliant jungles and gleaming waters of Costa Rica fall away beneath us. Her memory pops into my brain like she's still mine. "Um... she had some sea turtles to photograph for a project she's working on. She had to go."

"Tell me you at least tapped that," Pete whines. "I mean... at least one of us has to have gotten laid on spring break."

Flopping my headphone back over my ear, I don't say anything, because that's so not the point. Stella means more to me than a cheap hook up. What happened between us was nothing short of magical.

She's *special.*

We'll find each other, I promise myself. *An experience like that has to mean something in the grander scheme of things. We'll come back around. Life is cyclical like that.*

CHAPTER ONE

Anders

"Twenty-eight... twenty-nine... thirty." Noah helps me rack the barbell. "Not bad, Anders. We'll make a man out of you yet."

"Screw you," I pant. I've been upping my weight for training this season, and my buddy Noah never hesitates to give me shit about the fact that I still haven't caught up with him. It's not my fault the guy is built like a monster. And with his goalie pads on, he looks like one.

The newest member of the Vegas Venom overhears us and decides to add in his two cents. "These words are from song, yes? The cartoon, with the girl who dresses as a man, with fast-talking dragon who gives bad advice. What is this name?" Marco taps one finger against his temple, thinking hard.

"*Mulan.*" I sit up and roll my eyes at him, only knowing that because of Noah's daughter, Vivian. I love to babysit her whenever I can.

Truth be told, as much of a pain as Marco can be, the guy's growing on me. After all, it's not *his* fault that our team owner, Dante Giovanetti, is a total sonofabitch. Marco was a mediocre player when he first joined the team, but he's big and enthusiastic and he puts in the work. He's quickly become one of the most popular, especially with the ladies, due to his dark good looks, easy charm, and constant butchering of the English language. The puck bunnies fall all over him as they try to improve his vocabulary, although he's still second fiddle to Latham and me. Noah used to be a team heartthrob, too, until the dummy fell in love and got married.

He and his wife Molly, aka the little tater tot, make a disgustingly cute couple. I'd be jealous, but it's pretty obvious that love's not in the cards for me, all things considered. It's just something I've resigned myself to as the years have started ticking by.

"Ah, yes, the *Mulan*." Marco nods. "This movie, it was very inspires to me."

"Because it's what got you to start cross-dressing?" I ask.

Marco points at me. Surprisingly, his English continues to improve the longer he's in the States. At least, I can understand him a lot better than the day we picked him up at the curb at McCarran. "This comment is one of what we call *the toxic masculinities*. What is wrong with man wearing dress? The *pope* wears dress."

"I can't tell you how many times I've had to wear one," Noah says with a groan. "For Halloween last year, Viv wanted to go as characters from *Beauty and the Beast*."

Marco and I frown at him. "Why did you need a dress?" I ask. "All you need is tusks and bam. I wouldn't know the difference."

Noah flips me off.

"This is not insult," Marco insists. "Have you seen the TikityTok? All the ladies, they like Beast before he is Charming." Marco growls and waggles his eyebrows. "They like their mans like *wild animal*. Just like in other song, but not for children."

"You mean the one by Nine Inch Nails?" I ask, waggling my eyebrows.

Noah hastily butts in before Marco can start singing again. "Unfortunately, Biscuit got to be the Beast."

I frown up at him. "Was Viv dressed as Belle?"

Noah shakes his head. "She wanted to be Lumiere."

"Okay…" I wave my hand in a circle, urging him to explain.

With a long-suffering sigh, Noah pulls out his phone, pokes the screen a few times, and then holds it out for us to see.

An adorable girl dressed as a candelabra smiles in the front of the image. Behind her, Molly rocks a Cogsworth outfit. Biscuit, Noah's Cane Corso, sports a lion's mane, a cape, and a small crown. Noah's nanny-slash-housekeeper, Francine, makes an adorable Mrs. Potts. It takes me a minute to register that the figure at the back, dressed in a ruffly lemon-yellow tiered gown, is Noah.

Marco bursts out laughing. "See, see? Burly man can make dress look good!"

"Yeah, laugh it up." Noah glares at me. "I know you've got something to say, Anders. Out with it."

I try to suppress a full-blown laugh. "I'm too busy looking at Molly. Your wife makes a damn fine clock."

Noah pulls the phone back toward him and presses it to his chest, as if hoping to defend his beloved tater tot from my lecherous gaze. "Watch it, Beck. I don't want to have to throw down against my best friend."

"You dress this way again, and you invite me." Marco slaps one palm against his chest. "I will be Gaston. We are much alike."

I scratch my chin. "You know he's the bad guy, right?"

"Maybe so, but in Italy, we raise the chickens by hand. Every morning, I eat raw eggs to get big muscles like rest of boys. And the milkmaids, they love on me since I *thiiiiiis* tall." He holds his hand up to his hipbone.

"Dude, that's nasty." I fake a gag.

"Is joke." He lifts his hands to the top of his ribcage. "I *this* tall the first time a girl showed me her—"

My phone rings, and I dive off the weight bench to grab it. Bless whoever's calling to interrupt another of Marco's stories. Milkmaids went out decades ago even though they seem to reappear every holiday in the "Twelve Days of Christmas." I'm never sure if he's telling the truth or exaggerating, and either way, it's usually disturbing.

"Hey, Finn! What's up? What did I do this time?" I press the phone to my ear with one hand and scoop up my bag with the other. We're pretty much done anyway, and conversations with the team publicist tend to kill my adrenaline.

"You tell me," he retorts. "I was calling to ask how you'd feel about a modeling gig. Is there something else I should know?"

"I've been too busy to get into trouble lately. Although, if you think I'm due for a scolding, I'm sure I could make some." I push through the door into the team locker room. "What kind of gig are we talking? Clothing line? Workout supplements? Some kind of brand-name bottled water imported from Costa Rica?" I hold back a sigh at the memory of my trip to the jungle. Any mention of photography makes me think of her.

Stella.

The one who got away.

I wonder if she still wonders about me.

Wishful thinking, because in the seven years since we parted ways, I've finally had to get it through my thick head that everything I felt for her was a one-sided crush due to my raging hormones. If we were both looking for each other, we'd have reconnected by now.

I'm still hanging onto a connection I can't satisfy, and even though I know I should get over it... dammit, how am I supposed to do that?

Cheap hook ups with puck bunnies don't work.

Drinking myself into oblivion doesn't work.

Sculpting my body in the gym doesn't work.

Even winning the motherfucking Stanley Cup didn't work.

Finn pauses before answering. "Actually, no. It's more of an art project from a big-name photographer, S.J. Croft."

I peel off my sweaty tank and drop it on top of my gym bag. I've never heard of the guy, but that doesn't deter me. I'd rather participate in an art shoot than peddle sports drinks. "Interesting. Sounds pretty different from the stuff we normally do."

"If you're interested, I'll set up a time slot for the shoot." The keyboard clicks a few times on Finn's end of the line. "I'll send you the location and time once it's confirmed."

"Sounds good. Take care, man." I hang up and open a browser page on Safari. S.J. Croft has a well done website with a custom logo and samples of his work. The pictures are expertly done and they sell for a ton of money. There's also a tab dedicated to press. Seems legit. I drop my phone into my bag.

The locker a few slots down from mine slams open as Noah joins me. "Are you sure you want to be a hockey player? As many modeling gigs as you accept, I'm beginning to think you want to walk the runway."

My gaze snaps to him. "Says the guy who owns a custom-made Disney ballgown."

I try to keep my tone neutral so that he won't think too much about what I'm saying, but it doesn't work. Noah squints at me with his *concerned-best-friend* eyes. "What aren't you telling me?"

I throw my hands up between us. "Nothing!"

Noah considers my face for a moment before saying, "Bullshit."

I've never met a guy as stubborn as Noah, but he's also not

the type of person to give me shit about actual feelings. He was a philosophy major in college, and he's as smart about life as he is talented at keeping the puck out of the net. "Remember that girl from spring break senior year?"

"Ah." Noah nods. "*Stella*. THE Stella. How could I forget? You talked about her non-stop for months. You still never pass up the opportunity to mention her."

It probably doesn't bode well that a guy who never met her knows exactly who I mean. And he's not wrong, because I'm sure I've talked about her far too much over the years. "Every single time I get in front of the camera, I get nostalgic and think of her. It's like I feel closer to her when I get my picture taken for some reason."

Instead of razzing me about my unrequited crush, Noah just nods. "Have you looked her up? If she meant that much to you, you should. Reach out I mean."

"I tried. A couple years ago." *And pretty much every time I drink alone.* "But I don't know her last name. 'Stella Wildlife Photographer' isn't much to go on. She never even told me where she was from." I drop onto the bench and let my shoulders droop.

I'll never admit I even tried 'Bird Girl.' I'll also never tell Marco what came up when I took off safe search for that one. No need to get him asking questions about avian porn that I can't even begin to answer.

Noah stops his post-workout ritual to focus on me. "You should try one more time."

I don't have to stop to consider my answer. "It's not worth getting my hopes up again."

He pulls a face. "Why not? If she's still on your mind after all these years, it needs a dose of closure."

I give a flick of my wrist and hope he doesn't dig any deeper.

I don't like how vulnerable I still feel when even her name is mentioned. "We had two glorious days. It was a fling. We both moved on with our careers. What if I find her this time? I'm not quitting hockey to chase after lions and tigers and bears in Zimbabwe!"

Noah scratches his chin. "Do they even have bears in Zimbabwe?"

"You're missing the point. The point is... our paths haven't crossed again for a reason. We had our time together. I can't stop thinking about her, but I also can't see a way to be together. It is what it is. Besides, even if I *could* track her down, having some guy you slept with *a few times* in college slide into your DMs? That's a *Dateline* episode waiting to happen. I can almost hear Keith Morrison saying, 'It was a dark night in Las Vegas when Venom player, Anders Beck, at last found Stella...'"

"I'm hearing a lot of excuses," Noah deadpans.

Ignoring the pinging behind my ribcage, I say, "It happened, man. Nothing more—nothing less. But I'll never fall in love again. That was a frozen and perfect moment in time. It can never get better. Anything less would just be chasing it."

I probably shouldn't be spilling my guts where Latham might overhear, but screw it. Every time I think about Stella, my heart does this crazy thing in my chest. I can't count the number of times I've gotten myself off remembering the way she looked at me, the way she felt against me, the smooth lines of her body as she drifted through the water... But afterward, I always lie there and try to imagine what more I could say to her to hold her attention for another day, another hour, another *moment.*

And I can't think of a single damn thing. She's too smart for me. She's Belle, and I'm not even enough of a blip of her radar to be Gaston let alone Beast. I'm the creepy baker who tries to hit on her during her opening number and never makes it back on-screen. She's off taming creatures and winning awards. I bet *she's* never looked *me* up on Insta in a fit of desperation.

I bet she doesn't even know I led my team to a Stanley Cup and myself to a Conn Smythe trophy.

"You still hope to see her again," Noah observes. "That's your deal with the modeling gigs. You know that, right? Your subconscious is more honest than you are."

"I know." I glare up at him, because nothing's more obnoxious than when your best friend is right. "You of all people should understand grief and knowing your life isn't going to turn out the way you thought it would. Until I find a woman as exceptional as Stella, I can't get married and have a family. Maybe I'm destined to be alone."

Noah reaches into his bag, pretends to pull something out, and mimes laying it on the counter. He pretends to open whatever it is.

"Are you studying to be a street performer now?" I demand.

Noah lifts his hands to one shoulder. "Nope. I just figured you needed some accompaniment, so I got out the world's smallest violin to play you a little melody." He twiddles his fingers together and hums a sad song.

"Screw you," I snap, grabbing my towel and whipping it at him. "I was baring my soul."

"You were *whining*," Noah corrects. "If she means that much to you, make it happen. But do you want some advice?"

I sulk. "No."

"Too bad, I'm offering it anyway." Noah stops pretending to fiddle and places one hand on my shoulder. "Don't put her up on some impossible pedestal. If you act like she's the answer to all your problems, and you *do* run into her again, I promise that your relationship is going to buckle under the weight of all those expectations. When it comes right down to it, you don't really *know* each other. And a lot of time has also passed for both of you to change. You're not even close to being the same man you were back in college."

I snort. "Says the man with the perfect marriage."

Noah lifts one eyebrow. "Says the man who almost sabotaged his own chance at happiness by being an idiot. Remember? You were there. Riding me the hardest. You're part of the reason Molly and I got our happily ever after. Let me return the favor in your time of need."

I smirk at the recollection of all the pep-talks we had to give Noah last year. "True. But only because I know you the best."

He gives me a pointed look that I don't ignore this time. "Learn from my mistakes. Don't screw up the best thing that ever happened to you because you don't have the balls to risk getting hurt."

His monologue is cut off by the creak of the door and Marco's appearance. "What, you two are not showered yet? Were you waiting for me? I take longer, because I don't want you to be intimidated." He winks at us and gestures to his junk.

Unfortunately, he's not wrong.

Fortunately, that puts an end to the conversation, but I spend the rest of the day in a funk, remembering the best thing I never had.

One perfect summer fling. That's more than some people get. Why ruin the memory by getting shot down by the woman I can't forget? The one who still owns my heart?

CHAPTER TWO

Stella

"I can cancel the photoshoot," I tell Mom.

"Nonsense." She waves me away, but I don't like the way she sways as if a slight breeze could blow her over. "It's nothing. This happens all the time. I'm just a little lightheaded, that's all."

Her words are meant to be comforting, but they aren't. I just came back into town this week to learn that Mom's been having dizzy spells. She didn't mention it when I was traveling.

"To keep you from worrying while you were on the road," she said.

But she doesn't seem to understand that I'm worried *now*. Her not telling me the truth only delayed the inevitable.

"I can cancel the photoshoot," I repeat in a stronger tone. "I'll drive you to the doctor's. See? It's a good thing I came home. And it's another good reason for me to stay."

Mom shakes her head firmly. "It's just a test, Stella. I can go alone. It's all just part of getting older."

Every time Mom tries to convince me that her new bouts of dizziness aren't a big deal, she only makes me want to freak out. In my years of traveling, I've seen all kinds of horrible illnesses that start with lightheadedness. Lyme. Malaria. Concussions. Infections. True, all of these are a bit of a stretch, but this is my *mother*. She's all I have left. I can't imagine what I would do if something happened to her.

"I just don't want you to be alone," I fret. "You could

collapse. Hit your head. Break a hip. Maybe we should get you one of those devices that alert me in case you fall."

Mom places one hand on each of my cheeks and stares into my eyes. "Darling, you know I'm glad to have you here, but you have work to do, and I don't want to be late. Stop being such a worrywart. I'll call you after the appointment."

I know that tone. As far as Mom's concerned, this conversation is over. She plants a kiss on my forehead before grabbing her purse and sailing out the door, leaving me to get myself sorted out.

It's been ages since I came back to Las Vegas for anything more than a quick visit. To say the least, it's a bit of a culture shock. Many of the regions where I've spent most of my adult life and career photographing wildlife are rural. Even in the more built-up areas, my work takes me out of the usual tourist areas into locations that are either much poorer or relatively untouched by Westernization. I'm usually there for the animals, but getting to the next photoshoot always requires some level of human interaction, and I've met people from all walks of life. I've been up-close with hippos, lions, and chimpanzees in their natural habitats, and I've woken on more than one occasion to find my tent overrun with soldier ants, spiders, or, on one occasion, a king cobra.

I shiver at that vivid memory, but I've also gotten to photograph lions, hyenas, giraffes, and baby elephants. Basically, any and every exotic animal from A to Z.

And I've made a nice living doing it.

Give me a jungle over the Strip any day. It's nothing but concrete and bullshit facades. Looking at it just makes me lament what a waste it is. Do these people have any idea how much good they could do in the world with all the money that they choose to throw away on slot machines and bottom-shelf booze? They could feed an undernourished child in Africa for a whole year for what they drop on a long weekend.

Right after graduating from a private high school that Mom practically killed herself to send me to, I took off for college and never looked back. I honestly don't understand why so many of the locals hang around when they have the opportunity to leave.

I spend an eternity in traffic before I finally make it to my friend Eli's gallery. Until this new project, we hadn't seen each other much in person over the past decade, but we've kept up through social media. When I pitched him my new book idea, he offered to let me use his studio space for an extremely low fee. I'd feel guilty paying him so little if he wasn't my oldest and dearest friend.

"Hey, Stella!" Eli opens his arms for a hug the second that I step into the gallery. "How's your mom?"

"She's at her appointment now." I hold onto him for a little longer than usual. This whole health scare has me shaken, and I wish I could be there with her right now. "We don't know anything yet, but I'm trying to keep busy. Thank you for letting me use your space."

Eli clicks his tongue at me. "How could I not? You're back home, and that makes me happy as hell. I want to help launch you into the stratosphere. I want all your dreams to come true."

"The stratosphere, huh?" I chuckle at his hyperbole. "I think you might be overselling it. The book isn't published yet. And if I can't scrape up enough models, I won't be able to. Working with a publisher is different from freelancing and working for myself. What if I don't make my deadline?"

"I see your tendency to worry about *what ifs* hasn't faded with time." Eli places one hand on the small of my back. "First things first, Stel. Let me show you the space."

The main portion of the gallery is incredibly tasteful, with muted walls and clever lighting that makes the space feel even bigger than it is. Photographs and paintings in a wide variety of styles line the walls, and the three-dimensional art—mostly sculpture and pottery, with a few multimedia pieces by the well-known eclectic Jens Yenner—stand on tasteful tables and plinths. It looks like a museum. Eli's always been good at showing off every piece to its best advantage. He's sold a few of my pieces before, and they always command a fantastic price in his gallery.

He leads me to a door at the back, and up a flight of stairs to the second floor. I gasp when I see where he has me set up. One side of the room is dedicated to a photography space, with a spectacular lighting kit already assembled. A tall window on the other side looks out over an industrial portion of the city.

"*Eli,*" I breathe. "This is *amazing.*"

"There's a blackout curtain there, if you're worried about how the window will impact your lighting, and there's a small bathroom in the corner that you can use as your changing area." He shows me the switch that will bring it down. "I usually use this space for photographing pieces for the website listings, so everything should be good to go. You remember how to use this stuff?" The teasing lilt of his voice tells me that he's pulling my leg.

"I haven't been in the jungle *that* long," I scoff and immediately walk over to inspect the equipment. Elijah hasn't skimped on his gear, and I'm itching to try it all out. After such a long time, I feel like I'm that young college girl about to launch a real career—creating art from scratch that means something to me.

"You've got about half an hour before your guy shows up." Eli checks his watch. "Time to talk through your what-ifs, if you want."

My dream was always to photograph animals. I love the thrill of spending a day on the trail, or in the car, heading out to some remote location in the hopes of catching a one-of-a-kind shot. As a nature photographer, every single one of my photographs is candid. I get to see things as they truly are and to convey that unpredictable beauty through photos.

Sometimes, I'm able to catch animals doing something graceless. People love the signed prints of the bear I captured slipping over the edge of the waterfall when she lost her footing, or the mama chimp run ragged by her squabbling babies. Other times, I get to witness nature at its most majestic. Last year, I snapped a shot of a wolf pack along the Alaskan border, howling so that their breath was visible in the frigid air. I've preserved nature at its most beautiful and bizarre and brutal. My images are unique, but at the same time, they show things that are happening everywhere, all over the world, in places where humans rarely get to bear witness. I like to think that they demystify nature a little, while still celebrating its wonders.

I want my new book to do the same thing, but to the human form.

"Alright," I say aloud, "here's a what-if for you... What if I can't find enough people willing to let me photograph them in the altogether?"

Eli cocks his head. "Are you really worried about it?"

I tug my lower lip between my teeth. "I only have about ten models lined up. I'm going to need a lot more variety than that."

Eli nods thoughtfully. "Anything specific you're looking for?"

"I want to celebrate the human body in all of its shapes. I want to make people question their assumptions." I strike a pose against the wall. "We put so much of our energy into selling this very specific beauty standard." I change my pose, pretending to blow a kiss to a nonexistent photographer. "I want to shake it up. I want to make the viewer look at amputees, people with Down Syndrome, people with tattoos and scars and burns, in wheelchairs and braces, and ask them, *Is this what beauty looks like?* and I want to make it really damn obvious that the answer is *yes.*"

"In other words, you want to make people *think.*" Eli nods. "I like it. So who's coming in today? A war vet? A breast cancer survivor?"

I bite my lip. "An athlete."

"A Paralympian?"

I shake my head. "A professional hockey player."

Eli waits for me to elaborate, but I don't. That expression he's wearing sends me straight back in time even though he hasn't really changed that much.

"So, let me get this straight." He rubs one temple and shoots me a look of extreme disappointment. "You want to photograph the unconventional, so you've gone for... the most conventional possible version of male beauty?"

"I want the book to cover a wide range of body types," I say, with a twinge of defensiveness in my voice. "I don't want to do the thing some artists do and say, *No, that's not beauty,* this *is beauty.* I want to build on the idea of what beauty can look like."

Eli smirks at me. "Perfect people are people, too. I get it. You don't want to discriminate, even against people with pretty privilege."

"So you assume that just because a guy is conventionally attractive, he's automatically perfect?" I raise my eyebrows and plant my hands on my hips. "To be honest, I'm just starting with him because he was the easiest to book. I've never laid eyes on this guy. For all I know, he could have perfectly chiseled abs but a face like Walter Matthau."

"You don't have to sell me on it." Eli lifts both hands in self-defense. "I've dated enough beautiful assholes to know that the package doesn't always match what's inside."

It's my turn to smirk. "How many of those double entendres were intentional?"

Despite my friend's bland expression, his eyes glitter like jewels. "I can't imagine what you mean. Anyway, if you need me to stick around and help manage your hot guy, say the word."

I pinch my brows together. "I don't want to make him uncomfortable."

Eli pouts. "What exactly do you think I'd *do?*"

"I didn't mean you specifically. I just don't want him to be focused on an audience or worry what anyone will think." I assume that will be less of an issue for a guy like this than some of my other models, but that's what this project is about. Questioning assumptions. Why should I presume that this guy will want to show off his conventionally attractive body any more than I should assume that the other models will want to hide?

"Oh, I get it." Eli wraps one arm around my shoulders. "You want the hunk all to yourself. Heard and understood, loud and clear." He kisses my temple, then heads to the door. "Alright, Stella. Enjoy your alone time with the ambassador for perfect men. I'll see what I can do as far as hunting up some more models who aren't as traditionally beautiful, okay?"

"Thanks, Eli!" As he retreats to the first floor, I rotate on the spot, admiring the space all over again.

This is going to be the start of something special. I can feel it.

CHAPTER THREE

Anders

I arrive at the address Finn gave me ten minutes early and wander around the gallery. At first, I'm hoping to find someone who can tell me where to go, but then I end up just staring at the art. It's a cool space—I haven't been to this industrial part of town in a while. I had assumed there would be some kind of sports angle to the project, but if the display area's anything to go by, this really is going to be an art shoot.

I can't honestly say that I 'get' all the pieces. Take the giant pottery sculpture that looks like it's melting. What do people do with stuff like that? Just set it in the corner of the living room? Stick it in a glass case? What's the point?

But my eyes linger on a few of the others. There's a trio of paintings of ships at harbor, with a foggy sky that bleeds into a misty sea, and the distant hint of land in the background. They aren't photorealistic, but when I look at them, I'm transported somewhere else, with the smell of saltwater and morning mist strong in my nostrils. The sensation is so alarming that I have to look away. How can looking at something light up another one of your senses so vividly?

I love traveling and although I do it a ton for work, it's not the same as taking a vacation. And I don't get enough of those with the limited places I can go during my short summer break.

I rub my nose to get rid of the sensation and turn to a display wall that reaches the ceiling. It's about four feet wide, covered in black velvet, and this side displays a massive, brilliantly colored photograph so bright that it's almost blinding. A bird stares back at me, its eye expanded until the iris is almost as big as my head. Thousands of tiny green-and-gold feathers radiate out from the eye, almost obscuring the petite creamsicle-tinted beak. My heart aches as I realize that I know what kind of bird it is.

And I almost wish that I didn't.

"Resplendent quetzal," I murmur aloud.

Stella's bird.

"Stunning, isn't it?"

I jump at the sound of a deep voice. I didn't hear anyone come in. A man in his late twenties emerges from a door at the back of the room. Everything about him is as polished and deliberate as the space we're standing in.

"It's great." I hold out my hand. "Anders Beck. Any chance you're S.J. Croft?"

"Ah, you're here to have your portrait taken." The man's eyes slide over me, and the corner of his mouth turns up, as if he knows something I don't. "You must be representative of the perfect people."

I'm kind of taken aback. "Sorry?"

He shakes his head as he takes my hand. "Inside joke. I'm Elijah, the gallery-owner. Head upstairs. She's waiting for you."

She. I just assumed that S.J. Croft was a guy, although now that he says otherwise, I'm not sure why I jumped to that conclusion. I guess I assumed that this was going to be some athlete thing, and that world is still pretty male-dominated. If Marco were here, I'm sure he'd have something to say about my assumption. *Woman can be behind camera, Anders, just like man can wear princess dress. This is what we call in Italy, 'restrictive gender stereotype...'*

"I'll just go up then," I say.

I'm aware of Elijah's eyes on my back as I take the stairs two at a time. He didn't strike me as someone who would argue with a stranger, but he was definitely sizing me up.

She.

I bet the photographer's his girlfriend or something. For sure he's giving off that protective vibe that broadcasts S.J. Croft means something to him.

You've got nothing to worry about, buddy. There's only one woman I have any interest in sweeping off her feet. For me, this is just a job to pad my investment account. A means to an end since I know better than most that hockey doesn't last forever.

The room at the top of the stairs is brightly lit, with large windows on one side and a whole mess of bulbs around the area where I'm presumably going to have my photo taken.

The photographer stands with her back to me, and for a moment, I let myself imagine that it's going to be her. *My* photographer. We'll gasp and stare and after a few strangled heartbeats, our eyes will fill with tears. Then we'll pretend that time stood still and we'll fall into each other's arms. Our mouths will rain down kisses that last for treasured moments. We'll be reunited at last. I'll lay her bare and the only photographs that will be captured are the ones that will end up as sweet memories inside my mind.

Wishful thinking, but what can I say? I'm a romantic at heart, but only on my quest for her. The one woman who actually lit me up inside.

"Hey," I say.

She jumps before spinning toward me. "Oh, sorry! You're a little early, and I'm still getting set up."

I stare at her, mouth open in preparation for our introduction, but nothing comes out. This woman is *stunning.*

Not like a supermodel, but like a high-wattage light bulb. She's wearing the barest hint of makeup, and her russet hair falls just past her shoulders in soft waves. If I didn't know better, I would swear that it's her—but my Stella is overseas somewhere, photographing lemurs and aye-ayes and brilliantly colored birds.

Birds like the one in the photograph downstairs. The resplendent quetzal.

The pieces slide together, and just as I'm adding up two and two to equal four, she extends her hand.

"Stella Croft," she says. "And you must be Anders Beck."

"Yes," I breathe and extend my hand toward her.

Oh my fucking God, it's actually happening!

Our palms touch, and that spark of chemistry jumps between us, just as potent as it was years ago. It's a sign from the universe. A quantum leap. A manifestation. All that shit Noah was saying about keeping the faith was on-point. She's here. She asked Finn to set this up. She found *me*. After all this time.

My lip wobbles. God, I can't wait to kiss her. To press her up against the wall and tell her how much I've missed her, how much I've longed for her, how much time I've spent moping around and Googling art terms and taking notes on nature documentaries so that, on the off-chance we ever meet again, we'll never run out of things to talk about.

Our bodies connected in Costa Rica, along with our souls.

Now we can give our hearts and minds time to catch up.

My own heart makes a valiant attempt to launch itself out of my throat and land at her feet. It's hers. If I admit it to myself, it's been hers ever since that first afternoon in the jungle.

Stella nods. "Great to meet you! There's a changing room back there, and... oh, shoot." She pulls her phone out of the pocket of her fitted slacks and peers at the name on the screen.

Mom. "I'm *so* sorry, Mr. Beck, I've got to answer this. If you can get ready without me?" She points even as she lifts her phone to her ear and turns her back on me.

A phantom fist punches me in the gut. Words fizzle in the back of my throat.

And my nuts shrivel back into my body cavity. *Mr. Beck?*

No. No fucking way.

The girl of my dreams invited me into her studio by *accident.* This isn't fate. It's not serendipity. My brain swirls straight from 'it's happening' to 'this can't be happening.' She doesn't have a clue who I am.

I feel like I've stumbled into some alternate universe where my body goes numb, and the blood rushes through my ears until all I can hear is my own pulse as white orbs of light blur my vision.

Don't even get me started on the state of my heart.

"Hey, Mom," Stella says.

Her closed posture tells me that this call is important, but the longer I stand here like an idiot, the more humiliated I feel. Does she honestly not know who I am? Or has she forgotten about Costa Rica altogether?

Maybe it meant nothing to her. Maybe I meant nothing to her.

Now that I'm thinking about it, that kind of adventure might have been-once-in-a-lifetime for me, but for her, it might have just been an average Friday. She goes on all kinds of spectacular trips and meets all kinds of people. Why would I assume that she thought I was anything other than a run of the mill fling in a foreign country only because desire met opportunity?

Sign from the universe, indeed. Apparently the sign says, *Get the hell over yourself.*

As a professional officially representing the Venom, I have to make the best of a bad situation. I finally force myself to turn and walk back to the changing room, where another unwelcome surprise is in store for me. Instead of a jersey or a track suit or designer sweats, all that awaits me is a fluffy white bathrobe.

I stare at it for a long moment, wondering what the hell is going on. Stella's total dismissal has left a bad taste in my mouth, and the lack of appropriate and even semi-masculine clothing doesn't help. I change grudgingly into the robe, which barely comes to mid-thigh. As I step out of the changing area, I spot a fedora hanging from a peg on the wall and slap it onto my head, just so that I won't feel so totally exposed.

I can't remember the last time I felt this vulnerable. Not even on a breakaway in open ice with a huge defenseman on my tail aching to separate my head from my body.

"When will they have the results?" Stella asks into the receiver. After a slight pause, she sighs. "Alright. See you at home." She hangs up, then turns to me. "I'm sorry, I realize this is unprofessional. Are you ready to get started?" Her brow wrinkles when she spots the fedora on my head.

"Not really." I gesture to the robe. "This is all that was back there. Where's my gear?"

"Your... *gear?*" she repeats.

I put my palms up. "Well, yeah. Whatever I'm supposed to be wearing."

"Mr. Beck," she says slowly, and it hurts just as badly to hear her call me that a second time, "you're aware that this is a nude shoot, right?"

I gape at her as my stomach clenches.

"I was perfectly clear with the Venom's publicity department, and Dante Giovanetti signed off on it." She wrings her hands together. "Is that going to be a problem?"

Problem? Of course, it's a problem, Ms. Croft.

I grit my teeth at this fresh revelation. I wouldn't put anything past Dante, but the fact that Finn didn't warn me about this makes me want to put my fist through something. It's in direct violation of my morals clause that Dante himself put in my contract, never mind that it's a total fucking surprise that I didn't expect and don't want.

The last time this woman saw me naked...

God, all of a sudden, it feels like a lifetime ago.

Stella watches me with huge, nervous eyes, and that makes me mad, too. Not at her specifically, but on account of this whole situation. The woman I've been pining after for *years* made an honest mistake that has nothing to do with me and now she feels like shit *because* of me.

Why do you care?

Yeah, I've wished for a chance to get naked with her again, but not like this.

"It's fine," I grunt. "Are we ready now, or...?"

She checks her camera, a much fancier model than the one she used in Costa Rica, and nods. "I'm game when you are."

I strip off the bathrobe, like ripping off a Band-Aid, and toss it over the back of the only chair in the room. There must be more awkward situations for a guy to end up in, but nothing springs to mind. I use the hat to cover my junk as I shuffle to the middle of the set, surrounded by all the bright lights.

They bounce off every surface in the studio, almost blinding me as if they're mocking my distress.

Stella's eyes linger on the hat. "Are you planning to hold that the whole time?"

"Is getting a picture of my dick really part of the assignment?" I snap.

I almost wish I could yell at her. But even with my shattered heart, I'm not that big of an asshole. Christ, what happened between us happened seven years ago. Just because I'm the only one still carrying a torch doesn't give me the right to go postal.

She opens her mouth and hesitates before answering. I almost wish I could wipe away the slightly tragic expression she's now wearing while I'm wearing nothing. "No... but I'm a little surprised that you're this uncomfortable. I mean... aren't you naked inside the locker room all the time? Do you want to take a break so you can get more relaxed about the whole idea?"

I shake my head. "Let's get on with it. There's a draft."

"Mmm." Stella composes her expression and bends in front of the camera. "How about you turn to the side."

I do as she asks, angling my hips away from her but not letting her see my shoulders. I'm not ready to have *that* conversation with a virtual stranger. I doubt I ever will be.

Stella sighs and snaps a few photos. I try to angle my face away so that it won't be as obvious in the pictures.

"Could you please look at me?" she asks.

I turn my head slightly, but I can't make myself smile. Hopefully it just looks like I'm giving her a Blue Steel smolder. It's all I've got for the moment.

Stella's face reappears from behind the camera. "Why are you being so shy? I assumed this was par for the course for someone in your career."

"Not really," I inform her through gritted teeth. "In the locker room, I'm not the only one sans clothing and talking to the press is part of my job." *Since I work for one of the biggest dickheads in professional sports, this could, in fact, be career-ending.*

We try a few more poses, and I try to relax, but it's not

happening. Not with her. Not knowing what this could cost me. Dante excels at gaslighting. He calls players on the carpet for things he caused and that makes me nervous. The guy's a loose cannon, and he's sent players down to the minors for less.

"Maybe I could take a few from the back?" she suggests. "That way you wouldn't be focused on holding the hat...?"

Every muscle in my body tightens. Except *that* one. "No."

Her eyes widen at the continued waspish tone of my voice.

"No," I say again, less harshly this time. "I'm sorry, but this isn't what I was told would be happening today. Um... I never got to consult with my agent. I could get released over this."

"But the team owner approved," she says, her eyes bouncing between mine in confusion. "Why would he do that and then release you?"

I clear my throat of what feels like a furball. "Without my permission. If I'd known that you wanted me to bare it all for the camera, I'd have refused the offer."

Her jaw tightens. "Fair enough. I'm sorry that you were misled. That wasn't my intention." She backs away from the equipment. "If it helps, I'll get in touch with your publicity contact about the misunderstanding."

My lip curls involuntarily at the word. The *misunderstanding*, as she puts it, is a pain, but it's not the worst part of the day. The most painful part is having to look Stella in the eye and know that I mean absolutely nothing to her.

The only good news is that now that my dreams are shattered, I'll never have to see her again. The moment I get my pants on, she'll be out of my life for good.

Maybe since she's finally been knocked off her pedestal, I can move on and replace the long-standing fantasy with something real. Maybe fate knocking me right between the eyes will end up being one of those blessings in disguise.

CHAPTER FOUR

Stella

"What's got you so sulky?" Mom asks.

I stand on the edge of the Gnome Gloam, the backyard haven where my mother and her charge, Vivian Abbott, keep their ever-growing collection of lawn gnomes. "It's just the photoshoot today. The model walked out. I've never had that happen to me before."

Mom tilts her head to one side. "Hold on. What on earth?"

"I guess he didn't realize that it was going to be a nude shoot." I crouch down in front of one of the smaller gnomes, who appears to be walking a pet bee on a leash, and sigh. "I didn't realize how hard it would be to book models here."

I must be cursed. This is the third passion project in a row that I can't seem to get off the ground. I've gone from ten models to nine. That's not a book. That's not even a magazine. More like a brochure.

"I'm sorry, dear." Mom's busy clicking around on her tablet. "I know how tough it can be when things don't work out, but never fear. You'll get it sorted out. My daughter is talented as heck. I have faith."

"What are you looking at now?" I ask, nodding to her tablet. "Please tell me that you're not on WebMD again."

Mom sighs. "I might have a brain tumor."

Here we go. "You don't have a brain tumor, Mom. Googling your symptoms is the worst idea ever. Google is just like dealing with a contract—they throw everything in there but the kitchen sink because they're afraid they're going to get sued."

She narrows her eyes at me. "You mean the kind of idea that someone might have if they were suffering from a brain tumor?"

I struggle to keep my eyes from rolling skyward. "*Mom.*"

"Then I have MS. I know I do. God, I'm going to end up in a wheelchair and you'll have to push me everywhere."

I press my palms to my eyes and exhale slowly. "Mom. Please stop trying to self-diagnose. Remember this morning when you *assured* me that everything was fine?"

"Okay, okay. That was then and I might have been pretending to be less worried before. But only because I didn't want to worry *you*," Mom mutters. "I'm older and wiser now—with self-diagnosed medical trauma."

I bite my cheek, but fortunately, the sliding door at the back of the house opens and a tiny girl in a Wonder Woman costume emerges. An enormous dog lopes after her, dwarfing the girl by comparison. The dog is wearing a crown, and glitter-covered magic bracelets that match those of her mistress, the true ruler of the Abbott household.

"Nanny Frannie!" Viv cries. "Look! I'm Wonder Woman!" She spots me, and her eyes widen as she screeches to a halt. "Who're you?"

Mom waves to me. "This is my daughter. She's a photographer. I told you that she'd be staying with me for a while, remember?"

"Oooh!" Viv bounces on her toes. "It's nice to meet you! I'm Vivian."

"I remember you." At this height, I'm at eye-level with the little girl. "I met you once when you were itty bitty." I happened to be in town, and her uncle was at an away game, so I've never officially met Noah Abbott despite hearing about him often.

"I don't remember," Vivian says, but she hurries over to me. Behind her, the dog watches me suspiciously. "What's your name?"

"Stella," I tell her.

"Like a star!" Viv grabs one of my hands. Seeing that I've been accepted, the dog relaxes and busies herself with sniffing around the garden. "Stella, do you want to play Wonder Woman?"

"That depends," I say. "What are the rules?" My bad mood from earlier is already melting away. My lifestyle has never left much time for dating or planning for a family, so I have to take my kid-fix where I can get it, and Vivian is positively charming.

"Wellll..." Vivian lifts up her crown to scratch her head. "Biscuit wants to fly the invisible airplane, and usually I ride with her."

"I'm not sure there will be enough room for me, then." I rub my chin, pretending to think. "How about I take some photos to document your adventures?"

"Yeah!" Viv cries. "And they can go in Daddy's photobook!"

"Just a minute, then." I step inside the guesthouse to grab one of my smaller cameras before joining my mother on the garden wall where she's still ignoring my advice about waiting for the professional diagnosis. As Vivian and Biscuit zoom around the yard together, Mom sets her tablet aside.

"You're so good with her," she sighs. "You know, if it turns out that I *do* have a tumor, I won't have much more time to wait around for you to find someone..."

I roll my eyes and bump her with my elbow. "Are you really going to use your health to try to pressure me into having kids?"

"I'm just saying, you always think you have time until you don't." She smiles as Vivian and Biscuit collapse to the ground, breathing hard. "I can't remember the last time you mentioned anyone special in your life. Doesn't it get lonely, love?"

I fiddle with my camera strap. "Not really." Sometimes I wish that I had a special someone in my life, but I'm never in one place long, and I can't imagine giving up my career. When I'm in one place for more than a few months, I start to get itchy. Like my skin doesn't fit right. It would be nice to have a home base, but in my experience, guys don't like the idea of playing second fiddle to my love of photography.

Being with me would require a man with supreme self-confidence who had his own thing going on. One who understood the meaning of trust.

Mom hums knowingly.

Vivian scrambles to her feet and hurries over to me. "We're gonna do a new game. Want to play?"

"What are the rules of this new game?" I ask.

"No rules." She tosses her hair over one little shoulder. For such a tiny thing in possession of such fragile beauty, she's delightfully matter of fact. "I want to rearrange the Gnome Gloam. If we leave them too long, they'll get bored looking at the same thing every day."

I wink at her. "You know what? I feel exactly the same way. Let's mix things up a little." Leaving my camera with Mom, I follow Vivian over to the nearest cluster of gnomes and begin moving them around. It turns out, while there aren't rules, there are *guidelines*. Some of the gnomes like to stick with their specific set of friends, while others want to explore and meet new neighbors. Vivian is careful to correct any of my errors in gnome-placement, and we work our way across the yard.

When we reach the tallest part of the terraced rock garden, Vivian points to a special collection of gnomes. "They stay up here. These are the king and queen gnomes."

"Are all of the boys kings?" I ask. "They don't fight over the title?"

"No." The little girl tilts her head to one side. "They're co-kings. All of the gnomes that come from Miss C are *royalty*." She pronounces this last word carefully, as if it's tripped her up in the past. "Miss C is the best."

"Miss C?" I ask.

"Our neighbor." Vivian points to the fence. "She's very mysterious."

"Celine Dion!" Mom shouts.

"She's really nice," Vivian tells me. "Nanny Frannie says she's famous. She even has a helicopter."

"Nanny Frannie is a huge Celine Dion fan," I agree, not quite sure if I should believe them or if this is just part of their Gnome Gloam fantasy. "Very well, her gnomes reign supreme. Do they still get to move around the castle?"

"Of course. Put that one here, move her there, and... *oh!*" We both jump as a loud splash echoes across the yard. Biscuit has grown tired of the Wonder Woman routine and launched herself into the pool.

"No, Biscuit!" Vivian wails. "Your costume!"

"Oh, darling." Mom sets her tablet aside and hurries over to comfort Vivian. "Remember what we said about dogs having different priorities?"

"But the *glitter!*" Vivian rubs her eyes. "Daddy doesn't like it when he has to use those drop things."

Mom soothes her. "Biscuit must've been hot. You wouldn't want her to be uncomfortable, would you?"

"No..." The little girl hiccups. "I guess not."

Seeing my mom with Vivian really is sweet. I used to feel guilty about having left her in Vegas on her own, but I'm glad she has other people in her life, not just to take care of her, but who love her.

The back door opens, and a tall man emerges. He's handsome and clean cut, and although I've never seen him before, I know who he is immediately. He strides over to me and holds out his hand.

"You must be Francine's daughter," he says. Given how huge he is, I'm surprised by how softly he speaks. Then again, I do remember Mom talking about him being into philosophy and rare books with a stellar private library. I wouldn't mind checking that out while I'm here.

As my hand grasps his, I realize how cut he is. God, these athletes must spend hours in the gym at the expense of everything else. Maybe that's the kind of guy I could handle dating. I wouldn't see much of him and that would be okay by me. Maybe a professional golfer on the PGA tour. "And you must be Noah. The only time I was here, you were on a road trip. Thanks for letting me stay with my mom for a bit."

"Your mom is like family," he says, nodding to where she stands hand in hand with his niece, watching Biscuit paddle around in the pool in her water-logged costume. "That makes you family, too."

His instant acceptance warms me from the inside out. I've been wondering what would happen if Mom really did get a diagnosis of something more serious. What if she couldn't work for a few months? Would she still have somewhere to live?

I'm glad to know those fears are unfounded.

"By the way, I didn't catch your first name." He holds out one hand and chuckles. "Francine always just says 'my daughter this, my daughter that.' She's really proud of you."

His palm swallows mine. "Stella."

A strange, stilted smile crosses his face. "You wouldn't happen to be a photographer, would you?"

"Oh, God." I wilt. "That's right. You play for the same team Anders Beck does. I swear, it was all a misunderstanding. I told the publicity guy that it was going to be a nude shoot. I didn't realize it was gonna be an issue."

"I must've missed something." Noah crosses his arms. "Did you say nude? Anders mentioned he was going to do a shoot, but he didn't tell me how it went."

My face heats up, and I am suddenly tempted to follow Biscuit's swan dive into the water. "Yeah. That was so embarrassing. This is why I usually photograph animals. I probably shouldn't have mentioned it to you. He said it could be an issue for his career..."

"He'll bounce back," Noah assures me, a sudden grin stretching his face. "I wouldn't worry too much about it."

A curvy woman who barely reaches Noah's shoulder emerges from the house. Introductions lead to an invitation to join them for dinner, which is mostly taken up with casual chatter about work. Molly, Noah's wife, obviously adores both Vivian and my mother. It's one of the nicest evenings I've had in a long time. So nice, in fact, that it washes the bitter aftertaste of my encounter with Anders Beck out of my mouth.

I guess all hockey players can't be as warm and charming as Noah Abbott.

Too bad he was so grumpy and broody, because Anders Beck is just as chiseled as his friend.

CHAPTER FIVE

Anders

"So." Noah sidles up to me in the locker room before morning skate. "How was the photoshoot yesterday?"

I can't very well blame him for how wrong yesterday went, but that doesn't stop me from slamming the door of my locker. "Shitty."

"What?" His eyebrows snap together. "I thought you loved working the camera."

I lean my forehead against the cool metal door. "It was her, Noah. The person running the photoshoot. It was Stella. *My Stella*. And she didn't have a goddamn clue who I was."

Noah waits for a moment, but when I don't elaborate, he waves his hand. "Even when you reminded her?"

I eye my locker and consider giving it a swift kick. "Huh?"

Noah speaks slowly, like he's talking to a small child. "She didn't remember you, even after you reminded her that you'd met before?"

"I didn't remind her," I mutter. "She *forgot* me, man. And don't you dare pull that thing with the tiny violin again! I already feel like I got my balls sheared off."

Noah, halfway through gearing up, sighs. "What did you look like back in college? Since we didn't play for the same team, I don't really remember."

I whip out my phone to pull up an old photo. "Pretty much the same, you know." I hold it out to Noah.

One of his eyes twitches. "You think you still look like *that?*

You're, like, a twig in that photo."

"Nah." I examine the photo again. Sure, I've grown up a little, but I'm still *me*. "I was jacked back then. And my damn bone structure didn't change."

Noah abandons his preparations and grabs the phone. "Okay, let's play *spot the differences*. One, you had a derpy little babyface."

My eyes morph into slits as I consider throat punching my best friend. "Hey!"

"Now you've got a big ol' manly beard. Two, you've got mad lettuce now, instead of your Justin Bieber hairdo."

What the fuck is he talking about? He wasn't even there. "It was *not*..."

"Three." Noah holds up three fingers to silence me. "You've got a bunch of motherfucking *tattoos* all over your jacked-up body that was sculpted courtesy of high weight deadlifting, which are apparently a new addition. Of *course*, she didn't recognize you! Jesus, Anders, you're like two different people."

"You're exaggerating," I grumble. "Shouldn't she remember my pheromones or something?"

Noah makes a frustrated noise and pulls up my browser to a side-by-side of Jason Momoa from Baywatch and Jason Momoa from Aquaman. "You're saying that if you'd met little baby Jason once four years ago that you'd connect him with *this!?*" He jabs his finger at the *Aquaman* poster. "I get that your first name is pretty unusual, but come on. Did she even know your last name when you two met?"

"Um..." I scratch the back of my neck. "Technically, she didn't even know my *first* name. I went by Blaze back then. Remember? Everybody called me that back in college. I thought if I had a fast nickname, it might help me get drafted in the first round. And it worked."

Noah throws both hands in the air. "Hopeless!" he exclaims. He shoves my phone at me and lurches off the bench. "I give up."

His words reignite a spark of hope in my chest as I go through the motions. All through morning skate, I struggle to come to grips with the fact that I may have messed up irreparably. Now if I go back to the studio and try to explain things, Stella's going to know me as the guy who threw a mantrum and walked out of her photoshoot because he was embarrassed about being naked.

In her eyes, I must look like a total tool. An immature one with an inability to control my own emotions.

This leads me to another issue, however, one that's fallen by the wayside in my frustration about Stella. When we take a break, I skate over to Noah.

"Ready to admit that you goofed?" he asks. "*Blaze*?"

"Sort of," I admit, shooting him my 'cool it' look. "But there's something else. Dante signed off on some nude modeling shoot. I don't do nudity. Shit, there's a motherfucking morals clause in our contracts that he put in there!"

Noah razzes me about stuff all the time, but at this news, he looks genuinely pissed. "Dante's a douche who only cares about himself. If you don't want to do it, don't do it. Dante should get his nose out of player relations and the front office and stick to the board of directors where owners belong."

Technically, I agree, but we both know that Dante has a bad habit of swerving out of his lane when it comes to owning a hockey team. He bought the Venom for purely selfish reasons, mainly to one up Nixon Caldwell all while feeding his own ego. And that thing's like one of those Chinese Pandas that eat ten times their weight in bamboo, constantly needing more.

My eyes find Marco as he skates a drill. "I left early, and I'm not sure if she even wants a redo. But what if he loses it and trades me or something? He's vindictive as shit. My whole life is here in Vegas. I don't want to play for another team."

"No, what is this?" Marco skates over. "Are you being a trade?"

"You're getting *traded?*" Latham turns around and squints at us. "What the actual fuck? It's like we don't even talk anymore. Clue me in, man. You're my linemate. You're the team *captain!*"

"Nobody's getting traded, B-list," I growl, smirking when his face twists up at his new nickname courtesy of hockey podcaster Scarlett Stone. Who deliberately yanks his chain on the regular. "And keep it down. Let's not give Dante any ideas."

"Anders is just having a crappy week," Noah explains. Thank goodness, because if he started airing my dirty laundry on the ice, I would lose it. "He didn't want a wittle woman to see his wittle pee-pee. Maybe we should take him out to lunch and drown his sorrows in pizza and beer."

Cash nods as he shifts closer. "Lunch sounds good."

"Why your week filled with the craps?" Marco asks.

I exchange a glance with Noah. "The photoshoot I showed up to yesterday was a nude modeling gig."

Cash and Latham cough to cover their laughter, and Marco beams. "Ah, *mi amico*, how lucky you are!"

I shoot laser beams at him with my eyeballs. "Yeah? You want to take my place?"

"*Me?*" Marco presses one hand to his chest. "Of course! Like the Michelangelo! You can grate *pecorino romano* on these." He rubs his hand lower, over his abs. "Someone would be paying to see all this? I will show him everything with pleasure."

"Her," Noah says casually.

"Even better. For pretty woman, I will show for free." Marco holds out his arms. "Woman's gaze is like caress."

"Bad mental image," Cash mutters. I have to agree. The idea of him stripping down for Stella...

Whoa, there. My inner voice sounds suspiciously like Noah. *You have to stop caring about who she sees naked? What happened to giving up on her entirely? Moving on? Finding a relationship based in reality?* Noah's shrewd side-eye suggests that he's picked up on my conflicting emotions, but there's no way I'm gonna unpack this all right now, not with Marco waxing poetic about his abs and striving to flash Stella just to receive her visual caress.

"Talk to Finn," I say. I still haven't reached out to him, although at the very least I should probably shoot him an email before he has to hear the news from Stella.

"I will," Marco says. "As for lunch, I will do this, too. Although this one thing I do not like about America. Your pizza very greasy, and your pasta full of dusts."

"You eat dust?" Cash wrinkles his nose.

"Yes, yes!" Marco's usually easygoing face pinches into an expression of unbridled rage. "I try the Kraft. Orange dust not cheese!" He spits on the ice. "Mozzarella, burrata, fontina, gorgonzola! These are the cheese."

Latham shakes his head as he slams his stick down on the ice. "Yeah, but are they instant?"

"No instant!" Marco screeches. "These cheeses, they are made with love from happy cows over many years of error and trial!"

"Whatever," Latham says. "You sound like one of those lame Kemps commercials where idiots think Strawberry milk comes from pink cows. We still need to expand your pizza palette."

"Chicago deep-dish," Cash intones.

Marco's face turns beet-red, but before he can lose his shit, Coach asks us to skate a new drill. While my mind drifts back to Stella for the hundredth time since I saw her, Latham takes that opportunity to body check me and slam me straight into the boards.

"Pull your head out of your ass before it affects your game," he shouts.

I elbow him as Noah gives me a little poke check with his stick from the crease. "Fuck off, Newberry," I growl, skating back into position. Cash gains control of the puck and flips it toward me. I take his pass with ease, driving down the ice before flicking it to Latham, who has a clean shot on goal. He winds up and scores on our backup goalie before you can blink twice.

We skate back to the bench to guzzle some Gatorade and mop the sweat off our faces. Despite his poor delivery, Latham was right a few minutes ago when he read me the riot act. For as long as I can remember, hockey has been my safe place to fall. It's the only thing in my life that's never let me down. Being here on the ice calms me down and centers me the way nothing else ever has. The annoyance I have swirling in my gut starts to fade.

I feel a little better, but for the rest of the practice and all through lunch, I struggle to focus. I'm still worried about what Dante's response is going to be.

And I have no clue what the hell to do about Stella.

CHAPTER SIX

Stella

My next model isn't scheduled for a few days, and I haven't gotten responses to any of the emails I've sent out about lining up anyone new, but there's nothing more I can do at the moment. Rather than hover over my mom, who seems to need Vivian's particular brand of distraction from her health scare, I hunt down a can of tennis balls and a racket. I've never been particularly great at sitting still, especially not when I'm anxious. I need to keep moving. Getting my heart rate up will help release some of this nervous energy I've been carrying around ever since my plane landed in Vegas.

Fortunately for me, Noah's gated community has tennis courts. Smashing the shit out of the innocent yellow felt sounds like the perfect chance to decompress.

"Be back in an hour!" I call as I leave through the back gate. Mom, who is reading a book to Vivian in the shade of the little pergola behind the pool, waves to acknowledge that she heard me. At their feet, Biscuit lifts her head to see if I'm more interesting than her nap, and then immediately flops back down.

I sympathize with the dog. Trying to keep up with someone as energetic as Vivian is a full-time job.

The tennis court is only two blocks away, so I can walk there in just a couple of minutes. I'm still not used to the total lack of shade in Vegas. I've been to other places that are just as hot, and the humidity really isn't bad compared to the jungles where I do a lot of my shoots, but the only places to get out of the sun are man-made.

I'm still mulling this over when the tennis court comes into view, and I freeze. There, on the first court, is an uncomfortably familiar figure.

Anders Beck.

The walkout.

The man who made me fall into complete self-doubt when I was already teetering on the brink of that uncomfortable feeling. Now I associate him with that icky sensation that takes up residence in your gut and refuses to leave.

I spin my racket in my hand a couple of times, trying to decide what to do. I could try apologizing to him, although I don't know what the heck I'd be apologizing *for*. Still, he was obviously upset yesterday. On the other hand, if I approach him out of the blue, I'll look like a stalker.

He made his dislike for me apparent.

While I waffle between walking right up to him or running for the hills, my eyes linger on his exposed arms and his calves. I don't know much about hockey, but I have noticed that in general they seem to have incredible legs from all that time spent on the ice. Anders, however, has an incredible *everything*.

Beneath all of the ink covering his skin, every visible part of his body is muscular. Bulked up gym bros aren't usually my type, but Anders isn't just chugging whey protein shakes. The way his muscles shift beneath the skin is mesmerizing, and once again, I'm reminded that the body is, in essence, a machine, and Anders spends most of his day fine-tuning that particular machine.

I wish he'd let me photograph him.

I wish he'd let me...

He turns his head sharply, as if he can feel my thirsty gaze like an unwanted caress. I freeze, caught in the act of ogling someone who doesn't welcome it.

I expect him to get upset again, like he did yesterday, but this time, he catches the tennis ball, lowers his racket, and saunters toward me. His swagger and knowing smile are anything but shy. Where was this attitude yesterday, when I was trying to get him to make love to the camera?

"Hey, Stella." He crosses his arms and gives me a once-over that makes my skin tingle. "Did you remember me this time?"

"Um, yeah. *Kiiiiiinda* hard to forget the guy who got upset and walked out on me yesterday." I try to smile and make a joke of the whole affair. "You're the one who was really worried I was gonna snap a picture of your... butt." *Oh my God, Stella, do not say 'dick' in front of this guy who you have somehow already offended.*

"Right." His shoulders droop a little. "From the photoshoot."

I hurry to correct my faux pas. "I'm not making fun of you. I totally get that there was a misunderstanding. I already emailed your publicist to explain what happened. There must have been a breakdown in the Venom front office."

"Yeah. Same." Anders uses his racket to bounce the tennis ball off the court a couple of times. "And I'm sorry that I was so rude. I was just, you know. Surprised." His eyes flick toward my face again.

"I'm really not sure how it got lost in translation. I don't suppose..." I probably shouldn't even ask, but desperate times and all that. "Is there any chance you'd be willing to do it again?"

His self-confident air makes a reappearance. "*Do it* again?" I can't tell if he's hitting on me, or if he genuinely doesn't understand the question, so I decide to play dumb.

"To reschedule the shoot? Now that you know what the project is all about?"

His smile falters again. "Wow, you're really desperate to take a picture of my... butt."

He's not wrong. Not that I'm personally invested in his... butt specifically, but I'm not willing to let this project die without a fight. Something about him intrigues me. It's almost like I've seen him before, but since I don't follow sports or any of the guys in the NHL, that can't be true.

Setting down my racket, I meet his gaze. "Look, I know you think I'm just being thick, but I truly don't understand the problem. You're a professional hockey player. You can't be ashamed of your body, or even terribly self-conscious. I watch television on occasion. They show you guys being interviewed while practically naked in the locker room after every game. Give me a break. I'm not trying to take graphic photos, I promise. That's not at all what my project is about."

Anders shakes his head. "You really don't know me at all."

I lift my chin. "Am I wrong?"

He exhales sharply. "Let's pretend that the team owner really is fine with all of this. I still wouldn't be comfortable with the project. It's not that I don't want to be naked, per se. I don't want to be naked in front of *you*."

I bite back a childish response—something along the lines of *Well, I guess if you feel that strongly about it, I don't want to see your naked... butt, either!*—and settle for offering him a tight smile. "The body is a masterpiece, and I'm trying to showcase that in my book. This is a passion project for me, and I can only have so many models back out before I'm in real trouble."

"Sure." Anders hoists his racket onto his shoulder, which makes the muscles in his arm and shoulder do all kinds of interesting things. Mechanical things. Artistic things. Definitely not sexy things. "One of the other guys on the team mentioned that he might be interested. I can ask him to email Finn if you're that anxious to find a replacement for me."

"Really?" I can hear the desperation in my own voice but screw it.

"Yeah. I mean, it doesn't have to be me, right? Just a professional athlete of some kind?" Anders seems almost hurt, which is silly, given how adamant he's been about not wanting to appear in the book. I eye him up and down like a puzzle I'm trying to solve because he must have his reasons.

Even if they're not readily apparent.

I wave him off. "No, totally. It's not like there's anything personal about this. If your teammate is built anything like you, he'll do just fine for what I'm after."

What a relief. Since the owner of Venom was willing to sign off on one of his players participating, I'm sure he'll be open to pivoting to someone else. And since Anders will have already warned his teammate what he's signing up for, there won't be any more inconvenient surprises.

My day starts to look up as I realize my project is going to move full steam ahead and this conversation isn't going nearly as poorly as I thought it would when I first saw Anders standing on the pavement. Honestly, this is the best possible outcome, and I feel a little bad that I had to bully the man into it.

"He doesn't look *that* much like me." Anders closes his eyes and shakes his head. "But yeah, I'm sure you won't have a problem with him. He's definitely not gonna be shy about stripping." He tilts his wrist so that the screen of his smartwatch turns on. "I gotta go. I have plans later."

He starts to step around me, but I reach out to catch his arm. The moment my skin brushes against his, something like an electric current pops between us. Probably just static, but it leaves my heart racing and my mind swirling.

"Thank you," I tell him. "Seriously. This project is really

important to me, and it means a lot that you would be willing to put me in touch with someone who's willing to finish the shoot so that I'm not left hanging."

He glances down to where my palm is still pressed against his bicep. A flash of something unexpected enters his gaze before he shutters it, and I'm left wondering if I imagined it.

"Yeah," he says. "No problem."

After he leaves, I stick around the tennis court for a little while, practicing my serve. I'm not particularly good at tennis, but now more than ever, I need to burn off my excess energy. For some reason, Anders Beck is particularly good at getting under my skin.

It's just nerves. You're worried about the book, and he's one of the things holding the project up. And yes, I did see him naked yesterday. And yes, he's blistering hot. But the only reason I keep thinking about the parts of his body that I *did* see is because of how long it's been since I hooked up with anyone. It's easy to get me all hot and bothered at the moment. A stiff breeze would probably do it.

When my one-sided match loses its appeal, I head back to the house. As I slip through the gate, Noah looks up from the giant grill beside the pool.

"Hey, Stella. You're coming to the party tonight, right?" he asks.

I squint. "There's a party? Goes to show how much Mom tells me."

"There's an MMA fight tonight, and I'm having a couple guys from the team over. You're more than welcome to join us. Might be fun to mingle a bit. Your mom tells me you talk to a lot of animals when you're on a shoot in parts unknown. Of course, some of my friends are only one step above that so..."

I nibble my bottom lip. "I don't know jack squat about

sports. Is MMA a wrestling thing?"

He opens the top of the grill. "Mixed martial arts." When I stare at him blankly, he adds, "Cage fighting."

I crinkle my nose. "And that's different from wrestling?"

"Yes, it's... different." Noah is evidently not prepared to lecture me on the different scenarios in which people choose to punch each other on a mat. "You don't have to watch the match. I'm sure a bunch of people will end up out here in the pool. God knows Molly doesn't want to watch."

I could use a little distraction tonight, but Noah is another one of the Venom players, and he almost certainly has invited at least some of the team tonight. "Will Anders be here?"

I don't like the knowing look on Noah's face. "Definitely."

I lean against the metal fence that runs around the pool. That's what he meant when he said he has plans. He has plans right here. "In that case, I might have to make myself scarce. After what happened—or didn't happen—at the photoshoot, I'm pretty sure he hates me."

"Pretty sure he doesn't," Noah counters. "Come hang out with us tonight. You two can talk things out once and for all. Once he settles down a little, I'm sure it will be fine. He's usually not so prickly."

That makes one of us, but since Noah and his family have been so good to my mother, I don't want to be rude. "Sure. I'm gonna go shower and change. Then you can put me to work helping with the setup."

If nothing else, maybe I will be able to meet the replacement model that Anders was talking about. Noah might be right about his friend not actively hating me, but he made it pretty clear today that he doesn't like me in the least.

And I'm not sure why that bothers me so much. After all, I don't even know the man.

CHAPTER SEVEN

Anders

I spend way too damn long in the shower.

When I caught Stella watching me today, I thought for sure that things had finally clicked. That she was going to fall into my arms and apologize for not recognizing me, and we could pick up where we left off.

But no, she wasn't thinking about *me*. She was thinking about *the book*.

The worst part was watching her light up about the fact that I could connect her with someone else. Picturing her and Marco in that little room, while he whips his junk out and squeezes his butt cheeks... ahem... biceps for her or whatever, makes me want to put my fist through a wall. What if he starts talking about milkmaids and then asks her to milk his dick? She's supposed to be *my* dream girl. She's supposed to be the one who got away, not the one who doesn't give a shit.

You don't own her, Anders. She was never yours in the first place. I take a few deep breaths and try to relax into the flow of the water, letting it wash away my frustration along with my sweat. *What's with all the territorial posturing?*

The fact that I still wish that things could be different between us can't be a good sign. I finally haul myself out of the shower, dry off, and stomp over to my closet. I'm tempted to pull out a pair of tight, gray sweatpants. Maybe then she'd remember me. Why was she even at the tennis court today? We're a pretty long way from the studio. What are the odds that we'd run into each other again?

Unless she was following me...

"Says the guy who's been pining after her for over half a decade," I grumble.

I'm being ridiculous. This is a waste of energy. I focus on getting dressed, put up my walls, steel my spine, then head down the street to Noah's place for the party.

When I knock on the door, Biscuit barks once, and then small feet patter across the floor. The door flies open, and Vivian's face appears in the gap. She's wearing a romper with a matching robe, along with a pair of boxing gloves. Beside her, the Cane Corso wags her tail in greeting, content with her lot in life even though she's wearing the doggy-appropriate version of Vivian's outfit. Biscuit's patience never ceases to amaze me.

"Unkie Anders!" Vivian laughs in delight as I scoop her up and swoop her around.

"Hey, princess!" One of these days, she's going to be too big for me to spin like this, but we're not there yet. I almost wish she could stay four forever. Then something pinches in the vicinity of my heart when I realize I'll probably never be a father to an amazing kid like this. "Did you miss me?"

"Of course!" Viv giggles as I set her down. "Look at Biscuit! She's a ring dog, but not like weddings. Like at fights!"

My gaze takes in Biscuit's silk robe with her front legs coming through the arm holes. "So I see. Are you two planning to put on a show?"

Viv gasps and presses her hands to her cheeks. "I would *never* hurt Biscuit! She's my bestest friend."

"I bet she could flatten you," I say. "Isn't that right, big girl?" I crouch down to tickle Biscuit under her chin, and her mouth falls open, letting the pink tip of her tongue droop out.

"I don't know." Vivian lifts her little fists between us. "I've been working on my high kicks."

"Let's see what you've got," I say.

Viv kicks her foot up in the air and almost falls over.

"Wow, that's pretty good!" I applaud her efforts, and Biscuit nudges my elbow with her nose to protest the fact that I've stopped petting her. "Are you going to start training now? With your killer moves, you could go pro."

"No." Vivian rights herself. "I like swimming better than fighting. I'm getting super-fast! I can show you later, but I'm not supposed to wear costumes in the pool. Unlike *somebody* who forgets she's a lady." She narrows her eyes at Biscuit.

Biscuit nudges my arm again, and I scratch her ruff a few times before standing up. "I'm going to go out back and find your dad, okay?"

"Okay!" After a quick hug, Vivian zips away toward the screen door, with the big dog hot on her heels. "Love you, Unkie Anders!"

Since I spent so much time sulking about Stella instead of getting ready, I'm a little late. Most of the guys are already here, and Molly's sitting with Francine and a couple of other women at the round table off to one side; I recognize Mona, Molly's employee at *The Last Chapter,* but I can't tell who the other woman is from behind.

Cash, Latham, Marco, and Noah are clustered around the grill with beers in their hands. A folding table covered in a festive themed plastic cloth and filled with appetizers stands nearby, with a cooler underneath.

"Hey, guys." I lift my hand in greeting as I amble over. "What did I miss?"

"We're teaching Marco about American cuisine," Latham says.

"He hates Kraft," Cash reminds me.

"You say picky like it is bad thing." Marco squints down at one of the plates. "But picky good, eh? In Stone Age, picky man is long-lived men. The not-picky ones, they eat bad meat, they die."

Latham rolls his eyes. "You are *not* gonna die from trying pigs-in-a-blanket, Marco."

Marco lifts a pastry-wrapped cocktail weenie between his thumb and forefinger. "Where pig? Where blanket? Every part of this name is lie."

"The bread is the blanket," Latham explains.

"And the sausage is the pig," Noah adds.

"Why?" Marco waves his free hand at the pastry again. "Do Americans put blankets on pigs? They are smart animals, *si*, but blankets will get dirty. Better to heat the barn."

I sigh. "What would *you* call it, then?"

Marco examines the appetizer from a few angles. "Be more honest. *Pork in tart.*"

Cash chokes and has to thump his chest a few times. Latham closes his eyes and shakes his head but he can't stop the smile from busting loose on his face. "What are you, four?" he asks Cash.

Cash shrugs. "Pretty damn funny."

Noah points his spatula at Marco. "Whatever you decide to call it, don't knock it until you've tried it."

"Alright, alright, I try." The Italian lifts the tip of the sausage delicately to his lips and makes a big show of taking the smallest possible bite. As he chews, his face contorts in disgust. "This what Americans call *sausage?* No pig in here, no pig at all. Only salt and chemicals. You all come to Italy with me next summer. I show you true food." He throws a chef's kiss into the air. "Like from the gods."

"It's great stuff, right?" Latham nods eagerly.

"It certainly stuff," Marco says, and with a bit of urging he pops the rest of it in his mouth.

"Yeah!" Latham pumps his arms in a victory dance. "You're getting more American by the day!"

"One of us!" Cash claps his hands in time to his chant, clearly too exhausted and not inspired to speak in complete sentences today.

There's only so much interaction with these idiots I can take, so I crouch down to root through the cooler in search of a beer. I'm not gonna be able to deal with both Marco and Latham without some adult beverage assistance. If nothing else, they've at least managed to take my mind off of Stella for a few minutes, which is a blessing. She's been taking up far too much space in my psyche the last few days, and I'm ready to move on.

What if you can't move on? What if you never find another woman who even comes close?

Pushing those bleak thoughts aside, I stand up and pop the cap off of my beer with the bottle opener on my keychain. As I lift the bottle to my lips, I happen to glance over to the tableful of ladies talking by the back door. At that moment, the mystery fourth woman turns her head to say something to Mona.

I may not have recognized her from behind, but in profile, I would know her anywhere.

Stella has apparently taken stalking to the next level, because somehow, she's at Noah's party. Like what the actual fuck? I don't see this woman for almost a decade and now I see her twice in one day?

I manage to slop about a third of the beer onto myself in my surprise, and I'm so taken aback, I don't even bother to curse about it.

Cash points at me. "Whoop, party foul."

I block the side of my face with my hand and crabwalk over

to where Noah is just now taking the burgers off the grill.

"She's here!" I hiss. "Why the fuck didn't you warn me?"

Unfortunately, the rest of the guys are still standing right there. "Who be where?" Marco asks, in a voice so loud that the neighbors can probably hear him halfway down the street. Celine Dion's probably gonna sing about it.

Kill me now. "The photography lady," I explain, hoping that Noah will pick up on the context. "*Stella.*"

The sonofabitch has the balls to nod, like this is no big deal. Nice of him to have my motherfucking back when the walls are closing in around me. This is what I get for making fun of him and Molly, especially him calling her his little tater tot. If karma's a bitch, she's coming for me.

He flicks his spatula toward the women. "Oh, yeah, Stella. Francine's daughter. She's staying with her mom in the guest house while she's in town working on a project, so I thought it might be nice to invite her to the party. Wait, are you telling me that *photo* Stella and *Francine's* Stella are the same person?" He lifts one hand to his chest, the way a Victorian lady would if someone scandalized her. Like he's searching for pearls to clutch. "*No.* That's *crazy.* What a *coincidence?*"

In an instant, I shift from wanting the Earth to swallow me whole to hoping it takes Noah instead. His clueless expression almost fools me, but his eyes... The eyes tell me he knows more than he's letting on.

I'm gonna kill him.

Dead.

From blood to ash.

"Oh, this is woman who wants to take pictures of your *testicoli.*" Marco adjusts himself, in case any of us missed his very subtle word choice. "I will go to her and offer services."

"Just say ballsack," Cash deadpans.

"Marco, wait..." I try to block him, but he slips around me and fucking *prances* over to where Stella's sitting.

"Marco's on the prowl," Latham chuckles. "And that new chick? She's hot AF. This should be interesting. I might have to take a go at her when he crashes and burns."

Noah flips a burger. "She's my houseguest, so watch yourself."

Cash shakes his head but makes no attempt to hide his gleeful smile. "Poor photographer lady."

While the two of them revel in the glorious awkwardness of Marco's posturing, I slam the lid on the grill and glare at Noah. "Can we have a word?"

Noah gestures toward the house, but going inside would mean walking right past the table. I shake my head and point him toward the gazebo at the back of the garden instead. Fortunately, the gazebo is far enough away that I can't hear whatever Marco is saying, which means they can't hear us, either. My eyes narrow at his facial expression and wild gesticulations toward a woman I still consider mine—even if she doesn't feel the same way. With annoyance, shame, and disappointment swirling in my gut, I turn my back to the group and glare at Noah.

"You did this on purpose," I growl. "Stella is *Stella*. My Stella. She's been living in your fucking house and you didn't tell me?"

Noah takes a casual sip of his beer. "Funny," he says, "she didn't mention that she knew you until after the photoshoot. How was I supposed to realize that she was the same Stella from Costa Rica when she didn't mention ever going there? And she definitely didn't mention that she had met you twice." He taps one finger against the side of his face. "It's almost like she didn't recognize you. And if she wasn't able to put two and two together, why would you think that I would?"

"*Noah.*" I can't stop myself from whining. "What did you say to her?"

He lifts one shoulder and then lets it drop. "Not a thing."

I glare at him and try to work out if he's yanking my chain again.

Finally, he heaves a sigh. "Seriously, dude, *nothing.* I'm not trying to play matchmaker here. All I'm saying is that the two of you should talk. *Really* talk. It's like the blind leading the fucking blind here. Just take the blinders *off.*"

I bend my neck to try and crack away the pressure, but it doesn't move. "But she doesn't *remember me.* How can I possibly get over that?"

Noah pinches the bridge of his nose between two fingers. "Did you hear a word I just said, Anders? Why does it matter if she recognizes you right away? I wouldn't remember half the people I knew back in college on sight now. What do you lose by saying, *Hey, we met in Costa Rica seven years ago. Remember?* Maybe she does and maybe she doesn't. But if you confront it straight on, at least you'll know and you won't spend the rest of your life in a state of perpetual anger at everyone around you. You're gonna have to learn to coexist with Stella. She's Francine's daughter and Francine is family. Molly and I talked about this and we both agreed we shouldn't get involved, hence I chose not to tell you what I feel was not my information to share. She probably won't be here much, but with Francine starting to have health problems... Look, I'm not saying that you have to lay it all on the line, but—" He cuts off suddenly, and then adds, "It might be good for both of you. Enough said."

"*Enough said?*" I press my cold beer bottle to the back of my neck. God, I'm sweating like a pig in a blanket, or in Marco's case, a pork in a tart. "You make it sound so easy. But it's not like you and Molly; you two were so stubborn but at least you both *cared* about each other. For me, it's one-sided! And what if she doesn't remember me at all?" I slap my hand against my forehead as a jolt of humiliation overtakes me. "God, I can't take it anymore."

"Anders," Noah says in that soothing Goalie voice of his, but I refuse to be calmed, dammit.

My gaze locks with his. "And if she does, then what? Like at what point do I launch into this nutso confession about how I've spent the last few years..."

"Anders."

"...wondering if we'll ever cross paths again..."

"Anders."

"It was a magical experience, and I'm the only one who cares!" I bellow.

Noah stares at me as I stand there, panting like I just ran a marathon. He takes a long pull of his beer. "Are you done now?" he asks.

"Yeah." I rub my palm over the wet spot on my shirt from where I spilled my drink earlier. "I just don't understand how she could forget me."

"Well, why don't we ask her?" Noah uses the mouth of his bottle to point over my shoulder. "Stella, any input?"

A faint squeak emerges from behind me, and I turn on the spot to find Stella at the foot of the steps leading up to the gazebo staring at me like I'm a crazy person who just yelled the neighborhood down.

"Oh my God," she breathes, and this time, she's not just eyeing me up. She's pale and shaky, like she's just seen a ghost.

Our gazes snap together.

Then hers sweeps my body.

Her knees buckle, and she puts her hand on the wooden banister to steady herself.

Turns out, I was wrong. Apparently she remembers just fine, but instead of falling into my arms, she sways up the steps and all but collapses onto the bench around the edge of the gazebo.

Her obvious shock doesn't even begin to ease the ache in my chest because I've spent too many years pushing in the wrong direction.

When she's seated, she lifts her pale face to meet my eyes. "It's you. The guy from the waterfall. *Blaze.*"

CHAPTER EIGHT

Stella

My hair is absolutely going to catch on fire. My head might explode. I press my hands to my cheeks in hopes of containing the fallout.

Anders is Blaze. Blaze is Anders.

Back in Costa Rica, I never did ask for his last name. Like doing that would cheapen the most romantic moment of my life. I wanted to keep some mystery wrapped around it and weave that into my heart. And somehow, I didn't recognize him. Humiliation around that faux pas seeps into every pore.

No wonder he hates me.

"Hey, Stella." Anders takes a swig of his beer and doesn't meet my eyes.

"You've changed," I blurt, unable to bite back the words. "In a good way. I mean, you were hot back then, but now you're all man."

Noah chokes on his drink and backs away. "I think Molly might need me... elsewhere." He's enough of a gentleman to hold back his laughter until he's halfway down the walkway to the pool.

"This is so mortifying," I murmur. "No *wonder* you were so upset yesterday. And this morning..." A couple more pieces fall into place, little comments he made on the court. *Did you remember me this time?*

"Yeah, well." Anders fidgets and stays standing. "It's probably nothing unusual for you, right? You travel all over the world to lots of exotic locations."

I'm going to be sick. My stomach pitches and churns as runaway nausea bubbles up the back of my throat. Once I taste the bile, I rise on wobbly legs but almost fall down again.

"I should go," I say, launching myself toward the steps.

Anders winces. "Sorry, this is just... it's a lot to process. I'm not saying what I mean. Noah's right. We should talk. Clear the air. I mean... if you're okay with that."

I wrap my arms around myself as I try to calm my erratic breathing. "Are you sure that's a good idea? You must... you must... despise me."

"Nah, it was an honest mistake. Aren't you staying in the guest house? Noah made it very clear that he considers your mom family. You'll be here now and maybe in the future. A lot of the guys live in this neighborhood, and I'm within walking distance. We're going to run into each other. Besides, I've been in the guest house and there's not a waterfall in sight. You'll be safe."

I laugh a little too loudly. "Okay, yeah. Let's go inside." At least we're less likely to be walked in on if we're someplace a little more private. I don't want to have to explain this to my mom. I'm already going to have to live with the fact that Noah's in the loop. Ugh, that smile he gave me when I asked about Anders earlier. He totally figured it out even before I did, and I'm the one who spent two days being intimate with the man! Lord only knows how much Anders has told him, or what he thinks of me. Probably that I spend my life wandering around the world hooking up with hot strangers in waterfalls like on a regular basis.

When the truth is... not so much.

Anders remains silent as he follows me into the guest house. For all I know, Noah's going to think that we're using his property as a love shack. Since he's been so kind to my mom and now to me, I'll have to explain things to him later. The moment the front door closes behind me, I'm faced with a new concern. I'm alone in a quiet house with Anders Beck, who also happens to be the man I've always dreamed of meeting again.

The man who made me feel things.

Want things.

I spent so long hoping we'd cross paths again, and now that we have, I've completely blown it.

The guest cottage isn't large. There's only a small living room, a bedroom, and a bathroom. Mom spends most of the time in the main house, but she keeps this place nice and cozy. At the moment the living room is crammed with my stuff, since I'm staying on the pullout sofa-bed for the time being. Fortunately, I've been diligent about tidying up the bed every morning, so it's back in couch form at the moment. Anders and I sit down on opposite ends, putting as much space between us as possible.

"For what it's worth," I tell him, "there might be a lot of waterfalls in the jungle, but that's the only one where I... where anything like that has happened."

"Yeah?" Anders lifts an eyebrow. "Kinda hard to believe. The way you jumped right in and all."

"How many times have *you* done something like that?" I demand.

"Hook up? Maybe more than once." He shifts a little closer to me. "Like *that*? Just the once."

"Oh, right, because it was a *magical experience*," I argue, even though it was. At least for me.

He sets his beer on the side table. "I can't believe you heard all that."

I tug my lower lip between my teeth as my gaze sweeps his

body from his full beard to his new ink to his muscles upon muscles. He looks nothing like the youthful Blaze who stole my heart that special trip, but when I look deeply into his eyes, I can still see a sliver of the boy he was before.

And I realize I want to get to know the man he is now.

Déjà vu hits me in the feels, taking me right back to Costa Rica. To that waterfall. To him. I try to shake it off, but I can't. "I take it that means that you still think about it sometimes."

"Sometimes." He twists to throw one arm over the back of the couch, so that he's facing in my general direction. "It was kind of a unique experience. Do you ever think about it?"

"Once or twice." It's a gross under-exaggeration, but I can't very well tell him, *It was my peak sexual experience,* given that I hadn't recognized him. I sure as hell can't tell him that I think about him in my lonely bed every night. That I see his face every time I pleasure myself.

That I spent too much time thinking about what could have been—why I didn't get his name and number—why I pretended it was all just a college fling that could never turn into something more so it would be better to just let the past stay in the past and cherish the memories instead.

God, I can't believe that I found Blaze again, and I didn't know him on sight. I assumed that if we crossed paths again, I'd recognize him instantly. Although, given how my body responded when I touched his arm on the court this morning, my body remembered everything, even if my brain got confused by his mature new look.

He's a man now. All man. And his cool expression contradicts the heat rolling off his huge body in waves.

We're both silent for a minute, processing the conversation. I start squirming around—I don't do much better with awkward pauses than with living in one place too long.

"How come you told me that your name was Blaze?" I ask.

"Back in college, I always went by my nickname," he explains. "It sounded cooler. I thought it would help me get drafted higher."

"You thought *Blaze* was cool?" I ask. "It sounds like what a six-year-old girl would name her pet pony."

Anders slaps one hand to his chest. "Ouch. That hurts. Especially because all my friends used to tell me that *Anders* sounds like an old-man name."

"I like *Anders*. It's unique." I turn to face him, curling my legs between us.

"I didn't want to be unique. I wanted to be *cool*." He tosses his hair like he's in a shampoo commercial. "I'm known for my super-fast skating, and I wanted to sound speedy."

"You were a conformist!" I exclaim. "This explains so much. Hang on, did you even *like* birds?"

"I may have exaggerated how much I cared about birding," he admits. "But I wasn't exaggerating about my fascination with the *girl* doing the birding."

I rest my head on my arm. I know so little about him, and I've spent a lot of time imagining what happened to him after the week ended. I've also spent a lot of time imagining his face between my thighs. Now I can finally fill in the blanks. "Why? To get laid?"

"To get close to you." His eyes sparkle. "*Bird Girl*. I noticed you long before I ever spoke to you. I spent half my spring break moping around and salivating. My friends gave me so much shit about you."

"Are these the same friends who convinced you that Blaze was a cool nickname?" I ask. "Instead of the more obvious choice... Roadrunner?"

"On behalf of the Blazes of the world, it *is* a pretty sweet name. And I didn't just want to get laid." His eyes meet mine. For a heartbeat, it's like no time has passed between us. "I really liked you, Stella. I wanted to talk to you again, to get your number so we could stay in touch, but you didn't show. You didn't really even say goodbye."

"I was up late photographing the sea turtles hatching. It was *amazing*, by the way." At the risk of giving away how much I've thought about him, I decide to come clean. "I was upset when I realized that you were gone, so I tried to look you up a few times, but that didn't work. Obviously, since I was looking for a guy from Minnesota named *Blaze* and not a guy from Las Vegas named Anders. And without a last name..."

"You looked for me?" He reaches out to lay a hand on my knee. I stare at his skin on mine as heat flares anew. Only a small twitch of his lips gives him away. "Seriously?"

All my breath catches in my throat, but then I admit, "Of course. What we shared wasn't just a fling. At least not to me."

The warmth of his hand radiates out along my thigh, spreading higher until it pools low in my belly. It's a good thing we're in my mom's guesthouse, because waterfall or not, my body remembers his touch. I've spent years trying to tell myself that the place was what made the experience so special: the rush of the water, the cool droplets against my fevered skin, the remote location, the stunning views, the magical mist that seemed to distort reality. If I could find someone else I truly desired, we could recreate that thrill, maybe even surpass it.

Judging by how I'm responding to him, that's only part of the story. I realize with a start that I'd rather have Anders right here on this lumpy couch than any of my exes anywhere else on Earth.

Careful, Stella.

If we hook up again, I'm going to have expectations, and

apparently, so will he. As mature adults, it would be a lot more than causal sex for both of us, and I'm not ready to go there no matter how fierce the temptation. With that in mind, I force myself to remain perfectly still, even though I'm tempted to slide his hand higher so that he can feel for himself how his touch affects me.

"For what it's worth, I played college hockey in Minnesota, so I wasn't lying. And I looked for you, too," he says. "But I couldn't find Stella from Costa Rica. And I guess you go by S.J. Croft now?"

"It's the name I work under." I shrug. "Sometimes it's hard for women to break into the art world, and using your initials can make things a little smoother by not inviting judgment before possible clients even take the time to review your work."

"What would you have said? I mean... if you'd found me?" Even though I've tried not to encourage him, Anders is suddenly much closer than he was a moment ago. He shifts forward, closing the gap between us, and only then do I realize that I, too, am drifting. My nipples tighten, aching for his touch, and my lips part in anticipation of his tongue slipping between them. We're not even kissing yet, and I'm already itching to slip my hands under his shirt and feel for myself just how taut his muscles are and how much he's changed over the years.

A lot has transformed along the terrain of his body, and I want to wander every path.

I'm not like this, I swear, I want to tell him, but apparently I am when it's *him.*

"I would have asked you if you wanted to stay in touch," I mumble. My eyes bounce from his eyes to his lips.

"I would have said yes." His hand is on my thigh now, his mouth only inches away from mine. There's something both tender and feral in his expression. I remember the hunger in his eyes from that day in Costa Rica like he wanted to devour my body, but the affection is new.

How much has he thought about our time together, really? Did it all come rushing back when he saw me in Eli's studio? Or did he fantasize about me as much as I did about him over the years?

"And now?" I ask, my tongue darting out to moisten my lower lip. I hold my next inhale as he stares. "Do you still want to stay—?"

"In touch?" His other hand settles onto my cheek. "God, yes, Stella. I want to pick up right where we left off. Please tell me I'm not the only one who feels this crazy... God, I can't even explain what the fuck it even is!"

"It isn't crazy at all," I murmur, leaning into his touch. "I missed you, Blaze."

He laughs softly as he leans in to kiss me, and this time when our lips meet, there's more than a spark. It's as if I've been struck by lightning. It's stronger. Bigger. It fills the room and then overflows.

Time stops, and the only thing that matters is his mouth, and my mouth, and our hands, and the heat of his skin against my palms. Since we were together, I haven't gotten off with a guy. Thank God for vibrators, especially the waterproof kind. I've wasted more water than I care to think about standing in the shower, gripping the safety bar for dear life as I try to put myself back in that grotto, with this man who made it look easy.

My body remembers, and it craves that sweet release. I want his fingers to do to my body what his tongue is doing to my mouth. I want him to pull me into his lap and fuck me until I can't see straight. And I want him to keep doing it, not just today—maybe even forever.

My body screams at me to accelerate even as my brain warns me to pump the breaks.

You can't be with him, Stella. Sex doesn't make a relationship, and you're only in Vegas until you finish this new book. You're not going to give up your career to be with someone, no matter how good he makes you feel. And he's not going to give up professional hockey and you would never ask him to!

Fair enough, my body replies, *but we can have him right now.*

I'm on the verge of making some very questionable choices when the front door opens and my mother steps through. Anders and I jump apart to opposite ends of the couch.

"Hi, Mom," I say, trying to play this off casually. "How's the cage fight?"

"Not nearly as interesting as what's going on in here," she says. "Should I go, or...?"

Anders gets to his feet, taking his beer with him. "No, I should get back. Noah's gonna think I disappeared and then Latham will start riding me." He keeps his head down as he shuffles past her and opens the door. Before he steps out, he turns back to me, and his face lights up in a dazzling smile. It's somewhat hidden by the full beard he's rocking, but I know what he looks like underneath it. "See you later, Stella. Let's... keep in touch."

"Bye," I squeak as the door shuts.

"Well, well." Mom strokes her chin as she stares at the door. "Isn't *this* an interesting development?"

"*Mom*," I groan. "Please don't make me feel even worse."

"What?" She shrugs but her eyes twinkle with renewed vitality. "Honey, if you think I'm *not* going to tease you about the guys you like, you don't understand motherhood at all." She sits down on the side of the couch Anders just vacated. "I raised you, so it's only fair that I get to live vicariously through you from time to time. That's Anders Beck, Noah's best friend since high school. So, what did I miss?"

I pause. "It's personal."

Mom sticks out her bottom lip. "I'm sick, and you're really going to keep secrets from me? What if I drop dead tomorrow, and I go to my grave with no idea if my daughter is going to spend the rest of her life alone..."

"Okay, okay, enough with the guilt trip." I straighten my slightly rumpled clothing. "So, uh, remember when I mentioned that I met someone on that trip to Costa Rica back in college?" I didn't reveal *all* the grisly details of our fling, but after graduation Mom and I celebrated with a couple pitchers of margaritas, and we both ended up oversharing, so she knows more than she should.

"Of course," she says. "What was his name, Bolt?"

"Blaze," I correct. "Blaze Beck, also known as Anders."

"Ooh!" Mom's eyes widen, and she claps her hands together in delight. "Juicy! You two have a sordid past. That's wonderful! Totally has my stamp of approval. Are you going to start dating?"

I slump back against the cushions. "I don't know, Mom. We just opened the door but only a crack."

"All the more reason to strike while the iron is hot!" Mom slaps her palm against her thigh for emphasis. "Ask him out to lunch. Ask him to give you a tour of Vegas. Go out for cocktails! It's *Sin* City, Stella. The sky's the limit!"

My mind flashes with lurid images of all the filthy things I could get up to in Sin City with Anders Beck. And my body quickly follows. But since it's my mother sitting in front of me now, I tamp it all down.

My sigh is heavy, and Mom is good at reading between the lines. "I dunno, Mom. I kind of messed things up the other day."

She smirks and pats the seat of the couch. "Judging by what I just interrupted, I'd say he forgives you. Go on, Stella, live a little. And then maybe you won't want to leave again. You need a reason to stay besides me. If you only stay in Vegas to look after me, the guilt will eat me alive."

She almost convinces me, but with those words, I snap back to reality. "It's too complicated. I don't want to get his hopes up." Or mine. "Besides, I don't date. My career doesn't allow me to. No man wants to traipse around the world after a woman. Not if he has his own thing going on."

"Put on your big girl pants. The daughter I raised can do anything. She's fearless. Besides, you like him more than you've ever liked a man before. A mother knows these things."

In the face of her enthusiasm, I dig in my heels. "I'm not going to rush into anything. If he makes the first move, I'll think about it. Either way, I'll play nice, I promise. Out of respect for you and Noah and Molly."

"Oh, is that what you kids are calling it these days, playing nice?" Mom gets up again. "Whatever you say, Stella, but don't blame me if you wait too long and you two lose track of each other again. Lightning rarely strikes twice."

To my great annoyance, she has a point. I've spent years thinking about this guy, only to have him fall into my lap a second time.

Is it a sign from the Universe?

Maybe she's right. Instead of worrying about all the ways this could go wrong, I should open myself to the possibility that they could go *right*.

CHAPTER NINE

Anders

It's probably crazy, but I don't care. I spend the whole MMA fight thinking about it, to the point where I completely miss the action. Everyone else is cheering and booing and yelling their heads off—even Mona, Molly's store manager, gets into the spirit of things albeit in a monotone type of way—but all I'm doing is amping myself up for the conversation I'm going to have before I leave.

I'm going to do it.

I'm going to ask Stella on a date.

You only live once.

"This is exhausting," Marco says when the fight wraps up. "So much food, adrenaline, so much yelling... is very tiresome."

"*Tiring*," Latham corrects. "*Tiresome* would mean you were bored."

"This another thing I do not understand." Marco shakes his head. "English has so many words that are the same but mean differences. I cannot always keep straight."

"Hey, your English is a hell of a lot better than my Italian," Latham says. "Stick with us, we'll make an American out of you yet. You're already doing way better and it hasn't even been six months."

Marco frowns in thought. "I do not know. America has been good to me, but then I eat your pizza and your cheese dust and your pig blankets and your terrible coffee, and I am not so sure I want to give up Italy."

"What's wrong with the coffee?" Noah asks.

Marco twists his lips. "It because of this coffee shop, with the mermaid, who sells coffee so big."

Cash shakes his head. "Lay off Starbies."

Marco sighs. "Listen, when I come to America, I see your coffees and I think, *Ah, Americans, they are so bold! To drink this much coffee, they must be very busy. Have so much energy. Nothing can stop them.* But then I taste it, and, *pah.*" Marco pretends to spit something out. "I still not understand how you can drink this much. Is like wet dirt! Like... what do you call when you have scraps from kitchen, and you throw them outside to make new dirt?"

"You mean compost?" Cash asks.

He claps his hands together. "Yes, yes. Is like compost, but soup. No coffee! No goodness! Now I see why America is sometimes sad, because you pay so much for *this* and think it best."

"He kinda has a point," Mona says, staring at her black nail polish.

They start squabbling about what makes a good coffee, and while they're distracted, I get up and act like I'm headed to the bathroom. The moment I'm out of sight, however, I change directions and head out back.

As the sun started to dip below the horizon, Molly turned the back lights on, and the pool is lit up, too. Molly and Francine are drinking ciders with their feet up, while Stella sits on the edge of the pool, watching Viv swim in circles with her floaties. Biscuit lies next to the poolside, apparently asleep, but I know that if anything happened to Viv, she'd be on her feet in an instant all teeth and snarls, ready to save the day.

As I approach Stella, Francine catches my eye. Instead of glaring daggers at me, however, she lifts her bottle in a toast.

Apparently, I have Francine's blessing to ask her daughter out.

I sit down beside Stella and kick off my flip-flops, dipping my feet in the water. "Hello again."

"Hey." She tucks her hair behind one ear and looks up at me from under her eyelashes. "How was the game?"

"The match, you mean?" I grin. "No idea. For some reason, I was a little distracted." I brace my hands against the pool deck, and my left pinkie brushes hers. I pause while my next inhale creeps into my lungs. "So, I was thinking. You're gonna be in town for a while so you can finish your book, right?"

"Yeah, I should be around for a couple of months." Her finger twitches, as if she wants to take my hand and has just barely stopped herself from doing so. My heart breaks into a gallop when I hear her little pants of breath. Something tightens in my chest—something I'm not ready to feel. "So we should figure out how to coexist peacefully in the meantime, don't you think?"

I nod. "Then you should get yourself reacquainted with Vegas while you're here. Do some of the touristy stuff, you know?"

"Like what? Go to the Strip?" She shakes her head. "No, thanks. It's not my kind of place."

"How about something a little more photogenic, then? Have you ever been to the Neon Boneyard?"

Stella shakes her head. "I've heard of it, but I've never been. It's where they put all the old signs, right?"

"Yup. It's pretty cool. Lots of photo-ops." The itch to say something reckless bubbles just below the surface, clawing at me to let the words bust loose. *Play it cool, Anders.* "I could take you sometime, if you want."

"O-oh." Stella stutters on her answer and falls silent.

She's going to say no. She's trying to let me down easy. She doesn't even want to use me for sex this time. I swing my feet back and forth in the water, and I'm unspeakably grateful when Vivian comes to the rescue.

"Unkie Anders!" she calls from the far end of the pool. "Wanna see how fast I can swim? It's even better than my high kick!"

"All right. I'll time you." I pull out my phone and open the stopwatch feature. "Are you ready? On the count of three. One... two..."

"Three!" Viv hollers and pushes off the side of the pool. Dammit, she's too cute. Her course is a little erratic, but for a kid her age, her form is actually quite good. I'm sure that she and Noah have spent hours out here swimming around. He's such a good dad, even though Vivian came into his life under such awful circumstances.

Sometimes—not very often—I'm jealous of Noah. Not just because he has a family, but because they all get along so well. It's not like my family and I don't get along, but we're not close. I'm a kid from the wrong side of the tracks. A little rough around the edges and I haven't been able to shake that off no matter how much money I make in the NHL. Molly and Noah are so perfect for each other. I know that he's got a couple of years on me, but when I think about it too hard, it starts to feel like Noah's managed to put his whole life in order, and I'm lagging miles behind.

And now Stella's going to shoot me down, and I'll be back at square one, holding my heart in my hands.

Viv reaches our end of the pool, and Stella applauds while I stop the clock.

"Impressive!" I exclaim. "Sixteen-point-one seconds."

"Time me again!" she insists and takes off for the other side. "I can beat my own record. I know I can!"

When her head pops up on the far end, I shout, "Fourteen-point-eight!"

Vivian yelps and waves her arms around in a victory dance, which Biscuit misinterprets as a medical emergency. In an instant, the dog is on her feet and hurtling face-first into the pool. She hits the water with a splash that sends a tidal wave of pool water up over the deck.

"Biscuit!" Vivian screams. "You got water in my eyes!"

The dog swims to her side, and the two start playing around, distracting Viv from her race against herself.

Stella bursts out laughing, and I can't stop myself from staring at her from the corner of my eye. The way the waning light casts shadows on the planes of her face. The way the soft wind ruffles her silky hair. The way her eyes sparkle when she laughs full on. That was one thing I never got to experience with her years ago. But I am now. My heart squeezes in my chest. She's so beautiful, it isn't fair.

"Anders." She turns toward me, still smiling. "Let's get something straight. I'm not going to be in Vegas forever. I'm not sure about going on a *date* with you, but I'd be more than happy to spend some time getting to know each other better for the sake of our friends and family. If you're okay with that, then so am I."

"Yeah." I let out a sigh of relief. "That's all I'm asking. We kind of skipped the *getting to know each other* part in Costa Rica. It wouldn't be a bad idea to circle back around."

"We should exchange numbers," she says.

I hold my phone out toward her, and she enters her number, then sends herself a text from my messages. A second later, her phone chimes from her back pocket. "There. Now we can plan a night that works for us both since I know you're often on road trips for days a time. Maybe we could get some dinner, too? I don't know the Vegas food scene these days."

"I can recommend a couple of places." I take my phone back. "I'll text you tomorrow?"

Her fingers trail through the water. "Sounds good."

Molly appears on Stella's far side and sits down, still clutching a sweating bottle of hard cider. "Hey, while I have you two here, do you mind if I join you?"

"Not at all," Stella says. She leans back so that we can all see each other more easily. This all feels like a dream. Not just finding Stella again, but the fact that she's already friends with *my* chosen family. It would be so easy to get comfortable with this arrangement. Let it percolate naturally despite her warning that this can only last until she's ready to head off to her next project.

She's already warned me off her—told me she's leaving me. I'm not sure why it hurts so damn much to even consider why she needs to be proactive about not being with me.

"Christmas Eve is coming up," Molly says. "And I'm hosting a Christmas Eve get-together for all the single players and people who don't have family plans."

"For the strays, you mean?" Stella teases.

"I didn't say that." Molly giggles. "But it was strongly implied. Anyway, this is going to be my first time organizing a big event like this for our friends, and it would mean a lot to me if you'd both come."

"Of course," I say at once. "Let me know if you need anything. I'm always happy to help."

"That sounds like fun," Stella agrees. "Anders and I are going to spend some time together before that, so it'll be nice to know someone else at the party besides my mother." She shifts her weight and moves her hands to support herself. As she does so, several of her fingers come to rest over mine. "It's a little weird to have friends, actually. I'm so used to not putting down roots anywhere."

"Nice-weird, I hope," Molly says, raising her eyebrows in question.

Stella turns her head to meet my eyes for a fraction of a second. "Nice-weird," she agrees, and my heart skips a beat.

If I only get a couple months of this, I'm determined to enjoy it to the fullest. When she says goodbye, my heart will shatter again, but I'm not even going to think about it until it happens.

Because after finding Stella again, I think I might believe in miracles.

CHAPTER TEN

Stella

Anders and I set a date for a few days after the MMA party, and I agree to swing by his place at six o'clock. I'll be walking over, so that we can take an Uber. Apparently, the place where he made our dinner reservations serves amazing cocktails and I'm okay with indulging a little.

"Well, look at this." Mom corners me as I step out of the bathroom. "A new dress. Makeup. *Jewelry*. Who are you, and what have you done with my daughter?"

I fuss with my hair. "It's not like you've never seen me dressed up before. And I didn't buy the dress for this occasion. I picked it up when I first came back to town. I figured I should have some nice clothes for photoshoots and meetings with my agent."

"Mmmhmm." Mom gestures for me to spin in a circle, and I reluctantly obey. "Lovely. And that color suits you."

She touches the sleeve of my red dress. It's not so vibrantly red that I'll stand out in a crowd, especially not in Vegas. Instead, the color is a little muted. Darker. More like crimson. I don't get to wear stuff like this when I'm on location, but the moment I tried it on at the boutique, I knew that I wanted to wear it again.

I sweep her into my arms for a quick hug. "I like red. It's my favorite color."

"Anders will appreciate it," Mom says, nodding to the V of the neckline.

I immediately wrap my arm over my chest. "It's not that revealing!"

"No, dear, it's very tasteful." She kisses my cheek. "Have fun tonight, and text me if you plan to stay out until morning, so that I don't worry."

"I can't believe my own mom is trying to pimp me out," I grumble, but I kiss her cheek before I leave. I guess I should be grateful that she treats me like an adult at my age and not a teenager. I am in her house after all, and she wouldn't be out of bounds to give me a curfew and other boundaries. And with her health, I don't want to pile more stress on her by staying out until all hours.

Anders' house is just a short walk, even closer than the tennis court. He's already outside when I show up, standing on the sidewalk next to a rideshare.

"Stella, you look amazing." The way his eyes travel over me makes me blush almost as red as the dress. When he helps me into the backseat of the car, his hand lingers on the small of my back.

A feeling hits my core. It's the one I used to have but thought I lost so long ago.

Resurrected.

His touch electrifies me, brighter than all the neon lights of the Strip.

That's when I know that I'm in trouble.

* * *

I expected that we'd have dinner at some upscale, exclusive restaurant in one of the luxurious resorts, not because I particularly *wanted* to go someplace like that, but because in my experience, that's how most guys with money operate. Anders finds every possible excuse to brush against me, so assuming that he's taken my warning to heart, he isn't seeing this as a date so much as foreplay.

In short, I'd expected a flex of some kind, but instead, he leads me to a little hole-in-the-wall restaurant far away from the main drag.

"I hope you like Brazilian food," he says.

"Because it was the closest thing you could find to Costa Rican fare?" I tease.

He lays his hand on the small of my back again, and my knees wobble. "Not specifically. I'm showing you the best of what Vegas has to offer, remember? And this place is one of my favorites. I come here a lot with the guys."

Under his guidance, we order a sampler for two and a couple of the restaurant's signature cocktails. As we eat our way through a variety of slow-cooked meats, we do exactly what we had planned to do: get to know each other.

"Where-all have you traveled?" Anders asks.

"I've been to forty-three countries so far," I tell him. "You should see my passport. Do you want the list?"

He whistles. "I'll settle for a top five."

"If you'll accept territories, Bonaire makes the list. I got some incredible underwater pictures there. The reefs are *stunning*." I consider my next answer as I cut a piece of unbelievably succulent beef. "Indonesia, but the flight's a killer. New Zealand..."

He rattles the ice in his glass. "Is everything poisonous there, too?"

"No, it's basically the nerfed version of Australia, so the endemic species are a little less venomous as a rule. But the landscape is incredible. Some of my favorite pictures I've ever taken are from Ghana, and for number five..." I sip my drink and smile at him over the rim of the glass. I remember why I liked him so much back then. Why we had such an amazing connection. He actually listens to a woman. "Costa Rica."

"For the birds?" His hand inches across the table toward mine.

"No," I tell him. "For the turtles."

He laughs so loudly that people at the other tables turn to look.

Leaning back, he admits, "Even though I travel a lot for hockey, that's work. I've never really been many exciting places. Nothing like you."

I take a sip of my drink. "Good thing I love to travel and check out new places."

When we're finished, Anders pays the tab, and we catch another ride over to the Neon Boneyard. Whenever people described it, I pictured a giant pile of junk. I don't care much about neon signs, so why would I care about them when the lights don't even work anymore?

As we wander through the rows of defunct signs, however, I can see why people come here. There's something a little bit sad about walking through signs from the past, like visiting a dinosaur display at the Met. It's history. It's nostalgic.

It makes me feel things just like any other form of art.

"This isn't depressing, is it?" Anders asks when we stop in front of a tall display that wouldn't be out of place in a production of Aladdin. The words at the top read, *Lost Vegas*.

"Not really. It makes me think about what Vegas will be like if nature ever takes over again. Can you imagine the archaeologists of the future digging this up?"

"You mean when humans disappear?" Anders chuckles. "And you're saying that's *not* depressing?"

I shake my head. "We wouldn't have to disappear. There are plenty of cities that have come and gone in the time since humans started building them. Like Machu Picchu, or Angkor Wat. Even Vegas won't last forever. Seeing all this is like looking at the past and the future at the same time. It'll all end up like this. We have to enjoy things while they last. Change always steals everything away in the end."

Am I talking about me and him?

"You've got an unusual way of looking at things," Anders says.

"Good-unusual?" I ask, echoing Molly's question from the other night.

"Definitely. Refreshing." He takes my hand, and exactly at that moment, all the display lights in the Neon Boneyard flicker on, as if our touch alone was enough to bring all these old dead dinosaurs back to life.

Anders leans over me. "Do you wanna get out of here?"

I tug the collar of his shirt, and he bends willingly, brushing the softest of kisses against my lips. Even with that small contact, my whole body hums with energy.

"Definitely," I whisper. "All in the name of enjoying things while they last."

There's no point in fighting it. Ever since he eyefucked me on his sidewalk, I've known how tonight was going to end.

* * *

Before the front door of Anders' house shuts behind us, our mouths smash together.

"That car ride," Anders says between kisses, "was... excruciating. I have a flagpole in my pants."

I wrap my arms around his neck and pull him against me as our ride's engine rumbles outside. Anders kicks the door shut, never breaking contact.

"I know," I say, even as I untuck his dress shirt from his

slacks. My hands roam over the muscles of his back, following the dip of his spine upward. He moans against my mouth and stumbles toward the wall of the living room, catching himself with one hand so that I'm pinned against him.

One hand dips low again so that I can tug on the buckle of his belt.

"Stella," he groans. "*Bedroom*."

I shake my head, and my hair tumbles free around my shoulders. "Uh uh. Can't wait that long."

He groans deep in his throat. "The bedroom is literally *just up the stairs*."

I only had one drink hours ago, but I feel inebriated, dizzy with kisses and the promise of genuine satisfaction after almost a decade waiting for some random man to fill the hole he left inside me. I press my palm alongside his zipper, caressing his erection through the fabric. I talk slower this time, so there's no chance he'll misunderstand what I'm saying.

"Anders. *I. Can't. Wait.*"

He sucks in a breath and nods. "Fuck, Stella. Okay. Anything you want."

I tug his belt again. "I want it like before. Just like before. God, I hope you remember."

He lowers his head to kiss my neck. "That'll be a trick, since I'm not hiding a waterfall in my living room." His voice is low and husky and filled with all the promises I want to hear but he's never actually said.

"Not the place," I say, tripping over my own words in my desperation to make him understand. "Not the *waterfall*. The *man*. I want you, Anders, right now, just like you were with me then. You... I mean, it's kind of always been you."

His breath is hot on my collarbone. "Ask and you shall receive."

The next thing I know, his hands are behind me, lifting my dress so that he can push my panties down my thighs. I unbuckle his belt with shaking fingers and pull his cock free from his fly. The sound he makes when I wrap my hand around him goes straight to my needy core.

Anders hisses in a breath as his fingers hover ever so close to where I want them most. "How long have you been wet like this for me, Stella?" His words unleash a torrent of heat through my veins, and I realize that the boy I had before has been replaced by a man. Dammit, I might not survive his transformation.

"Since Costa Rica," I admit.

The way my body pitches and fires makes no sense. How come, with anyone else, all the foreplay in the world can't get me going, but after less than two minutes of kissing Anders, I'm already slick with my thighs clenching?

I slip my hand up his sinewy forearm and then around his back, pulling his lips to mine. I kiss him hard. Deep. Like the past melded with the present.

My mind goes blank when his strong hands slide behind my thighs, and he hoists me against the wall so that we're eye to eye.

"Condom?" I sigh as he pushes one, then two fingers inside of me. The sound of my little pants and Anders ripping open the condom and sheathing his cock are the only things I hear for a few seconds. "You knew this was going to happen, didn't you?"

His chuckle rumbles my chest. "I hoped."

As he drops a kiss to my forehead, then my nose, then my lips, I whisper, "Don't make me wait a second longer then."

"Say it again first," he says on a groan. "That part about what I do to you. Only me."

His dick rests in the V of my thighs, right against my entrance.

I wrap my legs around his hips, clinging to him as if he might somehow change his mind and leave.

Our breath and electricity intertwine until I shudder. I'm not sure which part, exactly, he wants to hear, so I tell him the first thing that comes to mind.

My hips tip toward him. "Anders, *please*. I want you. I need you. *Now*."

One of the things I remember most clearly from that day behind the waterfall was our urgency. For me, at least, it was something I had never done before, something that I wouldn't have imagined myself wanting much less acting on. That's what I crave now. I don't want the chance to think things over or change my mind.

But of course, things are different this time. We're different people, in different places in our lives, and this means more to both of us than it did back then. Instead of fucking me senseless, Anders enters me slowly, his eyes never leaving mine. His movement is gradual, sliding him deeper until my ass is pressed against the wall and the jut of his hipbones meets my skin.

"You're so fucking *lovely*," he whispers. "Your face. Your body. Your mind. I've missed you, Stella."

Presumably he means that his *dick* missed me, but I don't correct him. This man—a professional athlete—gets his dick wet on the regular. I try not to read too much into his words and just enjoy lingering in the present moment. He's already moving, sliding out slowly. The next time he thrusts, he moves faster, entering me so deeply that I swear he brushes a part of me that's never been touched before. I'd started to wonder if the G-spot was a myth invented by sex toy companies.

Apparently not.

Anders dips his head in for a quick kiss. "Like that? Don't

hold back, Stella. I want to make it so good for you."

"Mmm." I draw in a sharp inhale and lick my lips. I'm gonna come and come hard. The best part is I'm not even gonna have to chase it because I already know Anders can deliver. I rest my forehead against his as my eyes flutter closed and allow myself to surrender to the pleasure and let it sweep me away. "Yes, like that, it feels... *ahh!*"

He thrusts again, and this time he keeps his rhythm, a slow withdrawal followed by a deep thrust, awakening the sort of need that I thought I could never feel again. My fingernails dig into his back, urging him on, and his breathing turns ragged.

"Stella," he groans against my ear. "Are you getting close?" A blinding light flashes before my eyes. Just like he asked back then.

"Yes," I whimper.

"Then let me hear you." He kisses my throat. "I wanna hear how good I fuck you."

Years of self-pleasuring in close quarters with other people have taught me to be quiet; no guide wants to hear the photographer gasping out an orgasm in the next tent over. But I have a human body—as much as I always wanted to push that aside—and that human body has needs. It takes a conscious effort for me to let my head roll back and my mouth fall open, even to cry out the next time he pins me against the paint.

Any sense of self-consciousness is short-lived. At the sound of my voice echoing through the rafters of his huge two-story house, Anders' fingers tighten on my thighs and his cock jumps inside me.

"Music to my fucking ears," he growls. "Keep that up and this'll be over too soon."

With a challenge like that, I don't stop. My voice resembles a feral lion like the ones I photographed the last time I was in the sub-Saharan. His laser gaze meets mine as he slides his palm down my body to land between us, caressing my aching clit just right. I cry out again and again until my back arches away from the wall and I tighten around him in one of the most intense orgasms of my life. Anders almost drops me as he finds his own release, and if his hips weren't pressed so tightly against mine, I would probably fall as a rush of heat spills through me.

Once we finally manage to untangle ourselves, we stand there for a long time, using the wall for support as we try to catch our breaths.

After this, I know I have feelings for him. Real ones. And I'd admit it in a heartbeat if I thought words had the power to guide the future.

He pushes back from the wall and looks down at me, shuttering his expression. "This doesn't change anything, does it?"

"Right." I press my hand to his chest, where his heart still races. "I'm still leaving Vegas."

I try to ignore how I'm being cradled in his arms. Like I weigh nothing. Like I belong there. "And I'm still staying. But you're not leaving for a few months, though?"

An ache throbs behind my ribs. "Exactly. And in the meantime...?"

"It's casual," he says firmly. "But exclusive. When it comes to you, Stella, I don't share."

I stand on my toes to kiss him. "I wasn't planning on doing this with anyone else, that's for sure." *Not that I was planning on you, either.*

"Okay." There's something akin to resignation in his tone, or maybe I'm projecting.

"Do you want me to go?" I ask, testing the waters of this new territory in our friendship.

Anders tilts his head to one side. "Are you willing to stay the night? Because you're welcome to, but no pressure."

I gather my panties from the floor and tuck them into my purse before taking his hand. "Come on," I say, giving his hand a gentle tug. "Let's go to bed."

Between his answer and walking inside the master bedroom, I fire off a quick text to my mom so she doesn't worry. Before we even get completely undressed, Anders is hard as fuck and ready for round two. This time, we take it soft and slow, getting to know each other's bodies in the way we should have so many years ago. By the time we're finally done exploring—learning all our pleasure zones and tells—hours have passed and I'm exhausted and sated.

But my muscles sag with the good kind of tired. Being with Anders is natural, like picking back up right where we left off even though it's been years and what seems like a lifetime of milestones. I haven't slept beside anyone since him—since a room inside a resort in Costa Rica—but as I drift right to sleep, I can't deny how right it feels.

CHAPTER ELEVEN

Anders

I wake up the morning after my date with Stella feeling utterly content. Every muscle in my body is perfectly relaxed. It's been so long since I've experienced anything like that.

Years, in fact. I've been telling myself that the waterfall is what made our first encounter so special, but I was wrong. The setting was great, but what made the moment unforgettable was Stella herself. Having her here, in my house, in my bed, is every bit as good as time-traveling back to that remote jungle pool.

I roll over with a sigh and wrap my arm over the woman next to me.

Then I open one eye. My room is flooded with sunlight.

Shit.

I immediately roll onto my back again and pull the covers up to my chin. No way in hell am I letting Stella see my back, not with our current arrangement. That's something I'm not ready to face since I already feel vulnerable as hell when it comes to her.

All my thrashing and flailing wakes her up, and she stirs a few times before opening her eyes.

"Hey, hot stuff," she murmurs.

"Hey, yourself," I grit out.

She sits up in bed, giving me a full-frontal view of her incredible body. The sight of her is enough to make a grown man weep. She's a fucking work of art. Her curves have filled out completely and combined with the self-confidence she wears like a cloak, the woman slays me in the best way. Combined with the memory of how she clung to me last night, her presence sends my sex drive from zero to sixty in two seconds flat.

I'm not exactly being subtle with how much I'm eyeing her up. She shimmies toward me and grabs at the blanket while flashing me a wicked smile. "Here's an idea. Why don't the two of us hop in the shower and experience the water together? I know you don't have a waterfall, but it wouldn't be a bad starting point."

My body is all in, but there's one little problem. Or rather, a medium-sized problem. One that could compromise our whole situationship. And I'm not ready for that. Now that I've found her again, I at least want to keep her for as long as I can.

No way am I letting go of her or allowing her to let go of me.

Stella doesn't know about my tattoo, and I plan to keep it that way.

Before she can kiss me, I slap one hand over my mouth, clinging to the sheets with the other.

"Sorry," I mumble into my palm. "Morning breath. Haven't brushed my teeth yet." If I start kissing her, I can't imagine that I'll stop, and then my brain will go out the window. It's just a fact: when it comes to Stella, I'm a horndog with a one track mind. Couldn't change if I tried.

"Right." She sits up, eyeing me strangely. "Well, maybe you could do that in the shower?"

"Yeah. Right. Why don't you start and I'll... catch up." Damn, can I make this any more awkward when just a few short moments ago all I could think about was how glorious it was?

Yeah, I could make it more of a clusterfuck, if I had to explain that stupid tattoo right after our casual hookup.

That's all this is for Stella, after all. Casual sex. I have to keep reminding myself.

But it's not for you. And that damn tattoo proves it beyond a shadow of a doubt.

I'm so screwed.

Stella's once-saucy smile has turned a little melancholy, but when she slips out of bed, she turns her head to watch me ogle her backside. I could be sudsing that ass underneath a stream of hot water in ten seconds flat.

Even as my entire body hardens, my mind screams that it's not worth the risk. I lie perfectly still until she sashays off to the master bathroom. The moment the water starts, I launch into action.

This is all Xena's fault. I could be in the shower with Stella right now, kissing her and flirting with her, watching water run down her skin in soapy rivulets. It's all I've ever wanted. Only, I *don't* want to have to explain the stupid tattoo, which I never intended to get in the first place. I don't relish the idea of telling her that particular story. Not that it really pisses me off having her name etched in ink on my body like I belong to her, just how it happened. Instead, I get dressed.

And pout the entire time.

When I step through the bathroom door, Stella peers around the edge of the beveled glass at me. "I just got it warm, would you like to—*oh.*" Her face falls. "You're dressed. I thought...?"

"*I* thought I could get us some breakfast, since I'm starving." I squirt some toothpaste onto my brush and immediately start scrubbing my teeth somewhat more vigorously than needed. This seems like a reasonable excuse for my strange behavior, and it's true, I'm ravenous. Not hungry enough to skip a chance at shower sex, certainly, but it's not a lie.

"Um, yeah, okay." Stella raises a skeptical brow. "I can work with that."

I spit into the sink, then point to her. "How about this? You finish up, I go on food recon, and we meet in the middle?" I return to brushing.

"Sure." She doesn't seem thrilled as she disappears behind the glass, but I don't have a lot of other options. If lukewarm acceptance is the best I can get, I'll take it for now.

I finish brushing and bolt for the front door, stopping just long enough to don some sneakers, my favorite Venom hat and a pair of sunglasses. Instead of heading for the driveway, however, I loop left and jog toward Noah's house. None of this feels real yet. I'm just floating through the day on a cocktail of oxytocin and endorphins. Eventually, the truth is going to sink in, and I'm going to come crashing back down.

Hard.

It's still pretty early, but when I climb the steps to Noah's front door, I can see figures moving around inside. I knock, and there are a series of loud thumps followed by a collision.

"*Look out, Biscuit!*" Vivian's little voice cries. A moment later, the door swings open. "Oh, Unkie Anders! You're here for breakfast! Could you smell the pancakes?"

"I sure can now," I say as I step through the door. "Is your dad here?"

Viv nods and turns in the spot. "*Daddy!* Unkie Anders is here!"

"You could try coming through to the kitchen and using your inside voice," Noah says.

Vivian huffs and flounces off in that general direction. She's four going on fourteen, apparently. I follow her through to where Molly and Noah are in the middle of cooking up a feast that smells so good my stomach rumbles.

"Hey, Anders." Molly grins at me and waves. "Want to stay for breakfast?"

"I'm okay. Actually, I was hoping to talk to Noah for a

second." I pull off my sunglasses and tap them anxiously against the counter. I don't know what I was thinking coming over here. Noah's living the life that comes together when your romance actually works out. That's no surprise—he and Molly are perfect for each other. And now I'm standing in his kitchen, watching him live his best life, while the woman of my dreams stands naked in my shower.

Alone.

For a man who leads one of the top teams in the NHL, it's not lost on me that my personal life is a hot mess.

Noah looks up from his position at the pancake station. "Hey, Anders, what's up?"

"It's kind of..." I shift from one foot to the other and glance at Molly. "Private?"

Noah tilts his head before holding out the spatula to his wife. "Can you take over for a minute?"

She doesn't ask a single question as she accepts her new role as head pancake flipper.

"Hey, Viv?" Noah waves his niece over. "Could you keep an eye on Mommy and make sure she doesn't keep all the chocolate chips for herself?"

"What?" Molly's face pinches up in an indignant frown. "I'll be fair!"

"Then you have nothing to hide." Noah kisses her forehead before leading me out back. My last glimpse into the kitchen shows Molly, Viv, and Biscuit huddled around the stove, the latter anxiously awaiting any morsel that hits the floor.

"No pancakes for you, Biscuit," Viv says. "They'll give you runny poops—"

Noah closes the glass door behind us and waves me toward one of his cushioned patio chairs. It's a grim, overcast morning better suited for staying in bed or snuggling on the couch than for hanging around outside, but I don't want to drag Noah's wife and kid into my personal drama.

"What's the deal?" Noah asks. "You never wander over here this early. Must be serious."

He's wearing an old Vegas Venom t-shirt and pajama pants decorated with a garden gnome pattern, which I happen to know were a Father's Day gift from Viv.

I flop onto the chair. "Stella's at my house."

Noah draws a deep breath and steeples his fingers, channeling some big therapy energy. He still asks the question even though we both know how ridiculous it sounds being spoken aloud. "For how long?"

"Since last night." I set my sunglasses on the table and clutch my head, tugging on my hair. "We went on a... a date."

"And that's... bad?"

"She's going to see!" I hiss as I point frantically toward my back.

"Your tattoo?" Noah rests his pointer fingers against his upper lip. "Well, I *do* have some advice for you, if you want it."

I groan. "I already hate your tone."

He pauses before asking, "Have you considered telling her the truth? Just like you should have done the day of the photoshoot? Seems you keep withholding information from the woman you're supposed to care about."

We lock gazes. "I *knew* you were going to say that."

"In that case, you could have saved yourself a trip." Noah seems amused by my distress.

"I was hoping you'd have something... more. There was a while when things with you and Molly were all weird. How'd you get past that?"

Noah stares at me with hooded eyes, as if the sight of me exhausts him. "This is going to blow your mind..."

I press my lips into a thin white line. "Don't say it."

"We told each other the truth."

"*Uurgh.*" I slam my cap on the cushion next to my thigh and muss my hair up even worse than it already is. "But that's so *hard.* I could have gotten better advice from Marco, probably even Cash. How is that going to help? She's going to think I'm a freak."

"You are a freak," Noah deadpans. "So, counterpoint. Do you genuinely think lying to her is better?"

"I didn't lie. That's the whole point." I wave my hand over my shoulder. "So long as she doesn't see it, I don't have to explain how it happened. Both the fact that I have it and how I got it make me look like a total tool. Not the vibe I'm going for here. This is *Stella* we're talking about."

"Uh huh." Noah slow-blinks at me, totally unfazed. "And she didn't ask any other questions this morning that you had to answer with anything other than complete honesty? Questions like, *Oh, Anders, why are you wrapped in the blankets like a giant weird burrito? Where are you going?* She's still in your house by herself, dude. Alone. Most guys want to kick the woman out of bed in the morning and send her on her way, not do it to themselves. You think she hasn't noticed that something's up?"

I lift my fingers as I count all the ways he's wrong. "One, she doesn't sound like that. Two, she didn't call me a burrito. Three..."

Noah waits for me to say something else, even though he must know that I don't have any other arguments to make. He's right. This should be our first morning together, and instead, I cut and run because I'm scared to lose her, which might cause me to lose her. I feel like I've wandered into the bowels of a self-fulfilling prophecy.

Someone taps on the glass, and we turn to see Molly beckoning to us through the sliding door.

"You should go home and talk to her," Noah says. "If you want a future with her? Tell her the truth. Trust me, Anders. Start off on the right foot. It's the only way things are going to move forward in your relationship."

I nod, because he's probably right. What if I don't want to move forward, though? Stella made it pretty clear that this thing between us is temporary. There's a definite end date. In our case, doesn't progress just mean hastening our race to the finish line? And when it comes to the expiration date, I'd rather hobble toward the tape like Derek Redmond than set a new world record like Usain Bolt.

Just the thought of losing her again before we even get off the blocks causes a wave of indigestion. I get up, but when Noah heads inside, I make for the side gate. My friend deserves to have a chill morning with his family, and I can't just leave Stella hanging around in my house by herself forever. Still, my pace toward the house is much slower than when I made my hasty getaway.

Stella's on the couch in the front room when I step inside. She's smiling to herself as she flips through pages of a magazine I left out. When she looks up at me, however, her smile fades.

"I thought you went to get us breakfast," she says.

"Oh. Uh." I glance down at my empty hands. "Right. The place I was planning to order from was closed."

"You didn't have a backup?" She isn't buying this story. Of course not, because it's complete crap.

Shit, what am I supposed to say when I'm caught in a web of my own lies? *I panicked this morning because I've been in love with you forever and I'm terrified that now we're together but you don't love me back?* Stupid Noah and his stupid advice. *Be honest.* Now is not the time.

"I thought I'd better come back," I tell her. "To get you, so that we could go out together. You know, since my usual place is closed."

I'm saved from my incoherent babbling when someone knocks on the door. I hurry back over to answer it, praying that it's someone who will be able to help me extract my foot from my mouth.

No such luck. Francine stands there looking confused.

"Hello, dear." She extends her hand, offering me the sunglasses that I left on the back patio. "Noah said that you forgot these just now."

"Thanks." My soul shrivels a little. Being called out is bad enough. Being called out by my lover's mom? A thousand times worse.

"Just now, huh?" Stella closes the magazine and tosses it back onto the coffee table. "I didn't know that Noah Abbott ran your favorite breakfast joint."

I grimace as I wave Francine through the door. "He doesn't."

"Good morning, Stella." Francine smiles at her daughter.

"Morning, Mom." Stella waves one hand at me. "We're about to go to breakfast. Want to come?"

"I would love to. Noah and Molly wanted a family breakfast today, so I've only had a cup of coffee. If you're sure that's all right?" She glances up at me.

I nod. "Of course, that would be fine, Francine. Come on, I'll drive."

Stella takes her mom's arm and leads her out to the car, while I follow. Noah's advice keeps playing through my mind again and again. On one hand, I see his point—but I'm also worried that the truth will be enough to sink this relationship before it's even had a proper chance to get off the ground.

Then again, lying doesn't seem to be helping my case, either.

CHAPTER TWELVE

Stella

This is not the sexy morning brunch I was anticipating. I'd entertained vivid fantasies of Anders hand-feeding me fresh fruits while we sipped mimosas, and then crawling back into bed with a squeeze-bottle of chocolate syrup or a canister of whipped cream. One way or another, I figured we would end up back in bed, not in a diner in the Vegas suburbs with my mother.

"I got my results back," Mom says as she holds up the laminated menu for *She's Wafflin'*, the breakfast joint where we're now squeezed into a red vinyl booth.

"From your doctor." I put my hand on her shoulder. "When?"

"This morning. A nice young lady called to let me know that I have *diabetes*." Mom wrinkles her nose. "I wish she could have waited until Monday to call. It's pancake day, but according to the internet, I shouldn't be having pancakes *or* chocolate chips *or* whipped cream *or* maple syrup. I'm not sure what I can ever feed Vivian again. She turns up her nose at bacon. I mean... who doesn't like bacon?"

Across from us, Anders lifts his head. "You just found this out? Should we be making sure that you're getting insulin or checking your blood sugar or something?"

"I have a follow-up appointment on Monday to get more information," Mom says.

"I can go with you." My concerned gaze meets hers. "I'm sorry about your pancake plans, but this is good news, right?

Better than a brain tumor."

Mom gives me a sheepish smile. "Yes, it's better than the alternative."

Anders extends one hand. "Can I see your phone, Francine?"

Mom hands it over, then frowns down at the menu. "How am I supposed to know what I can and can't have? Diabetics can't eat *anything* good, you know."

"I'm sure that's not true. You just have to be careful with your carbs and your sugar intake." I scan the menu. "Look, there are some combination plates that I bet would be just fine..."

"Us athletes have to worry about our macros all the time so I'm an expert. Fiber is important because it slows down the blood sugar spikes. And always eat your veggies first and your carbs last." Anders returns Mom's phone. "I put a couple of apps on there to help with carb counting and meal plans. You can see what you like and then talk to your doctor about other options during your appointment."

I've been ignoring Anders since his weird behavior at the house before we left. He was being super sketchy, and the fact that he lied about going to Noah's only confuses me. Did he go there to brag about his conquest? That's the first thing that comes to mind, but it doesn't mesh with what I know about Anders *or* Noah. It seems far more likely that he was asking for advice about something. My gut tells me he didn't want me to stay the night, so he wanted to get rid of me and didn't know how.

Well, it worked because he turned me down when I practically begged him to have sex again. Maybe he's already done with me. Maybe I don't live up to my own memory.

And then my mom stopped by and basically invited herself to breakfast so he's still stuck with me hours later. Unease swirls in my stomach along with my food.

I'm not that worried about what he got up to this morning—if he needs to talk to someone about what's going through his head, I'm glad that he's got someone around that he can trust. I just wish he would have waited until I left. But what's more worrying is that he felt the need to lie about it. If he's lying about stuff like this, what else is he hiding?

The server comes to take our drink order, and while he's getting our coffee, Mom and I go through the menu using one of the apps he downloaded. As for Anders himself, he seems distracted, like he was this morning. I wish he'd just tell me what's going on. If he's changing his mind about this—about us—he just needs to tell me. It will be hard to walk away from him, but I don't want to be with a man who doesn't want me back.

Once our food order is in, Mom has me get up from the booth. "Thank you for the help. This is going to take some getting used to, but in the meantime, I need to use the little girl's room."

As Mom heads to the back of the restaurant, Anders smiles at me. "You're a really good daughter."

I shrug. "Anyone would do this. I'm just glad that this is happening while I'm already here so that I can make sure that she gets to all of her appointments and then gets settled in to some kind of doable routine."

"I'm allowed to be impressed that you're doing the work, even if you don't think it's special. There are plenty of people who have to go through this kind of thing on their own, especially when their kids could be traveling around the world, taking pictures of sloths and stuff."

I open a packet of creamer and stir it into my coffee. "I do love sloths. They're my favorite. And they're so *slow*." I lift my eyes to his as I stir my cup. "You must think I'm slow, too."

Anders frowns and crosses his arms on the table. "Not at all. Why would you say that?"

"Because you lied about where you were going this morning, and you didn't even bother to make it a *good* lie."

Anders flinches. "I don't like lying to you, Stella. It's just... complicated."

"More complicated than being friends and neighbors who sleep with each other?" I indicate my outfit, which is the same one from last night. I'm the only person out and about this early on a Saturday with mussed hair, no makeup, and a first-date dress. "All I know for sure is that there's a reason you didn't want to join me in the shower. I know it's not my body. I'm hot as hell. All that traipsing through jungles and Serengetis has paid off."

Anders examines me as he lifts his coffee cup to his lips. "That it has."

My breath hitches in my throat. "Are you having second thoughts about our arrangement?"

"No!" Anders reaches for me with a stricken expression. "God, no."

Leaning back in the booth, I regard him. "So why don't you just tell me what's going on?"

Anders rests his head against his fist and stares at me. It's obvious from his expression that something's bothering him, and judging by the way he's staring into my eyes, that *something* has to do with me. "Because I don't know what you'll think when I do."

"Would you like to know what I'm thinking right *now?*" I cross my arms. "Because I should warn you, it's not flattering."

Mom returns to the table, and I get up to let her have her seat back. All the while, Anders watches me with that pained expression on his handsome face. It's driving me crazy. Last night, he was passionate and sweet and desperate. What happened while we slept? Did he change his mind? Did the reality of being with the adult version of me not live up to the expectation? Or has it just now occurred to him that carrying on with me could compromise his friendship with Noah if things go south with us?

Inspiration strikes, and I turn to my mom. "I don't suppose you know why Anders decided to go to Noah's this morning, do you?"

Mom nods. "I do."

Across from us, Anders sinks down in his booth.

"And I'm thinking that he'll talk to you about it when he's ready." Mom pats my hand.

The food arrives, and as we take our first few bites, a strained silence descends over the table. I don't like being on the outside. The fact that Mom knows more about my boyfriend than I do is a problem.

Boyfriend? I'm not sure where that came from. Anders isn't my boyfriend. That's too official a word for what we are. But he's not really my ex either. We're stuck in relationship no man's land.

"So, Anders," Mom says, "I take it that you're still coming to the Christmas party."

Anders nods as he takes a bite of his bacon. "Yup. I know Molly's really looking forward to it."

She takes a sip of her coffee. "Noah's promised to help with the outside lights, but if you'd be willing to help him with the ladder, we'd all appreciate it."

"Sure. I can talk to him about it when I drive you home."

"Have either of you thought about presents?" Mom scoops up a spoonful of her Greek yogurt-smothered fruit salad. Her eyes bounce between us as she waits for an answer.

"Oh, we're not doing that." I shake my head. "I need to be able to travel light, and Anders doesn't need presents. Right?" I gesture to him, hoping that he'll chime in.

"I'm not big on Christmas, either," Anders says. "We're keeping things low-pressure."

"And we're so new. I wouldn't even know what to get him." I eye Anders up again. "There's a lot that I don't know about him, actually." *Like where he was this morning when he should have been in the shower with me.*

"You will," Anders says.

"Good." I lean forward. "And I hope you're ready to tell me more soon. I'm not sticking around forever, and there shouldn't be any secrets between us."

Anders blanches, but he nods. "Soon," he agrees.

I wish I could believe him.

CHAPTER THIRTEEN

Anders

"So." Noah leans against the locker next to me after practice and eyes me up and down. "How did it go?"

"She knows something's weird," I tell him. "But she doesn't know what. We agreed this was going to be a no-strings-attached situation. How am I supposed to casually bring up in conversation the fact that I have, you know...?" I point over my shoulder at the design on my back. "This. She's gonna freak out. Guaranteed, she's going to cut and run. I can't risk that, I just got her back, and I'm not ready to let go, dammit!"

Marco lumbers over behind me and digs the tip of his finger into my back. "This is problem? I thought women like when the man gets tattoo of name? Like to say, *I am marking property, hands off, this* cazzo *is only for mine.* In *Italia,* the women are loving commitment."

Cash looks up from his gear. "Not all women."

"But all this!" Marco waves to encompass my whole body, which I suppose I should take as a compliment. "Other women pay good money for man who looks like this. Why rent bull when she can have the cream for free?"

"Jesus fucking Christ, dude." I shove Marco away. "That's not how the saying goes."

"No, am pretty sure." Marco spins his jersey up into a rattail and smacks my ass with it. "Because they call it beefcake? Because man is bull and woman is..." He makes it complicated series of gestures with his hands, which only serves to give me a series of truly disturbing mental images. "Milkmaid. Sucking the milk from the body. Is a metaphor!"

Latham stares at Marco in utter disgust. "This dude kills me. Like deceased to the point of rigor mortis."

The Italian waggles his eyebrows at us. "How many times I say? Have known *many* milkmaids."

"Wow." Noah scratches his jaw, trying to work out what to say in response. Evidently, he fails, because after a long pause, he turns back to me. "This gives new meaning to the eight maids a milking thing. I'm not sure why he keeps talking about them. Must be an Italian thing, or I'm missing something."

Cash points at Marco. "I can't even."

Noah nods. "What I'm wondering is how Anders is going to keep hooking up with a woman and not reveal the fact that he has an obvious back tattoo with her name on it."

Latham cackles. "Wait, she doesn't *know?* Dude, you're in so deep already. Sucks to be you."

Marco lifts both hands in an attempt to slow us down. "Wait, am very confuse. Stella not know about her name on the beefcake?"

I stick my head in my locker so that I won't have to meet anyone's eyes. "Pretty much."

"Hmm." Marco ponders this with a loud hiss of air. "How I get one?"

Latham throws an arm around Marco's shoulder. "All you have to do is date and break up with a tattoo artist. Then you have to win the Stanley Cup. For the *Stallone Italiano*, that should be easy-peasy-lemon-squeezy."

Marco's intense expression suggests that he might be taking notes. "Okay, cow metaphor is end. What is this squeezy? Now is lemons. Life gives them to me, and then I get..." He mimes twisting a lemon onto a juicer. "A tattoo? Your American sayings like grasshopper. I try to catch them but they hopping all over the place."

"It's not the sayings that are confusing." Latham jerks one thumb in my direction. "It's this dipshit's love life that's the problem. Or lack thereof."

"He dates tattoo artist. What wrong?" Marco looks around at us helplessly.

"Nothing wrong with a breakup," Noah intones. "But I maintain that a guy has to be pretty foolish to go back to a woman's tattoo parlor after dumping her when she didn't want to be dumped."

"Foolish? I know not about this." Marco gestures to his groin. "My ex, she gives me Prince Albert after breakup. But maybe is different when piercing, not tattoo?"

Cash and Latham exchange a bemused glance.

"Just shut up," Cash pleads, putting his palms over his face.

Latham shakes his head. "I'm sorry, man, but I gotta know. Is this another translation thing? Please tell me you didn't let your ex pierce your dick."

Marco raises one eyebrow. "Why not? For ex, is already familiar territory."

"Guys, *please*," I groan. Ten minutes ago, I would've said that the last thing on earth I wanted to talk about was my situation with Stella. Now I have a new low bar.

Latham wags a finger at me. "We can get back to your fucked up love life in a second, Beck. I'm still trying to wrap my head around this new development. Like why haven't we *seen* it?"

"Is not new," Marco says. "I have had this every time I know you, but ring small. Now you know about my royal *cazzo*, but I still want to know about this tattoo."

"For the love of God, let me tell the story," I plead as I tent my hands together.

"Always I love the stories." Marco drops on the bench and gets situated. "You may begin now."

"*Thank* you." I rub my forehead between my eyebrows where it just started to throb. "So, you know how three seasons ago, Venom won the cup? Well, in the off-season, we decided to get commemorative tattoos. We all have the same design."

Latham coughs and points significantly to his bicep, which shows the tattoo in its original form: the Stanley Cup, with a hockey stick in front of it that says *Venom* and his number.

"Not exactly the same," Noah clarifies.

Cash smirks at me. "It went South."

"They *would* all have been the same design," I correct through gritted teeth. "Except I got stuck with Xena."

"Ah, yes!" Marco flexes. "Warrior Princess! We have this, too, in *Italia*."

"Not exactly. We'd slept together one time. She wanted more. But I was still hung up on Stella." Xena and I hooked up less than eight months after my return from Costa Rica, when the memory of my time in the jungle was still so fresh it hurt. I hadn't yet realized that I was comparing every girl I met to *her,* which in hindsight wasn't fair to anyone. In Xena's defense, I was kind of a dick about the whole thing. She could have done way worse to me and been justified.

"From what I see, you never *stop* being hung. Even now, you wrap around her ring finger." Marco lifts his fingers and blows a chef's kiss toward the ceiling. "She *bellissima*. I get hung, too, on girl like that."

Latham, like a prepubescent teenager stuck in a man's body, snickers at our teammate's word choice.

"I wouldn't advise it," Noah interjects. "Anders will kill you if you try anything with her."

"I will," I agree. "Anyway, when we went into the shop, I

whisper to *this* asshole," I point at Latham, "that one of the tattoo artists is my dirty hookup from back in the day and that I should probably leave. And he pretty much hollers, *Oh, is that the famous Stella? The one who got away.*"

"I didn't holler." Latham lifts his nose into the air. "She just had vindictive puck bunny hearing. Like Spidey senses. Look it up, it's a thing."

"It is thing?" Marco asks, looking to us for confirmation.

"Not a thing." Cash flicks Latham with one finger. The finger.

Marco frowns. "Why so crabby today, *Il Denaro?*"

I unzip my bag and shove a few things inside. "Long story short, I got stuck with Xena, and she ended up writing *Stella* on the blade of my hockey stick instead of the team name."

Cash clicks his tongue. "Should have sued."

I roll my eyes at the four of them and pull on a shirt. The rest of the guys have already cleared out of the locker room. "Yeah, I would *love* to get in a legal battle so that it can be splashed all over the headlines and documented on the internet for all eternity. Pass. She was moving to LA and already had a job lined up—the shop fired her, but she had no skin in the game. Hence, she botched me. On purpose."

Marco giggles. "*Skin.* I see what you do. This saying make sense to me."

I stare Marco down until he clamps his lips together. "Anyway, the moral of the story is..."

"Never date warrior princess." Marco taps one finger to his temple. "I will remember. But this Xena, I think she agree with me. Tattoo, like brand, yes? If you are bull, and Stella milkmaid, now you have brand so that all the other girls know whose you are. No one will pull the wrong teat."

"This conversation has gone straight into the shitter." I slam my locker door and lift my bag onto my shoulder. "That's it. I'm out. I should have known better than to expect support from this crew." I push past the guys toward the locker room door. I hear Latham ask Marco something about his piercing and if the chicks dig it, but I don't stick around for the details.

"Hey, Anders!" Noah jogs after me. "Wait up. I wanted to ask you about the game tomorrow."

I slow my pace and let him catch up. As the team captain, usually I wouldn't let these guys get under my skin so much, but I'm on edge these days. The whole situation with Stella has me keyed-up and nervous. The way she looked at me over breakfast the other day made me appreciate just how much I have to lose. If she leaves for work, fine, I know that's part of the deal. But if she dumps me because she thinks I'm disrespecting her? I'm gonna be a wreck for life because that's on me.

"You have some strategy in mind?" I ask.

"Sort of." Noah winks. "Why don't you ask Stella to come as your guest? She can sit with Molly. It's a chance to impress her with what you do best."

"Oh, um." I clutch the handles of my bag tighter. "I dunno, it sounds like she doesn't know jack squat about hockey. I doubt she'd want to."

"Seems like a good time to learn," Noah points out. "Besides, don't you want her to see you on the ice? Cheering for you? Screaming your name from the stands? Rocking your number for all to see?"

I step out of the stadium doors. December is one of the few months out of the year where Vegas actually gets cold enough to require layers, although all my time getting acclimated to the ice means that I can usually get by without them. Up North where I went to school, this time of year is freezing cold. Due to my lack of an inner circle outside my Venom brotherhood, it's been easy to avoid getting in the holiday mood, but this year, I'm wishing for chilly nights where I can curl up in bed with Stella or drink cocoa on the couch under a pile of blankets and watch Christmas movies. It's true, something about her presence makes me all soft and nostalgic.

And Noah's right. It would be nice to have her at the game, even if it's only once, just so that I can get a taste of what it would be like if we were together for real.

Almost like creating a core memory.

I pull out my phone, and Noah claps me on the back. "You're texting her right now, aren't you?"

"Yeah." I shrug. "It would be a shame to let that guest ticket go to waste." My voice sounds indifferent, but my hands are shaking as I type out my invitation. *Got a comp ticket to tomorrow's home game. Any interest in seeing what I do for a living?*

Her reply comes only seconds later and any further words for Noah dry on my tongue. *I'd love to.*

* * *

My nerves have me climbing the walls all day, but when the time to take the ice finally rolls around, I'm unstoppable. The rest of the team is in rare form, and Marco even manages to make an assist. When the puck is in play, I never take my eyes off it, but between shifts, my eyes drift upward to where Molly and Stella sit, along with the rest of the friends and family. She made it pretty clear that hockey isn't her forte, but every time I catch a glimpse of her, her eyes are bright and her cheeks are flushed pink. The only other times I've seen her like that are during exercise or sex.

And I'm going to get to see that face again, because we're together now. Maybe she'll let me drive her home after the game tonight. Of course, her mom's at her place, and if she spends the night with me again, I'll run the risk of her seeing my tat.

I really need to figure out how to handle that. Maybe I could put a bandage over it for the time being and fake an injury.

When we finally win, two goals ahead of the Redhawks, I can't get off the ice fast enough. The sooner I get changed and showered, the sooner I get to see Stella.

As we leave the locker room and head out the player exit, we're mobbed by a crowd of the usual fans. Only a few steps from the door, a bottle blonde with D-cups holds out a sharpie. She's got the Vegas Venom logo stamped on each cheek, and my number marked out in painter's tape on her skin-tight camisole.

"Anders, will you sign my boob?" she asks, pressing her hands up under her chest to give me an even better view of the proposed canvas.

"Oh, um..." I stare down at her ample cleavage in dismay. "I'm not doing that anymore."

The puck bunny sticks out her lower lip. "Aw, why not? You signed my friend a few weeks ago."

Latham appears behind me and throws one arm around my shoulders. "Because Anders has a *girl*friend. But I don't. Why don't you bring your perfect tit over here?"

She giggles and immediately peels off the tape, then hands Latham the pen as she does a complete one eighty. He takes his time cupping her boob, ostensibly to hold it in place while he signs.

To my left, Cash sighs. "Newberry needs therapy."

I sigh. "This is probably why Scarlett Stone hates him. I mean... he does this kind of shit all the time. You should read the blogs. I think he might need more than therapy at this point."

I duck around the scene Latham is causing that's borderline public indecency and follow Noah to where Molly and Stella are waiting for us.

"You won!" Molly squeals, lifting her arms in the air as she launches herself into Noah's embrace. "Way to keep all the biscuits out of the basket, Flopper!"

Stella's a little more subdued, but her eyes are still bright with excitement. "That was more fun than I expected," she said. "It's really high energy in here. Thanks for inviting me."

"You're welcome any time," I tell her, feeling unexpectedly grateful that she wasn't around to see the puck bunny throwing herself at me. "Want me to drive you home?"

She shakes her head, reading between the lines. "I can't tonight. I've got an early shoot scheduled. But I'll see you at the Christmas party this weekend."

My heart sinks a little. "Sure."

"Maybe before I leave, you could give me a kiss?" She steps closer and presses her hands to my chest, standing on her toes to reach me. "That seems to be what everyone else is doing after your victory."

I bend down to brush my lips against hers. I don't know how it's possible, but one kiss from Stella is better than signing every breast in the stadium.

When she leaves Vegas, I don't know what I'm going to do without her.

CHAPTER FOURTEEN

Stella

"What am I forgetting?" Molly frets as she spins on the spot, critiquing her decorated kitchen.

I follow her line of sight, taking in everything from the strings of silvery lights to the paper decorations, from the elegant party spread to the crockpot of mulled wine on the counter. Molly has opted for a charming mix of classy decorations and whimsical nostalgia that fit her personality to a tee. A stack of foil-wrapped Christmas crackers stands in the middle of the dining room table next to a tray of hand-iced gingerbread men. Vivian helped with the cookies, and it's obvious which ones she did because they're just the slightest bit off, but their crooked smiles and uneven cinnamon Red Hots I can't tell you a single thing out buttons only make them more endearing.

This party has Molly written all over it, and it's the sort of domestic endeavor that I will never be able to replicate. She loves this kind of thing, and it makes my chest ache and my ovaries squeeze to realize that I'll never feel fully at home in a place like this. A man like Anders Beck deserves a warm home and a family, and I can't give him that.

It's like a scene out of a Norman Rockwell painting. It's nice to visit, but impossible for a wild heart like mine to stay.

"I can't see a single thing out of place," I tell her. "It's *beautiful,* Molly."

She beams at me and wraps one arm around my waist. "It's

so nice having you here, Stella. How much longer are you sticking around? A while, I hope."

I lean into the warmth of her friendship, wishing things could be different. "I'm not sure. Until the book's done, and Mom's figured out how to manage her diabetes, I guess. A few months, maybe?"

"Even when you're not living here, you'll always be welcome." Molly jumps when the front door opens. "I hope you won't be a stranger. This can be your home base."

"The lights are done!" Viv exclaims as she hurries inside. "They're so sparkly, Mommy."

Her cheeks are flushed from the cold. She's wearing a pink plaid jacket, and behind her, Biscuit is wearing a matching doggie coat. I don't know where Noah found that sweet, patient animal, but her tolerance for clothing, especially headwear, is legendary.

"Take off your shoes before you go running around, Viv," Mom calls. Viv doubles back to extract herself from her gear.

"Did you see all the decorations, Nanny Frannie?" Viv cries. "Mommy made it just like in the movies. It's magical!"

"Yes, and everywhere there are treats that I can't have." Mom sighs theatrically, resting the back of her hand against her forehead.

"There are a few things you can eat." Molly points to the spread, which includes a massive charcuterie plate, a fruit tray, and an array of tiny finger-foods that are way more upscale than I've ever encountered. Molly went all out.

"Are those miniature loaded baked potatoes?" Mom asks in wonder. "You're a wonder, Molly."

Molly holds up a hand. "I've already learned the basics. Fiber, low-glycemic carbs, and healthy fat."

The back door opens, and Noah and Anders step through.

Just the sight of him causes my heart rate to kick up.

"Ladder's put away," Noah says.

"And nobody fell off the roof," Anders adds.

"Victory!" Viv lifts her arms in a V and runs around the room, while Biscuit chases after her. "Way to go, Daddy!"

The guys take off their coats, then wander over to join us. "Just in time, too." Noah checks his phone. "We've only got another twenty minutes or so until people start showing up." He scoops up a cup of mulled wine, then circles around to where Molly is standing. He drops a quick kiss on her lips before turning to me. "So, Stella, how's the book coming?"

Anders clears his throat significantly.

"It's going okay. I mean, one model backed out..." I wink at Anders so that he'll know I'm just yanking his chain. "And I'm having trouble finding the perfect plus-sized model, but it'll come together."

Anders retrieves his own cup of wine. "Looking for a plus-sized model, huh? Hey, Noah, isn't Silas McKay's sister a famous model? Madeline or something?"

"The one who works with the athleisure wear line?" Noah frowns at the ceiling. "They did the new uniforms for the Rochester Riot and a bunch of other teams. I think you're right about her being a model, but Madeline doesn't sound right, though."

Anders snaps his fingers. "*Madison.*"

"There you go." Noah turns to me. "Have you ever heard of her, Stella?"

I shake my head and whip out my phone. "Madison McKay, you said?"

"Yeah, the clothing line is something like CoachB." Anders sips his wine. "Her brother's a great player. I wouldn't mind having him on our team."

"CoachB+," I correct. "Oh my gosh, look at her photos!" Madison McKay's socials are overflowing with incredible photos. In addition to being a model, she's also a body-positive advocate. "She's *amazing*. She'd literally be perfect."

"I can text Silas and see if he can get you in touch," Noah offers. "We used to play each other a ton back in college. Good guy. Of course, he's the enemy now, but I can still drop him a line."

I nod enthusiastically as I continue to scroll, my heart pounding at the prospect of working with Madison. "Would you? That would be incredible."

He taps out a message while Molly and Anders exchange a knowing glance.

The doorbell rings, and the Abbots scatter, welcoming the first round of guests. I scoot around the kitchen island to get closer to Anders. "Thanks for thinking of Madison. If she's down to take a tasteful nude, It'll help a lot."

"I'm not sure he'll respond on Christmas Eve, but Noah will forward her contact info when he does. I'm sure she'd be down with the message of your book. I don't know why I didn't think of it sooner." Anders points to the ceiling. "By the way, you approached me just now, so I can only assume that you know about the dead weed overhead?"

"Huh?" I mutter, glancing up. A few sprigs of mistletoe dangle from the ceiling. I have just enough time to register them before Anders dips in to plant a kiss on my lips.

"Stella loves Unkie Anders!" Viv screeches. I'm not sure where she came from, but apparently she arrived just in time to witness the impromptu liplock and exploit it.

Anders swallows the rest of his wine as Vivian runs off to tell everyone what she just saw. *She's not wrong,* I think as Anders takes my hand.

"Want to slip away for a few minutes?" Anders whispers, his fingers inching along my waist. Now my heart is galloping for another reason. "Everyone will be so busy with the food and the guests that they won't miss us."

I'm suddenly aware of how short my gold skirt is. Besides, I did wear my sexiest thong. Not because Anders would be here, of course, just because it felt festive to wear a matching red bra and panties. In the spirit of Christmas, after all.

"Just for a few minutes," I say.

With one raised eyebrow, Anders leads me to Noah's library, locks the door, and presses me against the shelves stacked with first editions.

"We shouldn't be here," I pant as Anders tosses my nicest bra into a heap on the floor. "These books look old."

"No, definitely not. There's like a million dollars' worth of rare books in here." He lifts me up against the rolling ladder. "So we *cannot* get caught. We should stop. You should put your clothes back on."

"You suggested this. And you took them off," I protest. "And you should definitely—*oh!*"

"You like that?" Anders hooks my knees over his shoulders and kisses my belly as his fingers thrust into me without warning. There's nothing tender in his movements. He's eyeing me up the way a lion eyes up a gazelle, like he can't wait to sink his teeth into me. "You like it when I'm rough, don't you, my dirty girl?"

"Yes," I whisper as memories assault me from every angle. Of the first time he said that to me so many years ago. Of the way he played my body like a virtuoso at the strings. The way he's still playing it right fucking now until I lose all rationality.

He kisses his way down between my legs and laps at my clit, dragging his tongue roughly across me. I have to press my palm to my mouth and bite down to stifle my panting.

Anders lifts his head and rakes his gleaming eyes over me again. "Gotta be quiet, Stella," he breathes, twisting his fingers inside me until my hips buck. My sweaty palm slips on the rails of the antique brass rolling ladder. I'm completely at his mercy, and I've never been so turned on in my life. "If you make a noise, someone might hear, and what will they think if they hear you panting like that?" He winks and licks me again, sucking my clit between his teeth. "Spread your legs wider for me—that's it—use that ladder and hold on while I make that pretty pussy come all over my face."

Two can play at this game. While I use one hand to part my glistening folds even wider, I stare down into his face.

"There's a clock in the corner," I whisper. "If you can make me come in under two minutes, I'll let you do whatever you want to me. Otherwise, I'm going back out to the party."

His eyes widen.

"Two minutes," I repeat, watching the second hand tick toward the twelve. "Starting... *now*."

Anders growls against me and redoubles his efforts. I have to hook my elbow over one rung of the ladder to keep from collapsing entirely. I shudder and shiver against him, biting down hard on the tip of my tongue. It's almost good enough, but not quite.

The second hand returns to the twelve, and I exhale. "One minute left. You can do better than that, Beck," I whisper. "Just think what you could ask for? You could have me on my knees with your dick in my mouth. You could bend me over the table. Don't you want me completely at the mercy of your wicked imagination?"

He groans and shifts around beneath me, his tongue never stilling. I can't quite tell what his fingers are doing, but it feels fucking incredible. I'm so close.

Thirty seconds.

"You're not going to make it, Ander—*mm!*" I let go of the back of his head and stuff my knuckles into my mouth, biting down so hard I see stars. One of Anders' fingers teases my ass, pressing and massaging.

The effect is instantaneous. I shudder and fall apart, shattering into fragments as his tongue keeps teasing me. By the time he finally lowers me to the floor, the second hand has gone all the way around again, and I'm incapable of doing anything but gasping for air.

"Stella, Stella." Anders clicks his tongue and kisses my neck. "Who knew you'd be into that?"

I certainly didn't. My sexual experimentation has been fairly vanilla. But with this man, another side of me comes out and demands to be seen and heard.

Anders stands up and brace his arms against the ladder. "Well? Did I—scratch that, *you*—cross the finish line in time?"

I push away from the ladder, dizzy with pleasure. I would have thought that my release would satisfy me, but the opposite is true. I'm sensitive all over and desperate for more.

I'm addicted to him. There's no other explanation.

I loop my fingers through his belt loops and look up at him. "You did," I whisper. "But I still proclaim it was a team effort. Time to claim your prize. What do you want?"

Anders' eyes flutter shut. "Your mouth," he hisses. "I want to feel your mouth on me, Stella, and then I want to fuck you senseless."

It wouldn't take much. One could reasonably argue that my senses are already compromised when it comes to Anders Beck. My mouth drops open, and he guides me to him.

"Is it okay if I move my hips?" he whispers.

"Mmm." I wrap my hand around the base of his cock. "Mmmhmm."

He does just that, thrusting into my mouth. My pussy clenches and shivers, and I slide my fingers into myself, mirroring the pace of his movements.

When he sees what I'm doing, Anders makes a helpless little noise. He pulls away and scoops me up in his arms.

"What happened to claiming my mouth?" I whisper.

"Raincheck," he pants. "You do things to me. Now I can't wait." Instead, he helps me hook my knees around one rung of the ladder and brace my arms against the shelves beyond. Anders grabs a condom from his pocket and quickly sheathes himself. Then he thrusts into me. He tugs on my hair so that my head falls back, and when I arch my back enough, I'm able to meet his eyes.

"You're perfect," he growls. "You feel so fucking good, Stella. The sounds you make. *Shit*. Can you come again?"

"I... I don't know..." I'm not even sure we're being quiet anymore. The only thing I can think or feel is Anders, Anders, Anders, again and again.

"Hold on tight," he says. Somehow he manages to stay upright without dropping me. The movements of our hips never cease as he manages to work one hand between my legs. He grinds his palm against my clit, and it has no right to feel that good, but it does.

This time my orgasm hits like a runaway train, and I somehow manage to dislodge a whole shelf of books. They hit the carpet with a shower of dull thumps.

"Oh, *fuck*," Anders says, and at first I think he's referring to the fate of the books, but then he grabs the railing on either side of the ladder for support. "Stella." He kisses the back of my neck as one kind of need is replaced with another. "Are you okay?"

"I messed up Noah's books," I mutter, even as I slump against him.

"I noticed." He nuzzles me. "But how do you *feel?*"

I sigh. "Incredible."

It takes both of us working together to untangle me from the ladder. Our clothes are everywhere, and we hurry around getting dressed. It's a Christmas miracle that nobody hears us. But then again, Viv has decided to put a holiday Spotify playlist on the Bose sound system and it's blaring Mariah Carey louder than any scream I could make.

As Anders pulls on his pants, he smiles. "Oh, I almost forgot. Your Christmas present."

I stop midway through trying to tame my hair. "No. We weren't *doing* presents. We agreed!"

"Yeah, but I lied." Anders winks and holds out a small box.

For a moment, I'm irrationally terrified that he's going to propose, but he places the box in my palm and goes back to fixing and reorganizing the books. "You should go out first. I'll deal with this. Maybe we can still get away without being caught."

"I'll see you out there." I unlock the door and peer out into the hall. Fortunately, the coast is clear, so I make a beeline for the bathroom to salvage my post-coital appearance.

Down the hall, I can hear Marco's voice exclaiming, "Tater, this man of ginger has very good *sapore*! Here, I bring almond cookies like from home. Taste, taste!"

Only when I'm safe in the bathroom do I open the box Anders gave me. There's no ring inside, only a beautiful necklace with a little handwritten note that says, *Your favorite. Merry Christmas! Anders xo*

It's so perfect I could cry. Some women love diamonds, but this gift proves that Anders knows me all too well.

The dainty gold pendant is shaped like a sloth.

CHAPTER FIFTEEN

Anders

I'm in love with Stella Croft.

Before, I thought I was in love with her. I knew there was something magical between us. Now, there's no denying it. Only two things in life matter to me right now: hockey and *her*. When I'm not on the ice, I'm thinking about how to get back to her. How to claim her. How to carve out a future with her.

Noah can tell, and he keeps giving me funny looks, but he keeps his questions to himself for once. He doesn't even ask me why some of his books are out of order in the library, even though he must have noticed that some things have been moved around. That dude's anal retentive about his literary treasures. I did my best to put everything back in its proper place after the Christmas Eve party, but surely I didn't fix *everything*. He must have his suspicions. But I know Stella and I weren't the only couple to fuck like rabbits inside that damn library. I'm sure he's devoured Molly seven ways to Sunday right alongside his first edition copy of *Moby Dick*.

The season is going well—and so is my plus/minus ratio— but a sense of dread hangs in the back of mind, counting down the days until Stella disappears. Only, I don't *know* when she'll go. I'm living on borrowed time.

Which is why I call her the Thursday after New Year's with a proposition.

"Hey, babe," she answers. "Is this a booty call? I've never gotten one of those before."

Babe. I don't deny how much I like the sound of that falling from her lips. I drop down on the couch in my living room and kick my feet up onto the ottoman. "Would you like it to be?"

She laughs. "Give me one second." The sounds on her end of the line go muffled, as if she's covered the mic, but I can still hear her voice. "I'll be right back. Yes, it's Anders. *No,* it's not a booty call. If you're that horny, get your own significant other." Her voice returns to normal volume. "Sorry, I'm at lunch with Eli going over some of his contacts. Thanks for connecting me with Madison, by the way. We're doing a shoot in a couple of weeks, and she's been an amazing resource."

"Yeah? Book's going well, then?" I try to muster the appropriate enthusiasm, but in some ways that damn book feels like the enemy. The better it goes, the sooner she'll be on her way back to chasing animals and her dreams. I'm not petty enough to resent the project—I want Stella to be happy, but the book is part of her leaving me. Ideally, the project will go smoothly, but *slowly.*

I need to make this last, because I'm pretty sure that Stella's the one for me. Trouble is, I'm not the one for her.

Star-crossed love fucking *sucks.*

"Madison's connections with CoachB+ have been a godsend," Stella gushes. "I don't want to rely on all the same models the company hires, but she's opened some amazing doors for me. I swear, you saved the book when you and Noah put me in touch with her."

I pull a throw pillow into my lap and hug it, wishing she was here. "Glad to hear it."

"What were you calling about?" She must have stepped outside, because there's traffic in the background now.

"I was thinking you must miss all your adventures, since you've been stuck in one place for a while." I pluck the tasseled edges of the throw-pillow and then punch it like it's fate itself. "I'm off tomorrow. Do you want to go to Red Rocks with me? Snap a few candids?"

"Oh." Stella's reply is soft. I wish I could see her face right now so that I could get a sense of what she's thinking. Does she like the idea of spending some time with me? Or is she figuring out how to tell me no without ruining our situationship?

"Maybe taking some pictures in nature would help you get the creative juices flowing on your book," I suggest.

"Maybe," she agrees. "And I don't have anyone booked for tomorrow, so... yeah, that could be fun. What time?"

"I can pick you up around ten, if that's okay? And we could go to lunch afterward." I know that I'm pushing my luck, but I'd kick myself if I didn't try. All I have to do is remember she's not mine and my stomach clenches. This ceased being about sex long ago. Now it's just about *time.*

"Just lunch?" she asks.

"I'll bring you back after we eat. If you want, we can pick up something for your mom." Am I trying too hard? Possibly. But if we only get a couple of months together, I want to savor it.

"This almost sounds like a date." There's accusation in her tone but humor, too. "Are non-sexual dates allowed under the terms of our current agreement?"

"The contract doesn't specify," I quip. "Should I call my agent and get his opinion?"

"I don't think that will be necessary. It falls under the umbrella of our original agreement." An image of Stella swims into my mind, with her easy smile and bright eyes. Just the thought of living without her pings behind my ribs and settles. Dammit, I'm so screwed. I'm a changed man because she changed me, and I don't know how I'm going to learn to live without her. "I'll see you at ten."

After we hang up, I slump sideways on the couch and close my eyes. I grew up hearing stories about how *love conquers all*, but that shit is for kids. Kids that weren't me. Growing up on the wrong side of the tracks taught me a lot. Most of all, that only the rich get what they want and only the good die young. If there was a bad guy trying to keep me away from Stella, I'd fight him to the death. The real world, however, is much more complicated. Instead of a shadowy figure with a waxed mustache, the thing keeping us apart is our own personal values. I can't ask Stella to change for me. Not only would that be selfish, but it would defeat the purpose of loving her in the first place. She's like some sort of wild bird with brilliant plumage, and in order to keep her here with me, I'd have to clip her wings. You don't pull that shit with someone you love.

I don't want her if she has to be a captive to stay with me. A gilded cage is still a cage.

Just because my emotions are so deeply involved doesn't mean we could ever be true partners. She needs to travel, and I'm tied down to my work. If she asked me to give up hockey for her, we'd fail in the long run, because I'd resent her for making me choose between her needs and my own. It's obvious that she'd feel the same way if I tried to keep her in Vegas. Creative freedom is Stella's number one priority in this life and complete flexibility to travel on a whim is the one thing I can't provide.

It's a paradox, and the only obvious solution is to keep myself from getting in too deep. It would probably be wiser to call things off now, before she ruins me for life.

Who am I kidding? She's already ruined me. After all, I've pined for Stella for years. I'm hers until the day I leave this earth, even if she won't have me. And once she does, another woman might be able to have my body, but she'll never, ever have access to my heart.

Stella has it until eternity.

I'll have to take what I can get for now and hope that it will be enough.

* * *

"It's so beautiful out here," Stella sighs, as she lifts her camera to her eye.

Surrounded by the natural, rugged beauty of the sandstone cliffs, she's in her element. She opted for a pair of leggings that make her ass look fantastic and a light North Face jacket. Her hair is twisted up on her head in a messy bun, and her battered hiking boots have clearly seen more rugged terrain.

The scrub brush around us and the striated stone take my breath away almost as much as the woman by my side, but even amidst the incredible scenery, I can't stop staring at Stella. I'm going to keep this version of her in my memory forever.

Stella keeps her eye pressed to the viewfinder. "You're staring," she says.

I scratch my ear and turn away, embarrassed to be caught in the act. "Just seeing where this trail is headed," I lie.

She smiles and snaps another photo. "You want to see the map?"

I force myself to glance at the skyline. "Not necessary. We'll get there when we get there."

"How very Zen of you." At last, she lowers the camera and lets it hang from its strap around her neck. "Lead the way, then."

I didn't bother bringing a camera. I never do. Stella likes to capture the world in images, but what I want to remember is the *feeling* of the moment. A photo won't capture the burn in my thighs as I climb or the way my lungs expand as I push myself ever higher on the trail. I'll have to rely on memory to recreate the way my heart hammers when Stella scrambles over one of the larger rocks and almost trips, and the warmth of her palm on mine as I catch her hand to help her regain her footing.

She grins at me and holds on a moment longer than necessary. "You probably think I'm super clumsy," she chuckles. "Remember how I almost fell when I was trying to take pictures of that frog?"

"Of course." How could I forget? Every moment spent with her is forever burned in my memory. It was the first time I had an excuse to touch her. I can still remember that current of electricity running between us. Not much has changed in all these years. I still burn for her.

"I promise you, I don't go around falling all the time." She pulls her hand away and keeps moving, leaving me in the dust. "But I appreciate the save."

I follow her up to the next vista where we're met by a rock formation that looks like a crop of alien mushrooms has sprung up out of the desert. Stella whistles and takes a few shots.

"This is so wild," she says. "Just when I think I've seen everything the world has to offer, I stumble across something like this. And right here at home. It's incredible." She keeps her back to me and snaps a few more photos. "It's hard not to get carried away."

I'm so busy watching her that I don't notice anything else about our surroundings, at least not until a flash of movement catches my eye. I look down, and I freeze.

Uh oh. No. No. No.

Not now.

Stella keeps talking, ignorant of my current predicament even as my knees start to feel weak. My heart hammers behind my ribs as a light sheen of sweat breaks out across my forehead despite the mild winter weather.

She leans over. Snap. Snap. Snap. "So, I know that we said no strings, but would it be possible for you to, say... not sleep with anyone else while I'm here?"

I whimper, but other than that, I'm incapable of making a coherent sound.

"You can say no," she says, just as comfortable as you please in any surrounding. I guess that's an advantage of being so well-traveled. "I mean, even though we kind of talked about it before, you can change your mind. At least I'll know where I stand."

I hold perfectly still, staring down at the enormous black and brown tarantula that is slowly creeping toward my boot. I can't speak. I can barely breathe. Ever since I was a boy, I've had an irrational fear of spiders. Little ones, I can handle. Jumping spiders are even kind of cute. Anything bigger than my thumbnail, though? And with motherfucking hair like the kind you might find on an old man's balls? No way. I got caught in a spiderfest during tarantula mating season when I was about eight years old, and ever since, spiders have creeped me the fuck *out*.

"Stella," I squeak at last.

She sighs, and her shoulders slump. "Spit it out. It's not a big deal. I'm a mature adult, Anders. I'm not asking you to change for me. From what I hear, the puck bunnies are everywhere. I just thought that during the time we were together—it might be nice if we were monogamous."

I'd like to be monogamous with you forever.

But I don't say the words because fear sealed my lips shut the moment Hairy Ball Sack started his forward march toward my body.

I'm dimly aware that what she's saying is important, but the tarantula has just discovered my boot and seems fascinated. It probes the toe with its legs.

Just step on it. Squash it. Mash it to a pulp. My muscles won't obey me, and the next thing I know, the damn thing crawls all the way onto my footwear as if it has a right to be there.

"*Nooo,*" I whine. It's going to crawl onto my sock, and then right onto the bare skin of my calf, at which point I will either throw up or drop dead on the spot. And then Stella will know I'm a pussy when it comes to arachnids of the furry variety.

"Seriously, Anders?" Stella whips toward me. I can't look up to see her expression, because I'm locked in a staring contest with a desert pest, and I'm pretty sure that they don't have eyelids.

"Help," I squeak, breaking my gaze.

He wins.

"Ooh, wow, look what you found!" Stella hurries over and lifts her camera. I'm saved. She's going to exterminate it with her zoom lens, and I'll be able to move again.

Instead of rescuing me, however, she leans in so close she could kiss his tiny legs and begins to take photos.

"Wow," she gushes. "Look at that. It's the biggest one I've ever seen! Hold still. The note in the guidebook said that they'll bite if you startle them." She flips her camera sideways to get a better angle.

With my breath stalled in my lungs, I have never felt so betrayed in my life.

Maybe I don't love you, Stella Croft.

Maybe I don't even like *you.*

At last, when Stella has enough pictures, she scoots forward and gently shoos the tarantula away. Nobody gets bitten, and as it finally disappears into the surrounding scree, I finally relax.

"Poor Anders." Stella stands up and kisses my cheek. "Do you have arachnophobia?"

"Maybe a little." I wrap my arms around her. "Thank you for saving me."

"It wasn't *doing* anything but curiously existing!" she laughs.

I cling to her until my legs stop shaking. "Seriously, I can't handle those things. Childhood trauma. As long as you promise to keep me safe from the big, scary spiders of the world, I promise not to sleep with anyone else."

Stella frees herself and beams up at me. "Deal. Now, what do you say we head back to the car and get something to eat? I think that's enough nature for one day. If we stay out here any longer, you might encounter a gecko and pass out."

"Yes, please. Sorry for being a big baby." I take her hand, and we make our way back down the trail.

"It's not childish to be afraid," Stella says as a funny look crosses her face. "I hope that you know that you can be vulnerable with me. Even if you are a big, strong, professional athlete."

I lace my fingers with hers, conscious of how good it feels to be tied together. "Says you. I don't think you're afraid of anything. I bet there's nothing on Earth that scares you."

Her smile fades as she cuts her eyes away from me. "You'd be wrong," she says.

CHAPTER SIXTEEN

Stella

"When are you going to tell me where we're headed?" Anders asks.

It's my turn to drive, and for once, I've chosen the location of our date night. We've been doing this a lot since I've been in town and it feels so coupley. I'm starting to get attached to the normalcy of us being together. Anders keeps peering out the window in an attempt to pinpoint our location and figure out my plan for the evening.

"You can find out when we get there," I tell him.

Out of the corner of my eye, I see Anders reach for his phone.

"And no cheating!" I exclaim.

He laughs and puts his phone away again. "All right, I won't peek."

"Do you really hate surprises that much?" I tease.

"Depends on the surprise," he says. "When I was a kid, there were more bad ones than good. I'm trying to remedy that as an adult."

I frown at him. "That sounds crappy. Will you tell me more about it?"

He reaches out to rub my thigh as he says, "Another time. I'm gearing up for a nice night with my girl, and I'm not keen to shit all over it with tales of woe from my past."

That hand of his starts doing things to my body that only it can do, and just like that, all thoughts of vulnerability flee the scene.

Immediately, an intense sensation of desire warms my belly. After years of mediocre sex, I'd resigned myself to being a non-starter, but ever since Anders came back into my life, my libido has been off the charts. The memory of the Christmas party alone has fueled dozens of frantic, private moments while he was on the road.

Anders Beck has turned me into a sex fiend, and I'm not even mad about it.

I haven't been able to muster a witty retort by the time we pull up to the brightly lit arches outside our final destination.

"You brought me to a shady McDonald's?" Anders asks.

"No, goofball." I point to the sign. "It's the West Wind Drive-in."

Anders busts up laughing. "As in, drive-in movies? That's very Danny and Sandy. Where are we going next, the sock hop?"

I flick his knee. "If you don't like it, we can leave."

"I'm just kidding." He leans over to kiss my temple. "I'd be happy anywhere with you. But in case you were too busy exploring the jungle to keep up with modern technology, there's this thing now called *streaming*. Remind me to introduce you to the concept of Netflix and Chill. It's far more comfortable and climate controlled."

We inch forward a space in the entrance line. "I'm aware of the concept. But did it ever occur to you that I just want to watch a movie? Where's your sense of adventure and don't you ever step outside your comfort zone?"

"In that case, you'd take me to the theater," Anders points out. "There are only two reasons to go to a drive-in: you've got a screaming kid who can't sit still for a full two hours, or you're a closet exhibitionist who wants to fool around during the movie without getting caught."

I look away. "Is that so?"

We pull up to the window, and Anders sits quietly while I pay for the tickets. The minute I roll my window back up, however, he leans over the gap between our seats to peer at my expression.

I wonder how I'm going to manage if I can't wake up and see his face every day. Shoving that thought out of my mind for now, I let my eyes caress his chiseled jawline.

Anders waggles his eyebrows. "I was teasing just now, but it got me thinking. *Are* you an exhibitionist, Stella? Because a few out of the many times we've had sex, we've been less than discreet."

"And that's my fault, how?" I ask as I scan the lot. We'd have a better view if we park toward the middle of the lot, but I'd like a bit more privacy. I pick a shadowed spot on the opposite side of the lot from the concession stand and the bathrooms, where there's likely to be less foot traffic. "Maybe *you're* the exhibitionist and you're trying to pin the shame on me!"

"I'm not trying to shame you. If anything, I'm trying to encourage you." Anders reaches over and puts his palm on my knee. The moment he touches my skin, I shiver. It's warm inside the car, but the temperature outside is dipping toward chilly. The skirt I wore is not the least bit seasonally appropriate. Okay, I admit it. I might have been thinking about the easy access it provided when I picked it. Seems I can't get enough of this man no matter where we are.

I get out of the car and open the rear door before sliding into the back seat. "Come on," I tell Anders. "We've got the perfect setup here."

Instead of getting out, he climbs between the seats. It's a tight fit in my little car, and he has to practically crawl into my lap to wedge his body inside. He's much too big for that sort of thing, but I don't complain. Any excuse to touch him is a win in my book.

I brought a big blanket, and Mom packed us a picnic basket full of movie snacks. While we wait for the movie to start, I examine our supplies.

"I think Mom's trying to live vicariously through us," I say. "Look at this. Caramel corn, trail mix, Raisinets, sour gummies, Junior Mints... She can't eat any of this stuff."

Anders leans over me, his breath hot on my neck. "Did you say Junior Mints? Can I have some?"

"They're all yours." I press the box into his hand. "I've never really understood the appeal of ruining perfectly good chocolate by mixing it with mint."

He leans back against the seat and tears the box open. "These things are underrated. Any idea what we're watching?"

"*Two Weeks Notice*," I answer as I help myself to some caramel corn.

"Ah. The Hugh Grant movie." Anders pops another mint into his mouth. "Have you seen it before?"

Watching rom coms over and over in my various hotel rooms across the world provided a lot of comfort during those lonely nights on my own as I chased my dreams. But I'll never admit it. If I do, he'll have ammunition to argue against my leaving. "A couple of times."

"Me, too." He shakes a few more candies into his palm. "I can enjoy a good chick flick without letting it affect my masculinity. Since we've both seen it already, we're not going to miss much if we get distracted."

"See, what did I tell you? *You're* the exhibitionist." I grin sidelong at him.

"And you brought me out in public." Anders' eyes sparkle in the dim light. "What does that say about you?"

I shift closer to whisper in his ear. "Are you accusing me of trying to seduce you, Anders Beck?"

Outside, the screen flickers to life. Anders is still staring at me with rapt attention. "If you want to hear the movie, we should turn on the radio."

"I'm fine with just the heat," I say breathlessly.

"Yeah?" He leans over to place a minty kiss on my bare throat. "In that case, Stella Croft, I would say that you've got something on your mind besides the film. I kind of dig it. I should allow you to plan all future tarantula-free dates."

I glance out the window to see how much privacy we have. It's the middle of the week, right between the holidays; the lot is only half full, and the nearest car is a good twenty spots away.

"Look at you," Anders purrs. "I was right. Admit it, Stella. You love the thrill of wondering if you'll get caught in the act."

I open my mouth with the intention of saying something intelligent, but to my embarrassment, all that emerges is a little pant of longing. Seems I can't breathe anything but his air.

He nuzzles my neck. "Tell me what you want right now."

"Um." My mind spins into a jumble of thoughts wound as tightly as tangled fishing line. Is it his cologne? Is he emitting some sort of brain-scrambling pheromone? How does he have this effect on me? Worse yet, he's the only one who ever has. I've never experienced this before so I know how hard it is to find, which makes me wonder why I'm not grabbing it and holding on with both hands.

I know I'll never find it again. Which makes it that much more precious if I throw it away. We're caught in an impossible situation and in this moment, I make a conscious choice to ignore that.

"I want..." Under the blanket, my hand creeps between my

legs, and I rub my palm against the crotch of my panties.

Anders freezes. "Stella, are you *touching* yourself right now?"

"Maybe." I lift my head so that my nose brushes his earlobe. "Do you like it?" My panties are already soaked through. I don't know exactly what I want, but I can say with certainty that if Anders is the one doing it, I'm all in.

"Shit, *yes*." He shoves his box of mints into the door pocket and slides his own hand beneath the blanket. I imagine the curve of his cock, already hard beneath his palm, and my need leaves me trembling.

"Anders," I moan.

"Holy fuck." He sits upright, pulling away from me, fumbling with his waistband. "Are we doing this? Because if you're not comfortable with it—"

"I need you," I pant. "I've been thinking about you ever since the Christmas party. I've never come like that before. We didn't have enough time. And I had to worry about Noah's books. But I don't have to worry about anything right now besides being limber enough to pull this off. Can we do it again?"

Anders squeezes his eyes shut and mutters something under his breath, forcing his breathing into a steady rhythm. "We can damn well try. Can you get your panties off without too much trouble?"

I shimmy out of my underwear so fast it would make Houdini's head spin. Thank God we had the birth control/sexual health convo a while ago so we don't have to worry about condoms in this tight space.

"Impressive," Anders says as I drop them to the floor. "Come here."

He keeps the blanket over us as he shifts me onto his lap reverse cowgirl style. I gasp when the warm, smooth skin of his dick brushes against me. His sweatpants are slung low on his hips now. I face forward. If someone were to look through the window, they might think I'm just sitting on his lap to watch the movie.

"Is this okay?" he whispers against the back of my neck. His arms are around my waist, pulling me close.

I stroke him with one hand as I fix my eyes on the movie screen, where Sandra Bullock and Hugh Grant are arguing again because opposites attract. In the movie, they have to work together to communicate boundaries and actually adhere to them. So why do I feel like the little things are just as important? They make life rich. They make it worth living. Like making out at a drive-in with the man you always remembered and will never be able to forget.

I sigh and sag backward into his body heat. "I'll be better when you're inside me. Stretching me. Fucking me."

"Christ." He bends forward to rest his chin on my shoulder. "Was the Christmas party really that good for you?"

He asks the question like he can't figure me out and in that moment, I realize I must appear far more worldly than I actually am. "Yes. Wasn't it for you?"

Anders shivers and kisses my skin again. "Yeah, it was. It really was. Stella... it's you. The way you feel. The way you taste. The way you shiver and clench when you come all over me."

I brace my back against his chest and shift my hips forward, sinking onto him. His groan echoes through the small space, and I clamp down tight on him as I lower myself onto his lap. It's not the best angle, or the most comfortable position, but the urgency of the moment more than makes up for that. My nipples tighten and chafe against the cups of my bra, and I flex my legs just enough to raise me up and then drop down again.

Maybe he's right. Maybe I like doing this in public.

Or maybe I just need Anders so badly that I can't wait long enough to get him alone.

"Can I move you?" he whispers.

"Anything."

He lowers his hands to my waist beneath the blanket. "You should keep touching yourself." Then he lifts me up a few inches, as if I weigh nothing, and pistons his hips up against me.

Within seconds, I'm forced to bite down hard on the inside of my cheek to keep from crying out. My fingers flick between my thighs, circling my clit, driving myself toward the edge.

"You like that, Stella?" Anders pants. "Is this what you wanted? My cock stretching you as you touch your own clit?"

"Yes, yes..." I almost sob with relief. I can get myself off, and for so long that's been enough, but it's different with Anders. On my own, orgasms were one way to keep the pressures of the world at bay. With him, they're earth-shattering.

Because they're shared.

I'm not sure how much time passes, but the car windows are fogged with our frantic breathing by the time I clench up and then collapse against him in a boneless heap.

"Can I keep going?" he asks.

"Please." I'm still trembling with my release, although I know by now that it'll only be a matter of minutes until I'm ready to go again.

Anders' movements turn jerky and desperate until he, too, slumps back against the seat as a wave of heat rushes through me. He gasps for breath against my shoulder and engulfs me in an embrace.

In the quiet moments that follow, I find myself wishing that there could be more between us. I could almost convince myself that this is special to him, and I have to stop and remind myself our arrangement is temporary for a *reason*. I might have indulged in a little late night Google search after I found out who he was, and the stories swirling around this man are epic. Puck bunny after puck bunny used and tossed aside. Fans flashing their perfect tits and flat stomachs so he can sign them after games. The blogs are saturated with stories and photographic proof of him doing anything and everything. I'm not sure he's built for monogamy, and I'm not built to share. Besides, I've got a career that I love. I have goals of my own that don't align with his.

He loves hockey as much as I love taking beautiful photographs of nature and the wildlife I treasure. And those two don't mix.

The sex is fantastic, and the companionship is just as good, but it's not worth giving up my dreams over mind-blowing orgasms. If I gave up everything for what he wants, what kind of woman would that make me?

Not the one that Francine Croft raised, that's for sure.

Eventually, his grip eases. "Wanna turn on the radio now?" he asks, almost shyly. For a man who can talk filth with the best of them, his everyday golden retriever persona provides just enough dichotomy to make him irresistible.

But I have to resist him.

I will.

"Sure." I sit forward to fiddle with the speakers while Anders tucks himself back into his pants. We spend the next few minutes shifting around to get comfortable in the back seat and figure out where we are in the movie.

Anders' breathing deepens as the film progresses, and for a while I think he's asleep. It's not until Sandra Bullock barges in on Hugh Grant in the midst of his game of strip chess that he proves me wrong.

"Do I at least get two weeks' notice?" he whispers, lacing his fingers through mine.

I tilt my head and frown at him. "I don't work for you."

"Yeah, I know." Anders kisses my temple. "I mean, do I get two weeks' notice before you decide to ghost me?"

His question aligns a little too closely with my earlier train of thought. If I'm not careful, this agreement is going to bite me in the ass. I need to watch myself more carefully.

It's for his own good that I sit up and push him away. For a second, I almost thought he really cares about me. But that can't be true. He's a player. This is just another game to him.

"Careful, Beck," I tell him. "That sounds a lot like a string."

CHAPTER SEVENTEEN

Anders

"Remind me again why we're going golfing?" I ask.

Latham pipes up from the back seat. "Because Marco is learning to be an American, and what's more American than golf? Besides, there aren't that many chicks on the course, so he's less likely to get himself into trouble."

"Isn't golf a Scottish thing?" Noah asks as he rolls to a stop at the light.

"I'm not talking about its origins," Latham explains. "Most super-American stuff was borrowed from other places, but we made it bigger and better."

"I not know," Marco pipes up. "Sometimes you make bigger and worse. Like pizza. Or coffee. You should taste espresso back home." His eyes widen as he kisses his fingers and throws them into the air. According to Marco, everything is better in Italy.

Latham huffs. "Fine. At least we can agree that it's *bigger,* which is the point."

"Is that what you tell your hookups?" I ask. "Quantity over quality?"

Latham gives me the finger right over my shoulder. "If Marco's going to be in the NHL, he's gotta know how to golf. There are charity golf tournaments and just playing on a Saturday morning with your buddies to de-stress. He's learning. End of story."

Marco shrugs and leans forward between the seats to fiddle with the radio.

"Get your ass out of my face," Latham complains.

"And hands off the dial." I slap Marco's hand away. "That's not a thing. Shotgun controls the radio."

Marco's eyes widen. "In America, you shoot whoever touches radio? Actually, yes, I think this is very American. Guns, guns, guns. Everywhere the guns guns."

"Shotgun is whoever's riding in the passenger seat," Latham explains, pulling him back by his t-shirt. "In this case, Anders."

"Ah." Marco meets my eyes in the rearview mirror and frowns. "In *Italia*, we have no such rules. And no such guns."

Latham about launches himself toward the roof. "Seriously, Rossi? You Italians invented the *mafia*! Pretty sure you've got the market cornered on guns."

I place a protective hand over the radio dial. "When in Rome, do as the Romans do. But you're in Vegas now, baby! So mitts off."

Marco whines like a kicked puppy. "All I want is listen to Scarlett Sayzzzz!"

I sigh. "Fine. What station, since it means so much to you? Isn't she on Sirius?"

Noah snorts and glances sideways at me. "Here it comes."

"Absolutely not." Latham crosses his arms and glares out the window. "I hate her. I will *not* be listening to Scarlett Stone on my day off. That's a sure recipe for indigestion and a bad golf game. No way. Try again. I'd rather listen to Kenny G. than her."

"What?" Marco's hand flies to his mouth. "But her voice *erotico*, no?"

"No," Latham echoes, in a tone that leaves no room for debate. "She sounds like a cross between Harvey Fierstein and Marge Simpson. She's the worst, and I'm pretty sure I just made it clear that I hate her."

I twist around in my seat to study Latham. "Why? For a chick, she knows her hockey. I think her listenership is more male than female percentage wise. And that's saying something."

"I have the very best reason," Latham grumbles. He crosses his arms and shrinks back into the corner where the door meets the upholstery. "She. Hates. Me."

"It's true," Noah agrees. "I think he probably disappointed her in bed or something. Why else would she pummel one of the best players on the team? She's got a hard on for you and not in a good way."

"You don't know shit," Latham mutters.

"Well, she loves some Marco Polo," the Italian preens, smirking and wiggling his upper body in a little car dance.

"We've moved on from the *Stallone Italiano* thing?" I ask.

"Yes." Marco winks at me. "When you say Marco Polo, you want someone to come find. I want Scarlett Sayzzzz to come find *me*. She *bellissima*."

"Stop saying the name of her podcast all weird," Latham complains. "She doesn't deserve you stanning all over her. She's not worth the airwaves she's invading. In fact, let us never speak of her again."

After a healthy dose of Latham's bad attitude, I wait about two seconds before reaching for the radio and turning on Scarlett Says.

"Oh, come *on!*" he groans, flopping back into the leather like a dying fish.

"There is rule in America," Marco informs him by looking sideways and thumbing up a storm. "Shotgun controls radio. Is sacred law."

I lift my fist in solidarity, and Marco bumps his knuckles against mine, just like we taught him.

Sure enough, we tune in midway through Scarlett's commentary on Marco. "...one of the newest players, but with real raw talent reminiscent of hockey's glory days. He's a new fan favorite, especially with the ladies. Marco—"

"Polo," Marco whispers. *"Come to poppa, Scarlett Sayzzzz."*

"—Rossi has improved considerably since last season. At this rate, he'll be one of the best players on the team, something few people would have believed when he started last year. But Marco—"

"Polo."

"—isn't the only player whose game has gotten better this year. Noah Abbott, a long-time fan favorite, had a few rough games last season, but he's been steady and consistent in the net for the Venom. His save percentage is one of the best in the league." Scarlett chuckles to herself. "One might suggest that being in a long-term relationship can improve a goalie's game."

"Give me a break," Latham grumbles. Then I hear a grunt and a snort.

I lift a hand to stop him. "No, no, let's hear her out. She hasn't said anything about me yet. Maybe this thing with Stella is going to help my season."

I used to think the guys with wives and girlfriends had lost their ever-loving minds. Like why would you willfully settle down with one chick for the rest of your life? And then when you make that kind of extreme commitment, how do you then leave that woman all season long for practices, games, community outreach, and charity functions? During the season—which seems to be getting longer and longer—my calendar is rarely my own.

I used to tease and laugh at the guys who would hurry back to their room to FaceTime their family, especially Noah. I've never had an issue with my playboy reputation before, but right now I'm considering shedding it like a winter cloak. And instead of considering becoming a one-woman man an utter snoozefest, now I kind of understand it.

I might even want it.

"Yeah?" Latham grumbles. "You think getting your dick wet on the regular is going to improve your plus/minus? Guess the fuck again. Just wait until she figures out you're relationship averse and the whole thing goes stale like day-old bread."

He doesn't say it, but he doesn't have to, because I've been thinking about it nonstop. *What happens when she leaves?*

"To round out the dream team," Scarlett says, "we have to consider Anders Beck one of the finest players the NHL has to offer. His season-high goals scored make this hometown boy a favorite. Just like the Magic Wand, Anders always gets it done. Unlike Marco—"

"Polo."

"Will you friggin' *knock it off!*" Latham snaps, and I miss the next thirty seconds or so of coverage as the two of them wrestle in the back seat.

"Settle down, kids," Noah deadpans. "Don't make me turn this car around."

The scuffle dies down in time for us to hear Scarlett say, "Which brings us to the Venom's biggest, B-list fuckboy, Latham Newberry. In my personal opinion, he's one of the most overrated players in the sport today and should be demoted from the first line. Often affectionately called a grinder and held up as one of the hardest working in the NHL, Latham's obsession with scoring, both on and off the ice, is relentless. Too bad he's no good at either."

I whistle and point to Noah. "I think you're onto something with this spurned lover theory. This sounds personal. Latham, what did you *do* to her? Don't you know if you're going to go down on a woman you don't spell out the alphabet with your tongue anymore? It's all about sucking the clit and finding the g-spot at the same time. Read a book or something instead of spending all your time jacking off to PornHub, my dude."

"Are you fucking kidding me?" Latham snaps. "Like I would *ever* utilize my skill set on that witch. She probably paints her pussy in Belladonna just like her acerbic tongue. People are allowed to hate each other, okay? Everyone else loves me. Do you know how many boobs I'm gonna get to sign now that you two are going steady? Every hot chick with a great rack who used to fall all over Anders is going to gravitate to me."

"I have no *amore!*" Marco calls from the back seat. "I will sign boobs, too!"

"One angry sportscaster calling me a fuckboy isn't going to bring me down," Latham insists, despite the fact that his mood is, in fact, much lower than it was before. "I know who I am, and I sure as hell know what I can do. So let's focus on teaching this nitwit to golf. Haste makes waste. We can't teach him not to embarrass himself on the links and get Scarlett Stone off my back at the same time. Figuring out her deal is a challenge for another day."

I spin my head so I can look at him. "For somebody who takes his pregnant sister to Lamaze, you sure have a lot of chicks pissed at you."

He snorts. "I do that on the down low. Don't go shooting your mouth off about it."

When we finally make it to the green twenty minutes later, Latham gestures to his bag full of clubs. "All right, Marco, show us what you've got," he says.

Our Italian teammate hovers nervously over the array of options. "Which one I choose? I know nothing of golf."

"Don't worry, young Padawan," Noah says. "We will teach

that she's a seasoned professional.

"Nope. Every model's different. I'd like the photos to reflect that. If there are any poses that make you feel beautiful, or anything you'd like to show off, that would be my starting point."

Madison ponders this. "Beautiful? Or sexy? Because that would be completely different in my mind."

"I don't want this to be a *sexy* book, at least not in an erotic sense," I tell her. "More like... intimate. When people make assumptions about your appearance, what are they missing?"

"Ooh, I like that." Madison nibbles one fingernail, lost in thought. "I guess the big thing I hate is when they assume that my size means something. Like it says something about me. Fatphobic people naturally think that bigger bodies are attached to souls that lack morality or they wouldn't be big. But I live a very healthy lifestyle. So I'd want them to know that who I am isn't defined by my body, if that makes sense? I'm a confident person. I'd be confident if I were a size two, and I'm still confident as a plus size. How would you feel about trying to recreate some of my shoots for CoachB+, but minus the athleticwear?"

"I love it." I rub my hands together in delight. "Let's start there and see where it takes us." If only all of my models could be as self-aware as Madison, this book would be a slam dunk.

I'd almost forgotten that the guys were still here, but when Madison removes her robe and steps in front of the screen for the shoot, Marco pitches forward in his chair.

"*Bellissima*," he sighs, then his eyes widen when he realizes he said it aloud. He slinks back down and clamps his lips shut again.

Madison blows him a kiss before turning her back to me and falling into an effortless yoga pose. She stretches her arms behind her head and bends back in a crescent lunge.

Marco lets out a sigh that sounds more like he's about to expire.

"This dude is literally so extra," Madison tells us, but she doesn't seem annoyed anymore.

As we move through the shoot, I can't help but admire her approach. Every image is dynamic, and it makes me reconsider the stories that I want to tell in this book. I don't want to capture people's appearance so much as their *essence*.

It's the same with Anders. His body is amazing, obviously, but the reason I'm in trouble is the man inside of it.

I've never met anyone else quite like him, and now that I have, I'm afraid to lose him.

Because when I do, I'm going to lose a part of myself.

CHAPTER NINETEEN

Anders

Toward the end of January, Dante schedules a team dinner to welcome some new VIP skybox owners. I don't mind the events themselves, but any time I have to spend more than ten seconds in a room with my arrogant and rude boss, my skin wishes that it could crawl straight off of my body. I can't stand the guy on a good day, and this whole mix-up with Stella's photobook has only made things worse. I haven't spoken to him about it yet, in part because I'm afraid of what he'll say. Even the most basic conversations turn into confrontations with the Venom owner. According to Stella, Dante himself green-lit the project.

Either he's somehow forgotten about what's in my contract, or he's trying to get me in trouble. Is my boss just ignorant or a villain?

Even though I'm well aware it's probably a mixture of the two, I'm not sure I want to know the answer.

The seating arrangements have me between two of the wives. One is in her fifties, the other is pushing seventy. The younger of the two, Mrs. Zobrovski, is keeping things classy, but the older woman is going for broke. She introduces herself to me as Helena, and she's in that stage of life some people reach where their IDGAF attitude overrides their social niceties.

"My first husband looked just like you," she says. "Without the tattoos, of course, we didn't do that sort of thing back in the day. I like them, though." She runs her fingertips over my arm, tracing one of my sleeves. "It's pretty. Makes me wonder what you've got under your shirt. Or if you have one of those, oh, what do you call them. A tramp stamp?"

"You're awful," Mrs. Zobrovski titters, swirling her long-stemmed glass of rosé. "You can't ask people things like that. Anders here is a professional."

"Why not?" Helena demands. "I'm curious, and he'll tell me if it bothers him. Does it bother you, young man?"

"I don't mind you asking," I tell her. "I have plenty of tats you can't see. Got my first one back in high school."

"Ooh." Helena grins wickedly. "Is that so?"

"Yup." I wink. "I've got a few even my girlfriend hasn't seen."

Helena swoons, and Mrs. Zobrovski fans herself. Their husbands look over our way, but they're preoccupied talking business with some guy from the front office, and they seem resigned to whatever's going on over here. After all, mingling at these events is what the Venom players are here to do.

Helena turns to Cash, who's sitting on her far side. "What about you, young man? Are you tattooed as well?"

Apparently, the older woman hasn't noticed the gray peppering our veteran winger's beard lately. Or she just doesn't care.

"Sorry, no tats," Cash informs her, thumbing Marco's way. "He's got piercings."

Helena squints across the table at the Italian player. "I don't see any."

Cash smirks. "No, you wouldn't."

I wait for Marco to chime in with one of his usual off-color comments, but he just stares down at his plate and chases bites of crab cake around with his fork.

"Earth to Marco," Cash says.

"Polo," I add.

Marco jumps and glances around. "Sorry, am thinking."

"What's on your mind, honey?" Helena leans across the table toward him.

"The other day, I meet girl." Marco sighs dreamily and stares off toward the ceiling. "For me, is love at first sight, but my words get all tangled. I tell her she is angel, and she is offended. I tell her she is my destiny, and she turns away. And she so *bellissima*. So fierce, like tiger! I miss her already."

Cash and I exchange a glance over Helena's permed white hair. I can't begin to imagine what this woman looks like to have Marco so distracted. Since he got signed, I've literally never heard him talk about a woman this way. And since Marco doesn't spend that much time alone, I'm trying to figure it out.

"A hot young stud like you?" Helena asks. "There must be something wrong with this woman. Something you can't see. You're a catch!"

"I'm surprised you have any troubles with the ladies," Mrs. Zobrovski adds. Her cheeks are bright pink now, and her glass is empty. "I mean… just look at you."

"Usually, is fine. But is different." Marco gestures to his face. "One look in her eyes, and I know, she my *anima gemella*."

"I thought men didn't believe in soulmates?" Mrs. Zobrovski asks.

Cash shakes his head. "I sure don't."

I'm not so quick to answer. What is Stella, if not my other half? I've been chasing her from the beginning. Even in Costa Rica, I was the one in pursuit. She likes me well enough while I'm convenient, but I'm not sure she'd toss the word *soulmate* around. Then again, we're not discussing Stella's beliefs, are we?

"I think I do," I admit.

"You young people are so passionate," Helena says. "I believed in true love when I married my first husband. Then I found out that he was an ugly drunk who couldn't keep a job, and I got over *that* little fantasy. Take a well-intended piece of advice from an old lady who's lived a bunch. Love is work, boys, but in the end, it's worth it. You just have to hope both of you never fall out of it at the same time."

"A pretty face won't keep a marriage going strong." Mrs. Zobrovski nods over at her husband. "Anton and I were very clear on the terms of our prenup, and we weren't just discussing money. To hear some people talk, you would think that proper planning would take all the romance out of a relationship. I couldn't disagree more. Communication is the key to any partnership, marital or otherwise. Shared values and interests matter too."

Helena drinks to that, but I sit with it for a moment. Stella told me that she doesn't like having secrets, and yet I've been going out of my way to hide my tattoo. Not to mention my deep feelings. If I can't trust her with that information, why should I expect her to trust me with anything?

Maybe it's time to come clean and just let the chips fall. After all, this is Vegas and Lady Luck reigns supreme. Despite things rarely coming easy for me, in the end, I always come out on top.

I'm still pondering this when the meal ends, but before I can make my getaway, Dante slides over to me. He's wearing a sleek silver suit that makes him look like a poor man's Robert De Niro, and his tight smile doesn't exactly give me the warm fuzzies.

"Beck?" He gestures toward a small meeting room off the main ballroom. "A word if you will."

"Good luck, buddy," Cash murmurs, but he doesn't stick around to wait for me. None of us like being caught in Dante's crosshairs. It's much like being a spider entangled in its own web. And I've made it pretty well known how I feel about hairy arachnids.

As team owners go, Dante Giovanetti isn't the most likable guy to work for. Despite the fact that he doesn't know shit about the game, he's always up in our business, making decisions that would be better left to the front office or Coach Brenig. Of course, nobody likes to call him on it, because the dude signs our paychecks. The only good thing his meddling has ever done for this team was bringing Marco aboard, and that was a happy accident. Dante didn't hire him for his skill on the ice. He wants a team full of players who will ask how high when he says jump. Lord only knows what he's holding over Marco's head.

The man smells like money, dresses like a gangster, and has eyes as flat and soulless as a shark's. No, scratch that. The animatronic shark in *Jaws* possessed more humanity than the mafioso.

I'm gonna need a bigger boat.

He leans against the table and gestures to the chair in the corner. "Sit," he says.

I do as I'm told. It's a power move, of course. Dante's not as tall as most of the players, so he has to find ways to make himself feel big. If he's already doing that, I won't like what's coming.

"I wanted to ask you about the book." He crosses his arms and sneers down at me. In public situations, among people he wants to charm, he can make himself likable, but the people who work for him know what he's like behind closed doors.

"What book?" I ask.

He shakes his head. "S.J. Croft's book."

I immediately stiffen. "I'm sure it's coming out," I say. "But I didn't finish the nude shoot. It goes against the morality clause in my contract. You know, the one *you* had us all sign?"

"Don't be a pussy." Dante smirks. "Marco's happy to take your place. I just thought I'd give you one more chance to fix your mistake. You're the team captain. The younger guys look up to you. I don't like the fact that you refused the project. It's not a good look for you or the team."

I ball my hands into fists. "My naked ass isn't going in a coffee table book any more than it'll be going up on a billboard on Las Vegas Boulevard. The terms of my contract are pretty clear. Why would you blindside me with something like this without going through my agent to renegotiate?"

Dante's head tips to one side. "I own this team. And as a result, I own you. I don't understand why the ladies love a scruffy, wrong-side-of-the-tracks, inked up, little nobody like you. You've got no taste, no breeding, and no class. Even so, you're a fan favorite. Scarlett Stone talks you up, the press can't get enough of you, and every sweet piece of ass between here and Henderson is hot for you. So if I tell you to play hockey, you play. And if I tell you to show the ladies your cock for some famous photographer's coffee table book, you'll whip it out and fluff it up. So shut your ignorant pie hole and do what I tell you to. Never, ever question me again or we're going to have a serious problem."

I grip the arms of the chair so hard it's amazing that the wood doesn't splinter. "You don't own me, whatever you think," I growl. "If you're so desperate to trade me, go ahead. But good luck finding someone who can consistently score over thirty goals a season. You need me more than I need to live in Vegas. If you tell me to play hockey, I'll play. And if you tell me to violate my contract again? I'll move on, and your team will tank without me. No more Lord Stanley for you. You think those rich patrons out there are gonna stick around if you start racking up losses? All these new VIP skybox owners we're wining and dining tonight? Yeah, they won't renew."

Dante's face turns bright red, and he leans in toward me, hissing at me so that my face flecks with spittle. "You arrogant little motherfucker, you think you can talk to me that way? You think you can threaten *me*?"

"What are you gonna do?" I demand. "Release me outright? I'll sue you in court and in the press. Because I have the receipts proving you're in the wrong. How does that sound?"

A dark blue vein pulses in Dante's temple, and the tendons bulge in his neck. He swears at me in Italian, spewing a torrent of foreign words until spittle flies out of his mouth. My boss is probably threatening me with every ugly thing he can think of, but I hold my ground.

If he was going to pull this shit with anyone on the team, I'm glad it's me. What would Noah do if Dante threatened him? He's got a home here—not just a house, but a family network that extends from Molly and Viv all the way through Francine. If he was the one sitting in this chair, he'd have to be careful about how much he pushed back or everything that matters to him could come crashing down with a snap of Dante's stubby fingers. I wouldn't put it past Dante to take advantage of that.

How many other guys on the team have done things they're not comfortable with just to appease this asshat?

Dante steps close and sucks in a deep breath. "You really want to fuck with me, Beck?"

"No, sir," I growl. "I want to keep my head down and keep winning games for you, but apparently that's not good enough. So what'll it be? Are we going to stick to our own lanes, or do you want to make this a whole thing?"

Dante straightens up and runs his palm over his Armani

blazer, appearing ominously calm, but I know better. "I suppose you've made your point. Now, let me make mine. I don't take kindly to being undermined, and I'm not likely to forget this anytime soon."

"Right." I nod. "Noted. I'll keep that in mind. Can I go now?"

Without another word, he waves me through the door of the meeting room, then slams it shut behind me. On the surface, this looks like a win, but it doesn't feel like one. As long as I play for the Venom, I'm going to have to work with Dante, and I doubt this will be the last I hear about the book.

Or my blatant insubordination because of it.

Despite Cash's curious glance and Noah's pinched expression, I walk by the table with a little wave and head out. I can fill them all in when I've had a chance to cool down. It's still early, so as I head toward my car, I pull up Stella's number for a text. Helena's advice from earlier is still ringing in my ears, and after Dante's temper tantrum, I need to be near her.

My heart is in my throat as I type the words, *Can you come over to my place? I have something to tell you.*

It's time for some honesty. Stella was right. We shouldn't have any secrets between us.

CHAPTER TWENTY

Stella

I'm already waiting by Anders' front door when he pulls up. When he steps out of his car, I whistle. He's scrumptious from his tailored suit to his scruffy jaw to the tattoos peeking out from underneath his cuffs.

"You look nice," I tell him. "What's the occasion?"

"We had a welcome dinner at the Mona Lisa." He smiles crookedly as he approaches me. "You really think I look nice? You don't think I look like... how did he put it? *A scruffy little nobody with no taste, no breeding, and no class?*"

I balk at the bitterness in his words. "What? No. Who said that?"

"My asshole boss." Anders unlocks the door and ushers me inside.

"Oh my God." I pull a face as I kick off my sneakers. "*Dante Giovanetti* said that? Why?"

"Because he was trying to insist that I should go along with his plan to have me in your book, despite me being in breach of his own contract if I do it." Anders shrugs out of his blazer and loosens his tie. It's weird, seeing him all dressed up like this. He's hotter than hell, but he doesn't seem comfortable in formal clothes. I get it. Formal events are exhausting, and I personally hate having to act all proper in front of strangers, when that's not who I am at all. And I know Anders has to do it all the time. From traveling to and from games, to team events, to community outreach.

"He already sent Marco Rossi over to talk to me the other day. And Finn has been emailing me nonstop. He seems more excited about having you in the book than I ever was. I'm not sure why he's being like this. Any professional athlete is fine for that portion. It almost seems like Dante's being difficult on purpose." Mom usually handles my email correspondence, especially when I'm traveling, but she had to ask me to help draft a response the other day. The PR guy, Finn, is persistent, I'll give him that.

"You shouldn't be shooting Marco, either," Anders tells me. "Not naked, not clothed, not at all. He's got the same contract I do. And he's got way more to lose if he gets released because he'll immediately get deported back to Italy." He rubs the crease between his eyebrows and sighs. "Fucking Dante. Jesus, that guy doesn't know when to quit."

I bite my thumbnail. "Is this what you want to talk about? Because I'm not going to pressure you to finish the shoot. I'll figure things out with Marco separately. As far as I'm concerned, you're off the hook for all this. I'm not sure what I can do about Dante, but..."

Anders slides close to me and wraps his arms around my waist. As he looks down at me, some of the tension drains from his face. "No, that's not why I asked you to come over. I had something else I wanted to discuss. Do you want to come to the bedroom with me and I can show you?"

"Oh-ho." I bite my bottom lip and hook my fingers through his belt loops, pulling him against me. "I think I know what you want to show me."

"I'm not sure you do." He takes a deep breath and leans down to kiss my cheek. "Because I figure we should talk about the reason that I didn't get in the shower with you that day. And the main reason why I didn't show you all of me that day at the studio."

I swallow past the lump that forms in my throat. This doesn't sound good. "Oh. Yeah, okay."

"Is that a problem?" he asks.

"No." I search his eyes. "This just seems like it might be important, and I don't want to screw it up."

He bends down to kiss me, ever so sweet. "You won't. I trust you."

If he'd blurted, *I love you and I want to be together for real,* I don't think I would be more moved. Love is a thing that happens when you're not paying attention, but trust is something that has to be earned. Anders just gave it to me, even though I might not even deserve it yet. I don't take that lightly.

Anders takes my hand and leads me upstairs to the master bedroom. It's different, coming up here when I'm not crazed with lust. He walks me to the bed, but instead of hauling me into his arms, he perches on the corner of the mattress and starts to unbutton his shirt.

I sit in the middle of the bed with my legs tucked to one side, watching his movements intently. When he strips the crisp white cotton off at last, he pulls it away to reveal his back.

I've been braced for something horrible—scars are the first thing that came to mind. A deformity. Maybe healed scoliosis or something like that. Even a really terrible tattoo of a previous girlfriend. Instead, there's just more ink banding his ribcage, spilling like waves over one shoulder and rising like a phoenix up the other.

"I've never seen all your tats," I murmur. "Can I touch them?"

"Yeah." He shivers when I lay my palm against one shoulder blade.

"What do they all mean?" I follow the curves and lines of his ink across his bare flesh. Most of it's black, but there are a few places where the harsh lines fade into a gray stippling, and into brighter jewel-tones here and there. And if I know Anders, every single line means something to him.

"Most of them have to do with my family," he says. When he speaks, his voice rumbles through his chest and into my palm. "The ravens are for my grandparents on my dad's side. They pretty much raised me."

"Where are they now?" I ask, afraid I know the answer.

He stiffens. He inhales. "Gone."

My fingers flutter to a stop even as my heart squeezes. I pause. "I'm sorry, Anders."

He shrugs one shoulder. "It happens. They were old, and I got to be there for them in the end."

"And the wave?" I trace the whitecaps with my fingers.

"It has to do with how I felt when my mom left. I haven't spoken to her in, shit, fifteen years? She's remarried. Happy now, I guess, but." He shrugs again. "You know. She only contacts me when she wants money. My dad left us when I was too little to remember it. He tapped out when the going got tough. I don't even know if he's dead or alive."

It's been just me and my mom for a long time, but I can't imagine feeling so rejected by a parent. Who would I be without my mother's support? After my dad died, she's spent her whole life bending over backward to make sure that I have everything I need, and she's never held it against me even when her life would have been far easier without being a widow and a single mother.

Some of the pieces snap into place. "When you told me that you were impressed that I was helping my mom, is that because of what happened with your grandparents?"

"Hmm." Anders folds his hands in his lap. "Something like that."

My fingers start tracing the swirls again. "And the phoenix?"

"For the person who fathered me." Anders' voice comes out rough. I don't have to ask what he means by that. His tattoos are a map of his loss, a record of things he's loved that have slipped away in the night, whether by choice or not. "To remind me that I always have to rise. No one is going to do it for me."

"Oh, Anders," I breathe. "I shouldn't have pressed you so hard to talk about all this."

"That's not what I was trying to show you, actually." He gestures toward the middle of his back.

My gaze searches it out. "Oh, the cup. Is it, um, that thing from Harry Potter? The Goblet of Fire?"

"Are you shitting me?" Anders lets out a bark of laughter. "Oh my God, Stella, it's the Stanley Cup."

"Hmm." I clear my throat. "Right, *the* cup."

His entire body shakes with laughter. At least my faux pas lifted some of the lingering gloom. "It's the NHL championship trophy!"

I lean forward and rest my chin on his shoulder. "How many women have you slept with who have no idea what the heck that means?"

"One. Only one, and it's you. I can't believe that the biggest triumph of my life means *nothing* to you." He can't stop laughing, and I'm glad that I've eased the tension a little. "I'm not quite sure how I feel about that, but I do know it's funny as hell."

I kiss his neck and sit back. "Is that what you wanted to show me? You were afraid I wouldn't know what you were talking about, and—*oh*." My fingers pause on the handle of the hockey stick that cuts across the cup, where my own name is written out in jagged letters, in the style of his team's logo.

"I'm guessing you saw it?" he asks.

"Why would my name be on the tattoo?" I ask, holding my breath.

"It's kind of a long story." Anders fidgets. "Basically, the chick who did it knew I was still hung up on you, so she decided to get me back. Joke's on her, because I like it this way."

"You could have had it removed," I point out. "Or turned into something else. Like 'strength.' Because you, Anders Beck, have that in spades."

He turns his head to meet my eyes. "Why would I do that? It felt *right* to have your name there. Like, the Stanley Cup was my biggest achievement, and meeting you in Costa Rica was the best thing that ever happened to me. They make sense together. The other guys have the same tat, and theirs say Venom in the blade, but I guess as the team captain, I get to be extra."

"Are you serious? We hooked up *during spring break in college*." Despite my protests, I know what he means. I spent years thinking about him, even though I didn't know his real name. He was the standard by which I measured every guy I've been with since. I didn't know him, but I missed him. I pined for him and what could have been—what I thought could never be—even though I was certain that we'd never meet again.

I yearned to relive that one perfect moment that seemed suspended in time.

Anders' only response is, "I'm serious."

I lower my head to his skin and kiss the tattoo. Anders sucks in a breath, so I do it again, dragging my lips and tongue over the stretch of skin that marks at least this little patch of him as *mine*. Even though I might not deserve it.

"Stella," he sighs. "I was sure you were going to hate it. Then I thought you'd get mad. Then I thought you'd leave. Probably for good. During none of the scenarios that played out in my head did I ever imagine your lips on my skin."

"Why would I get mad?" I kiss him again, wrapping one arm around him and pressing my palm to his stomach. His ribcage heaves, and a soft moan tears out of him.

The truth is, as much as I pined for Blaze, there wasn't much between us. All I knew about him was that he was a good flirt and a great lay. When he touched me, he left my body satisfied for the first time. I put Blaze on a pedestal and turned him into a fantasy made up of all the attributes that the men in my life never had—those men who left me empty.

Meeting Anders now has meant so much more than that. Now I know how smart and thoughtful he can be, how voracious, how kind. I know that he can fuck me until my legs turn to jelly, but he also looks out for his friends. He's good with kids and animals, he has a strange sense of humor, and because of the trauma he's triumphed over, he can be so unexpectedly shy when he's not sure which way the wind is going to blow. I don't know everything about him yet, but I'm learning, and that's a hundred times better than imagining because it's real.

I might not have a tattoo of his name on my skin, but parts of me belong to him, too. I don't know how I'm ever going to walk away from this now that I know more, because the fantasy version of him is so much less compelling than the real man.

I shift closer still, so that my chest is pressed to his back, although I'm still fully clothed. I leave my left hand on his stomach and drop the other into his lap, palming him through the material of his dress pants.

Anders leans into me, reaching one hand back to caress my hair. We're folded together, without the frantic hunger of our previous encounters.

Things have shifted.

The air becomes thick with that knowledge.

"Stella." Anders twists around to kiss me, and in his attempts to push his way onto the bed, he ends up on top of me. His hands push under the hem of my shirt, caressing my belly and sides as his mouth covers mine. Even his kisses are languid and slow, almost drunk. They leave me intoxicated and greedy.

"Missed you," he whispers.

I turn my head to the side and scoff. "It's been less than a week since you saw me last," I point out. "Remember? Or is sex at the drive-in such a common occurrence for you that you forgot already?"

Without being able to reach my lips, Anders has to resort to kissing my neck. "Not common," he tells me. "Time isn't the issue. It's you. Even if I'd seen you before I left for that stupid dinner, I'd have missed you while I was gone." He pushes himself a little more upright. "Besides, you were avoiding me."

"I was not!" I exclaim. "I was busy!"

"And you weren't the least bit worried about the fact that I may have suggested introducing a single, solitary string into our relationship?"

He's got me there, I'm afraid. But not of our actual relationship, more of how I'm going to fall apart when I have to leave. I have indeed been busy, but not *so* busy that I couldn't make more time to text, or meet up with him for dinner. Perhaps sneak out of the guest house in the middle of the night for a secret rendezvous just a few doors down.

"I'm gun-shy," I tell him, before I realize how stupid it is to say something like that to a man who's lost as much as Anders has. "God, that sounded so awful. I'm not articulating myself very well here."

"Should we stop now, then? Because if having your name tattooed on my body *permanently* isn't a string, I'll be damned if I know what is." His hand rests on my stomach as he stares into my eyes. "I've told you all my secrets, Stella. Is there anything *I* should know?"

Three words rest heavy on my tongue, but damned if I'm going to say them now. Instead of spilling my guts in an awkward confession, I wrap my arms around his neck and pull him toward me. "I want you," I say, which is also the truth. It's just not the full truth. "And just how much I do scares me."

I want a lot more than sex and friendship from Anders Beck, and that knowledge is nothing short of terrifying. Because loving him—even thinking the thoughts—could blow my world apart. I could lose everything if I give myself completely to a man.

I could even lose myself.

He lowers himself onto me, pressing his groin to mine. His body is incredible—I can't imagine that I'll ever get enough of it. Warmth radiates from every inch of him, and his palms skate over my skin, upward to the bottom of my sports bra. I didn't have time to dress up before I headed over, so I'm just wearing the comfy clothes I was lounging around the house in, but Anders still caresses me like I'm wrapped in the finest silk. He peels off my shirt and bra in one fell swoop and tosses them aside.

Instead of teasing my breasts, however, Anders lowers himself onto me again so that we're skin to skin, and kisses me again. His movements are achingly slow, and the musky, masculine scent of him surrounds me, sharpened by the pine forest scent of a cologne I don't recognize. It brings me right back to our jungle. And the man who forever changed me while we were there. Did he choose that smell specifically for me?

He's claiming me, stamping my skin with himself. Even as I surrender, I wonder what it all means. He doesn't put his full bulk on me. Instead, he keeps himself lifted just enough that he feels like a weighted blanket. A warm, loving, slightly erotic weighted blanket.

Then he rolls his hips against me, and the whole tone shifts.

"Do you mind if we do something different?" he asks.

"No." I don't need to think about my answer before I give it. I trust this man to do something that will feel good for both of us, and if he wants me another way, I don't mind in the least.

"Come with me." He gets out of bed and shimmies out of his pants. I follow, shedding my leggings and panties as I go.

Anders starts the shower just as I step through the door.

"Oh." I bite my thumbnail as I ogle his naked ass. Holy shit, his thighs are incredible from all that skating. Men shouldn't be allowed to be this attractive. It's criminal.

"I have something in here you might appreciate." Anders grins as he gestures me inside the huge space. I swear you could park a car in here. "It's warm now. Ladies first."

I step in, sighing when the warm water hits my skin. "Why is your shower, like, a thousand times better than any other shower I've been in?" I ask.

"Water pressure. I have special showerheads. The main one is a rainfall, but there are five in total." Anders winks as he steps in after me. His shower could fit ten grown men and my feet enjoy the heated floors. "Turns out, after I met this absolute dream girl in Costa Rica, I developed *kind* of a fetish."

"Is that so?" Thank God there is some kind of treatment on the tile floor that grips the soles of my feet. Something tells me that this is all about to get extremely slippery.

"Yup." He pours a bit of a citrusy shower gel into his palm and rubs it to suds between his hands. The aroma hits my nostrils and then right between my legs. It smells... like him. "Mind if I...?"

I step forward to kiss him, and his hands instantly land on my breasts, covering me in suds. Bit by bit, his hands work their way over me, massaging the knots out of my back and shoulders, working out the tension in my wrists and fingers, and eventually working their way down to my ass. The pressure of his skin on mine leaves me feeling slow and sleepy even as my need throbs between my thighs.

"Shower gel is a terrible lubricant," I murmur as he massages the tops of my thighs; it's all he can reach without bending over.

"I know." He kisses my forehead. "I wasn't planning to use my hands this time, though." He shuffles forward and detaches the middle portion of the side showerhead. Water still courses over us, but there's plenty of pressure coming from the handheld portion as well.

"Oh." My eyes widen as Anders rinses me off.

He chuckles against my neck and pulls me against him. "Lean on me," he says. "I'll hold you up, okay?"

"I'm perfectly fine holding myself up," I protest.

"Sure." He doesn't sound like he believes me. "Spread your legs a little, Stella."

I do as he asks, and his free hand settles between my legs, spreading me open. The instant the pressurized water hits my clit, I shudder.

"Oh, *fuck!*" I yelp, arching against him.

"Is that a good thing?" he asks.

It's better than good. The warmth and the pressure combined leave my knees trembling. Anders adjusts the angle of the shower hose, and I let out a guttural cry.

"That good, baby?" he asks, holding me in a tight grip.

I can't speak. If I take even an ounce of focus off of staying upright, I'll become another statistic, a fresh victim of the slipperiest sex setting. So much for holding myself up. If Anders weren't here, I'd be down for the count.

Every muscle in my body shudders as I tighten around nothing, already pushed to the brink.

"Wow." Anders chuckles. "That's the fastest I've ever seen you come, baby. That was hot as fuck."

"Don't stop," I say. I cling to his arms for support. "I think I can—Oh, *Anders! Oh my God oh my God ohmygodohmygod...*" My words finally end in another wordless groan as I come even harder the second time. Apparently Anders isn't the only one with a water fetish.

He shoves the showerhead back into place and lifts me, just like he did in Costa Rica. He's even stronger now, and my feet don't touch the ground. With just a bit of shifting and stabilizing our bodies, he positions himself. I help out as much as I can as Anders thrusts into me, growling as he does so. There's more friction than usual, one of the downsides of water, but I'm still shaking with my second orgasm and I'm giddy with pleasure. Who knew being multi orgasmic was even a thing outside of romance novels and *Cosmo*?

I'm a believer.

Anders doesn't last long, either. Within moments, he sways, and he barely manages to put me down before he has to catch himself on the shower wall.

"Sorry," he says in a slurred voice as he rubs my shoulder. "It was just, you know, after everything, I wanted you so bad. And hearing you like that, feeling you against me, it's so fucking hot when you explode all over me."

"There's nothing to apologize for." I hold onto him to avoid slipping. "Although I *am* going to need you to carry me back to the bedroom."

"Yeah?" Anders grins. "And you're sure you want to do that now? You don't want to see how many times I can make you come with the showerhead?"

I bite my bottom lip and consider his offer. "Only if you can hold me," I say at last.

It's a treacherous endeavor, but a rewarding one. By the time Anders carries me to bed, I've lost count.

CHAPTER TWENTY-ONE

Anders

The moment I roll up to the stadium, a little kid runs over and throws his arms around me. "You're my favorite!" he tells me. "When I grow up, I wanna be awesome like you!"

"Is that so?" I squat down to his eye-level and quirk a brow. "And what would that look like?"

A couple years ago, Finn came up with the idea to get involved with the Make-A-Wish Foundation. Dante's such a loose cannon that he would never have come up with the idea on his own, but his personal motto seems to be *all press is good press,* so he signed off on Finn's idea.

Personally, I enjoy the Make-A-Wish days, so when Finn emailed me and told me that a kid with epilepsy and a major hockey obsession named Owen asked to spend a morning with me, I went all in.

Right from the get-go, this kid's a charmer. "I wanna be huge and rich and kick butt on the ice!" Owen flexes his little muscles.

His mom, the only parent there, stifles a laugh.

"Hmm." I squint, sizing the little guy up. "And how old are you now, Owen?"

"Six." He puffs out his chest, which is swimming in an oversized Venom jersey with my last name and number on the back. "But I'm gonna be seven real soon!"

"Wow, *seven.* When I was your age, I didn't know *what* I wanted to be. You're ahead of the curve, little buddy." I stand up again. "Do you know how to skate?"

He nods and points to the bag his mom is carrying. "Kinda. And I brought all my stuff, just in case."

"You don't have to skate with him," his mom adds hastily, stepping a little closer. She's about my age, which seems pretty young to have a six-year-old—not that I'm judging, I just can't imagine having my life together enough to wrangle a kid. Although Noah's managed pretty well, all things considered.

If you and Stella had gotten together after Costa Rica, you could have a kid Vivian's age by now. The thought pops unbidden into my mind. Usually, the idea of knocking up a woman I've casually slept with would give me a borderline panic attack, but I'm suddenly weighing the pros and cons of having a child with Stella. How would that even work? Long-term, it would be hard to balance both of our careers with a baby... unless Francine was able to help out. And why not? She's helped Noah out plenty, and I bet she'd be thrilled to have a grandkid of her own...

Before I can develop a full-on case of baby fever, I smile at Owen's mom. "It's fine with me, as long as he's okay to skate. I should warn you, though, I don't have a lot of medical training."

"His new medication has been helping a lot," Owen's mom says. "And if anything happens, I'll be right here, being a total helicopter mom." She laughs to herself and turns her face toward the floor, hiding a smile. She's a lot less outgoing than her kid.

"In that case, let's make a day of it." I hold my hand out for the giant duffle bag she's carrying. "Want me to haul that around for you?"

"Oh, thanks, Mr. Beck, but that's really not necessary." Her cheeks turn pink. She's not the usual overzealous female

Venom fan that I'm used to, but it's obvious that she's flustered.

"You can call me Anders," I tell her. "And it's not a problem, I have to carry gear around all the time. You and Owen should enjoy yourselves today. Let me be the sherpa *and* the tour guide."

She lifts the duffle strap off of her shoulder. "That's really nice of you. And you can call me Kelly."

I hoist the bag onto my shoulder and gesture to Owen. "Follow me. Let's go on an arena tour. After that, I'll give you some pointers on how to play."

"On the Vegas Venom *ice?*" Owen claps one palm to each cheek, and his eyes gleam. "Really? Mom, did you hear that? I'm gonna go on the ice! That's where all the magic happens."

Pretty sure most of the magic lately has been happening inside my shower.

"You sure are, baby." Kelly shoots me a grateful look. "Isn't that amazing?"

Some of the Make-A-Wish kids I've met with in the past have had pretty serious physical limitations. Not all of them are safe to skate, so I've had to figure out a tour route that follows the access ramps through the stadium. Owen, however, is rocket-powered, so while his mom and I take things a little slower, he zooms all over the place, checking out everything up close and personal.

"Do you come to a lot of games?" I ask Kelly.

She blushes again and shakes her head. "It's just me and Owen, so money's tight. This is his first time in the arena. Usually we just get to see it on TV. But that doesn't stop him from being your biggest fan."

"I know what that's like," I tell her. "We didn't have a lot of money growing up. You two live in Vegas?"

Kelly nods, and from the way she shrinks into herself, I can picture the kind of circumstances they go home to at night. Raising a kid as a single mom is hard enough, never mind the added stress of a chronic condition. They probably can only live in a bad part of town where she has to worry about safety along with insurance and medication costs. Hockey tickets don't fit in that scenario at all.

I can't fix their circumstances, but there's something I *can* do. "If coming to games wouldn't trigger his epilepsy, you know, with all the lights and noise, I can get you set up for a few games."

Kelly's eyes widen. "Are you serious?"

"Yeah. It's not a big deal. We get comp tickets, and I don't have a lot of people around to invite, so..." I trail off, realizing how this might sound. "Just so you know, I'm not trying to make this weird. I'm not, uh..."

"Hitting on me?" Kelly laughs. "I didn't think so. I'm sure you have no trouble scoring, and single moms aren't exactly a hot commodity."

The self-deprecating way she says that is a little bit heartbreaking. "Well, you know, my girlfriend isn't a big hockey fan, so she'd probably be happy to hear that the tickets are going to someone who can actually appreciate them. And I was raised by my grandparents for most of my childhood, so I get the single mom thing. It's a tough gig."

"You have a girlfriend?" Kelly perks up. "I thought you guys were all kind of, you know..."

"Slutty?" I smirk. "I'm not saying you're *wrong*. But a lot of the guys are married or coupled up. And I'm spoken for too. I take that seriously."

Kelly sighs and her eyes unfocus. I guess the idea of a professional athlete who's a voluntary monogamist is appealing.

Owen zooms back down the steps toward us. "Wow, you can see everything from up there!"

"The seats are even better up front," I tell him. "But you're about to get the best view in the house."

We lace up our skates together, and Kelly sits on the Venom bench to watch us as I take Owen out onto the ice. He's a little wobbly at first, but after a few minutes he finds his groove and begins to skate without relying on me for stability. I show him a couple moves and give him tips on how to stick handle, and then the two of us run some shooting drills. Within the hour, Owen's zooming around the rink like a seasoned pro. He even manages a decent shot that sends the puck sailing into the net.

From her vantage point as honorary coach, Kelly whistles and cheers and takes videos on her phone, while Owen skates a victory lap.

"Look at me!" he crows as he sails past me. "I'm an NHL pro!"

I toss my hair and wink at him. "Now you just need to grow out your flow and bulk up those muscles." I flex my arms. "Eat your veggies."

"Okay!" Owen skates back to the edge of the rink. "Mom, Anders says I gotta eat more vegetables! But not spinach. I hate spinach."

"Good advice." Kelly winks at me as Owen heads to the bench and bends over to unlace his skates. "Maybe you should start with an extra serving tonight."

"Okay!" he chirps. "I'm gonna grow big and strong."

"Ready to finish up your tour?" I ask.

Owen wriggles out of his skates and stuffs his feet back into his sneakers. "Yeah! And can you sign my jersey?"

"Heck, yeah." Kelly hands me a Sharpie, and I scrawl my name in giant letters across the back of his jersey.

Our tour ends outside of the arena, where Owen and I pose for a few shots together.

I should have asked Stella to come. She would have gotten some amazing pictures. Maybe next time, assuming she's still in Vegas then.

"Say cheese!" Kelly calls, aiming her iPhone.

"*Cheese!*" Owen's grin takes up his whole face. I'm a little more reserved.

All of a sudden, Kelly lowers it, and her face flames bright red. "Oh, wow. Anders, is that *you?*" She points behind me, and I turn, not understanding the question.

And then I see it.

One of the enormous billboards over Las Vegas Boulevard, which has been sitting empty for weeks, is plastered with a huge black and white photo of a mostly-naked man.

A *familiar* man.

"Yeah," I say in a strangled voice. "It is." Not only do I recognize the picture, I know exactly who took it. The fedora held over my junk is a dead giveaway.

It's one of Stella's pictures from that day at the photo studio before we gave up and went our separate ways.

"Wow," Owen says, shaking his head. "I'm gonna need to eat a *lot* of vegetables."

Thank goodness, none of my bits are on display. I wouldn't let Stella photograph my back, and the hat is safely in place. But the sideview puts my ass right out there. And my whole upper body and my legs. With a shake of my head, I stare. How the hell did this happen?

The script across the left side of the billboard read, *See most of Anders here in black and white.* To the right of the picture it adds, *See **all** of Anders in living color on Venom Ice!* with a huge arrow pointing to the rink.

I don't know how that picture got out into the world, but I know *exactly* who is responsible for that billboard. Dante motherfucking Giovanetti.

Then Dante's words from the dinner the other night send me crashing back to earth with a thud. *I don't take kindly to being undermined, and I'm not likely to forget this anytime soon.*

Seems he's a man who makes good on his threats.

I'm gonna kill him. Then I'm gonna call my agent.

"Well, that's it for the tour," I say in a strangled voice. "Did you have a nice day, Owen?"

"Yeah!" He hugs me again. "It was super fun!"

"Want to give me your email?" I ask Kelly. "I'll have someone from the front office reach out to you about that other thing we discussed."

Owen claps his hands and dances around his mom's legs. "More surprises?"

Oh, how I long for the days when normal team publicity was a *good* thing and not an indication that people in my life were betraying my trust left and right.

"Patience, Owen," Kelly says as she writes down her info for me. I must be doing a pretty good job of hiding my anger, because neither of them are in a huge hurry to get away from me. That's good, because if they could see how livid I am, how my insides have turned into a category five hurricane, it would probably ruin a perfect afternoon.

I manage to keep it together until they're safely in their car, driving away from the arena. The second they're out of sight, I hail a cab.

I hope I can get Owen and his mom some comp tickets, but it might be difficult to swing that if I'm in jail for murdering my boss. The worst part isn't Dante's behavior, because honestly, that's just the kind of asshole he is.

The thing that *really* bothers me is that I didn't sign a release on those photos, and yet somehow, they ended up in Dante's hands.

Which means that Stella lied to me.

I can't even begin to describe the pain that knowledge sends shooting through my heart.

* * *

It's only a few blocks to the Mona Lisa, where Dante's private offices are located. I don't visit often, since Dante's not the kind of boss I like to hang around with for fun. Still, all the security guards know me by sight, so nobody tries to stop me as I storm back to find him. His assistant stutters and tries to page him through the phone, but I wave her off.

When I slam open his office door, Dante doesn't even look up from his paperwork.

As I inhale, I seethe. "What the hell, Mr. Giovanetti? Why is there a naked billboard of me right in front of the arena?"

"Billboards are damn expensive," Dante observes, still scanning his papers. I doubt he's reading right now. This is just another one of his power moves. Ignore and throw your enemy off their game. "The empty space was costing me money, and the picture is already generating buzz. The women love it. Like I told you before, I do what I want. Thought I made that very clear during our last conversation."

I slam my palms down on the desk. "How did you even *get* that photo?"

Dante sniffs. "S.J. Croft—I'm sorry, Stella—sent it to me and told me I didn't need a release from you. I paid her handsomely."

A roar bubbles up but stalls in my throat as I swallow against it. "Bullshit."

Dante finally glances up at me. "Are you calling me a liar?" he asks in a deadly whisper.

I want to put my fist through something, but I can't cause a scene. If Dante trades me, fucking *fine*, but if I do anything to make myself look bad, I could sabotage my whole career. If I get released under the morals clause that *he* violated without my consent, other teams might not be willing to take a chance on me due to the ensuing drama.

I've been living my life for Stella and hockey. I'm not going to let Dante take both from me in one fell swoop.

He offers me a little shit-eating grin. "If that's all you needed, Beck, then now would be a great time to fuck off and think about how you can score some more goals." His smirk widens. "And you might want to do some more squats. You could have looked better."

Dante's right. There's no point in sticking around. He didn't even deny his role in putting up that billboard.

As tempting as it is to pound him into a pulp, I know better. Besides, there's someone else I need to see. I don't like, admire, or even trust my boss, so his betrayal means almost nothing.

Stella's means everything.

CHAPTER TWENTY-TWO

Stella

"Which angle is better?" Marco asks, rolling onto his side on the fur rug we're using as a prop. "You want jewels or cheeks? *Cazzo o culo?*"

I shake my head at his antics. Marco's not as professional as Madison, but he's a lot more comfortable in front of the camera than Anders was. He's goofing around, and since I'm trying to capture his personality on camera, that seems fitting.

"Let's try a few different angles and see what feels natural," I say.

"Which do you think Madison would like more, eh?" He lets me snap a few pictures before he sits up and crosses his legs, then braces one elbow against his knee and rests his chin on his fist. "Like Rodin's *Thinker*, maybe seem so smart? She like smart men, you think?"

"You're kind of hung up on Madison, aren't you?" I ask.

"*Si, si,* cannot stop thinking about my *bellissima!*" Marco sighs, staring off into the distance with a goofy smile on his face that makes him look almost blissful. I take a quick picture. I'm not ready to end the shoot yet, but something tells me that's going to be the one I go with for the book. "So pretty. No, not pretty, word not big enough. Need bigger word for so much the flesh, don't you think? I hope I see her again. To let woman like that leave forever would be very sad."

"Her brother's a hockey player, so—" I begin.

I'm cut off when the door slams open and Anders stomps

into the studio.

"Ah, *Capitano!*" Marco lifts his arms in the air, like a baby who's hoping to be picked up, but all that does is shift the rug so that Marco's junk is exposed in all its glory. And Marco, God bless him, doesn't even think he should move to cover himself. "Stella finally let me agree to shoot, and now you are here! Did you change mind?"

Anders' face turns bright red, and his lip curls back in a snarl. "What the *fuck?*" he snarls, lifting his arm and pitching forward like he's about to punch Marco. "Did Dante send you here?"

Instead of going on the offensive, Marco moves his arms to protect his face. "No hitting, no hitting!" he exclaims. "What I do now? She only looking for book, there is no touch! *La promessa!*"

"I can't fucking believe that you'd go along with Dante for this after I made it clear how I felt about it!" Anders bellows. I've never seen him like this, even on the ice. He's never, ever aggro. This sudden change in him is so out of character I'm speared where I stand. It's kind of terrifying.

I've never been *afraid* of Anders before. "Stop it," I say. "Stop this right now. Whatever's going on, let's talk about it."

"I only do what he tell me!" Marco shouts, keeping his hands up in a defensive posture.

"Sure, because you're his goddamn *pet*. And *you*." Anders spins toward me and points an accusing finger in my direction. "What the actual hell, Stella? Why would you send Dante that picture when I never signed a release? And why would you take pictures of Marco after I specifically told you not to? What are you trying to prove? That you don't have to answer to me? That you don't have to care about my feelings about anything? Well, you've succeeded. You've proven just how much I matter to you. Not one fucking iota."

I dig my heels in. "First, you don't get to tell me what I can and can't do. Marco insisted I take the photos, so I figured I might as well do the shoot and then sort out the details of the release after the fact—"

"Oh, like you give a single shit about whether or not he signs the release?" he snaps. "As long as the *book* happens, you'll be happy."

"Don't swear at me. Of course I care." I toss Marco the white terrycloth robe so that at least he won't be naked and even more exposed in the middle of whatever this is. A fight? That's what Anders seems to think, although I have no idea what he's talking about.

"Yeah, right. That's why you sold a photo to Dante without my permission. I should have known better than to trust you." Anders rubs his temples. "What kind of famous photographer does that, anyway? It's unprofessional and unethical. Probably illegal, even. I'm calling my agent."

I take a few steadying breaths. "I literally have no idea what you're talking about. Marco, why don't you go get dressed? We're done here."

The other player scrambles to his feet and hustles back to the changing area, keeping his eyes downcast. I've never seen him this defeated, but he seems just as shocked as I am by the way Anders is handling this situation. We're both in the dark.

There are a lot of firsts happening right now, and I'm not a fan of any of them.

"Now, what's going on?" I ask Anders. "And use your inside voice this time, please."

"Don't get condescending with me." Anders glares at me from under thunderous brows. "And don't lie, either. Where else would Dante have gotten the photos?"

"*What* photos?" I demand.

"Come the fuck on." Anders yanks out his phone and shows me the screen.

I feel the blood leave my face. Sure enough, one of my photos of Anders' mostly naked body is plastered on a billboard in the middle of the Strip.

"I didn't send him that," I say. "I don't know how he got it, but I didn't send it."

"Right." Anders rolls his eyes and shoves his phone back into his pocket. "Let me guess, Dante hacked your camera? And he hacked your bank account to deposit a huge check, too, I'll bet. Dante already told me the truth, and it's obvious anyway, so why bother denying it? I don't know which is worse. That you lied or that you're trying to cover it up."

I open and close my mouth a few times, and a tear runs down my cheek as I finally lose control of my emotions. I immediately wipe it away. "I wouldn't," I say again, feeling like a broken record. "I would never."

"I trusted you when you of all people *know* how fucking hard that is for me." The anger drains out of him, and he hides his face behind one hand. "I'm used to being betrayed by everyone I care about. I never thought you would be one of those people too."

A tense silence settles between us until Marco peeks out of the changing area.

"No more fighting?" he asks. "Lower the voices?"

"No more fighting." Anders takes a deep breath and turns to him. "I'm sorry, man. I shouldn't have come in hot like that."

Marco twists the hem of his shirt between his fingers. "Always, am confuse. I think you my true friend, Anders Beck. I think Stella your true *amore*. Trouble come when I call sexy *bellissima* round. Trouble come when I do what Dante says. To play hockey, I must golf. Cheese and dust are the same thing in this strange new world. Everything has become upside down. America makes no sense. Nothing easy squeezy lemony here. Maybe all would be right again if Marco go home."

"Marco—" I say, reaching for him. The poor guy looks like he could use a hug and Anders is the one who made him sad and blame himself for just being in the wrong place at the wrong time.

Before I get there, Anders intervenes and wraps one arm around his friend's shoulders. "I'm sorry I yelled. That wasn't fair. We are friends, assuming you'll forgive me for taking out my shit on the wrong person. And this time, it *is* upside down. You didn't do anything wrong." He shoots a nasty glare my way to make it clear exactly who he thinks is at fault here.

"We friends," Marco repeats, gesturing between himself and Anders. "And teammates. But Dante in charge, and when he tells me to take photos, I take. Not so bad. Fun, even. Until now."

Anders releases him. "I'm gonna go. But be careful, Marco. This kind of thing could really screw up your career, and you deserve better than that. If you're ever confused again, always ask your agent first." He turns his back on us and stalks out of the room still mad at me.

I don't try to stop him. What could I possibly say? I don't have an explanation for how Dante got his hands on those photos, and until I do, Anders has no reason to listen to me.

"I go, too," Marco says. "Sorry, Stella. I still not understand."

"That makes two of us," I tell him. "Are you going to be okay?"

"All fine." He manages a timid smile. "See you later, maybe." He follows Anders down the stairs.

I slump into the nearby chair and cradle my head in my

hands. How did any of this happen? I can't even blame Anders for being angry, although I wish he'd trusted me enough to give me the benefit of the doubt, even if the evidence is fairly damning.

There has to be a logical explanation. There just has to be.

I'm still sitting there in shock with my mind reeling when the door to the studio opens again.

"Anders?" I say as I look up, but it's only Eli.

"Hey." My friend peers around the room. "Everything okay? I was on a call down there when all hell broke loose. What happened? Shit, Stella, are you crying?"

"Can you... um." I wipe my nose on my sleeve. "Maybe. Would you mind giving me a ride home? I'm not sure I should drive right now?"

"Of course." Without any more questions, Eli takes my arm and leads me downstairs. It's a good thing he's there for support, because my legs feel like jelly.

It's only just now sinking in that Anders is gone for good. Without a solid commitment or even talk of a future, the tenuous connection between us was easily snapped in two. No matter what happens, I don't see us coming back from this.

We may have had an arrangement, but not long into it, my feelings got involved. Now, we're nothing. Less than nothing.

We're over.

* * *

Noah and Vivian are playing in the pool when I get home. Eli and I wave to them on our way through the backyard, although I have to avert my face so that Noah won't see how puffy it is right now. I cried the whole way back from the studio as Eli clucked his tongue and stroked my back as he drove one-handed.

I know Noah means well, but if I tell him what happened, he'll try to get involved, and I don't need that kind of help right now. Besides, Noah's a great guy and it wouldn't be fair to either him or Molly. When the rubber meets the road, he belongs to Anders. They're best friends and I would never come between them. To hear Anders tell it, he doesn't have many people in his corner.

When Eli and I enter the guest house, Mom lifts her head from the battered paperback romance she's reading. The instant she sees my face, her expression crumples, and she opens her arms. Before either of us can say a word, I'm sobbing all over again.

"S-s-sorry!" I bawl, burying my face in my mom's shoulder. "I just don't know where to s-s-start!"

Eli sits down on my other side and rubs his palm against my back. "It's okay, Stella," he says. "Take your time."

Little by little, I manage to unspool a garbled summary of our fight at the studio. "I don't even know how Dante got the pictures!" I wail.

"Oh, dear." Mom's face pulls into a guilty frown. "I'm afraid I do."

I look up and rub my eyes. "What?"

"Remember how I told you that I kept getting emails from the Venom representatives?" Mom winces as she strokes my hair. "One of the emails said that they needed the pictures for review, to see if they really did break the morality clause. The front office made it sound like the team could take legal action against you if they didn't verify it, so I sent everything over. They never said they were going to *use* them, just review them for compliance."

I hiccup as a new wave of horror washes over me. Anders has every right to hate me in this moment. On the way home, Eli and I drove by that billboard. I can't imagine how violated he feels.

"Damn," Eli breathes. "That's cold."

Mom's eyes well up with tears. "I'm so sorry, baby. I thought Dante was the big boss, and the email was so official sounding!"

"It's not your fault." I hug her, so that she'll know that I'm not angry. "He is the big boss. I just didn't realize how awful Dante could be, or I would have warned you. I mean, even though he's got ties to organized crime, he still has to play nice when it comes to the NHL. I thought he would do things involving the team by the book. I guess I've never been more wrong."

"He sounds like the kind of person who actually *might* take legal action if he doesn't get what he wants," Eli observes. "Using his stable of lawyers as greasy as he is."

"I'll talk to Anders," Mom says. "I'll explain everything. I've been handling your flagged emails for years, and I didn't know—"

"No." I shake my head and pull my knees up to my chest. "He wouldn't even listen to me. He yelled at me. He busted in on my shoot with Marco and caused an uproar. He was so mean Marco thinks he should go home before he ruins everyone's life. I'm over the whole damn thing."

"I understand that you're upset, but I can see his point, too. That billboard is huge and millions of people can see it. Having something like that happen would be like a nasty ex sending your private dick pics viral." Eli squeezes my shoulder. "Don't you think you should talk about this? Emotions only run this high for one reason. You obviously love him."

"That means nothing. I don't need a partner who doesn't trust me. Who throws a temper tantrum like a child instead of talking like a rational adult." I wipe my eyes. "Love should flow.

It shouldn't be this hard. Loving him isn't enough, Eli."

Mom chimes in. "You've been talking about him for years, Stella. Then, by the grace of God, you found each other again. Second chances are rare in this life. Don't you think that what you have is worth fighting for?"

"Not when I have to fight *him* to get it," I argue. "I knew that this had an expiration date anyway. We might just as well let it end now before either of us ends up more hurt than we already are. It's just not right."

I can tell that Eli and my mother are making eye contact over my head, but it doesn't matter. Anders and I were never meant to be. The sooner that I accept the inevitable, the better.

CHAPTER TWENTY-THREE

Anders

I have nowhere to go and no one to see. I can't talk to any of my friends about this. Cash and Latham don't give a damn about relationships, I already fucked up things with Marco, and Noah would just ignore my volatile feelings and give me some shitty advice about how love conquers all. I can't go to the arena to skate it out, and I sure as hell can't bear to be at home alone.

So I do what I usually do when I'm in a crap mood.

I head to the tennis court, and I smack the living shit out of an innocent little yellow ball fresh out of the can.

It's soothing to be outside, and working my muscles helps me unwind. This time of day, there's almost nobody at the court, so I can give it my all without worrying that I'll bean some soccer mom with a wild serve. I'm still mad, but every time I picture the looks on Stella and Marco's faces, I feel like an absolute asshat. What kind of friend scares his buddy like that?

What kind of man swears at his girlfriend, the only woman he's ever loved, without giving her a chance to tell her side of the story?

A man who had no role models growing up. A man who never kept a woman around long enough to learn how to communicate. A man who's not very good at expressing his feelings.

And despite all that, I still want to try. I want to become better. I want to step into my greatness and be the man that Stella deserves.

If she'll have me.

It makes no sense but part of me wants to believe that Stella's somehow innocent in all this. Even now, when logic dictates that she betrayed me, I want there to be another explanation.

I should talk to her and at least hear her out. That I know. It's just so damn hard for me to push my pride to the side when it's been my constant companion my entire life. Sometimes, it was all I had.

We're moving toward twilight now, but I don't even look at the brilliant sunset just over the red rocks, and my shirt is soaked with sweat. I keep thinking that eventually I'll get too tired to keep thinking about her, but evidently that's not a thing. I have nothing else to distract me, either. All I can do is bash the ball and hope that eventually something will give.

I've fallen into a rhythm when a voice behind me says, "Is it working?"

I just about leap out of my skin and whip around to see Stella's friend, Eli, leaning against the fence, watching me.

"Is what working?" I ask.

He gestures one finger toward the racket. "Stella's been crying her eyes out for hours. I can only assume that this is the macho-man equivalent of letting your feelings out."

"I guess." I tap the racket against my leg and watch the ball roll to a stop on the far side of the court. "Has Stella really been crying this whole time?"

"No offense," Eli says, "but *duh*. She's managed to convince herself that you two are terrible for one another. You know, doomed from the start because of your competing careers and whatnot. But I have to think it was you raising your voice at her that sent those thoughts reeling until they careened over the edge."

I wander over to retrieve my tennis ball. I'm finally too tired to be angry, so I guess this worked. "Listen, Eli, I don't know you that well, but... have you got a few minutes?"

"Depends what you have to say." He must have practiced being nonplussed in the mirror, because his expression is *scathing*. "Are you going to go all caveman on me?"

I grimace, remembering Marco's response to my tantrum. "No."

"Fine. Then I've got some time." He peels away from the fence and settles in on one of the nearby benches while I collect my stuff. Now that I'm no longer electric with anger, I realized that it's getting chilly out.

Eli sits back and lifts one leg onto the other knee. He crosses his arms, too. His posture couldn't be much more closed. All fair, I suppose, if Stella's as upset as he says.

"I've known Stella for a long time," Eli says into the uncomfortable silence. "Since middle school, actually. She's not just an amazing photog, she's an amazing human being. She was one of the first people I came out to because I knew I wouldn't be judged."

I cock my head to the side. "You're gay?"

Eli sighs. "Crazy, I know, since I don't shout it from the rooftops and call everyone *honey* all the time."

"That's not what I meant. I just thought you and Stella might have a history of some kind. Romantically speaking." I scratch my jaw. "Anyway, you were saying?"

Eli's quiet for a moment. It's that time of night where it's a little too dark to see clearly, but not bright enough for the automatic lights to come on. He taps his foot a couple of times.

"I didn't tell a lot of people, even in high school. Kids can be jerks, you know, and I didn't want it to become a whole thing. Then this guy that I'd been seeing threatened to out me to the whole school when I tried to break up with him." He chuckles. "Stella found out, and she went off on him. I don't even know what she said, but he avoided us after that, and he kept his mouth shut. She wasn't ashamed of me, but she understood how important it was for me to be able to decide who I told and when." He rolls his head toward me, making eye contact for the first time. "She respects people's privacy, is what I'm saying. What you're accusing her of is not even possible. I'd bet my life on it. But you didn't even give her an opportunity to explain herself, did you?"

"Then—" My voice cracks. "Then why did she give that photo to Dante?"

He pauses. "She didn't. You know that, right?"

"That's what she said." I rap my knuckles on my knee.

He blows out a breath. "That's not what I asked. Do you *believe* her?"

I turn his question over in my mind, trying to see the situation from another angle. Every time I do, though, the facts war with my instinct. "I don't think she'd do that. Which is why it hurts so much. I don't even get *why*, you know?" I rub one eye. I want to lie down and sleep for a couple of days, but as exhausted as I am, I doubt I'll get much rest tonight. Stella was in my bed only a few days ago. The sheets still smell like her.

"From what I'm told, your boss is a real piece of work," Eli says. "Manipulative. Is that right?"

"Yeah." That's one word for him. I can think of a whole list of much less flattering ones right off the dome.

He picks an imaginary piece of lint off his pants. "And you believe whatever *he* told you, but not what Stella said?"

"Wait." I ball my hands into fists. "Did Dante blackmail her or something?"

Eli snorts. "Your boss is that much of a tool, and you're only *now* thinking to ask if there's more to the story? With a man like that, the options are endless."

Around us, the lights click on, flooding the empty tennis court and the playground beside us in a silvery glow.

I rest my head in my hands. "Oh, crap. I didn't even think—what's he got on her? What did he do? Son of a bitch, I should have asked if she needed my help instead of running around like freakin' Donkey Kong."

"Yes, you probably should have," Eli says. There is zero sympathy in his voice. "And for the record, he didn't blackmail her. But there is more to the story."

I look up, waiting to hear his explanation.

"Oh, hell no, I'm not telling you." Eli glares at me. "If you want the full details, you've got to talk to her. I want my friend to be happy, Anders, and when she's with you, she's all sunshine and light. I'm willing to *help* you fix this, but I'm not going to do it for you. Stella's amazing. She deserves to be with someone who sees just how great she is and doesn't take it for granted. Someone who believes her when she tells the truth. She loves you."

I clear my throat. "I love her, too. I always have, I think."

Eli flaps his hands in the air and pulls a pained expression. "So why don't you *tell* her that, ding-dong!"

"Because I'm..." The word sticks in my throat. It's not the kind of thing I'd say to most people, much less a near-stranger. Then again, it's easier to risk Eli's opinion of me than someone who I care about. I don't want to lose the few people in my life who matter to me.

Which is the point, I guess.

"I'm scared," I whisper. "She doesn't want to stay here. She doesn't want to settle down. I don't want to be the one holding her back. When you love someone, you set them free, right?"

"That's a copout." Eli waves in the general direction of Noah's house. "So you're going to drive her away before she has the chance to reject you, is that it? Where there's a will, there's a way. You haven't even given it a chance."

"Uh." I blink a few times as his words sink in. "Well, it sounds stupid when you put it that way."

"That's because it *is* stupid." Eli holds out his hand. "Give me your phone."

I do as he says, because I'm still trying to catch up with this whole conversation, and he seems like he knows what he's doing.

"Here's my number." Eli mashes his thumbs against the screen, glowering the whole time. "When you figure out how to fix this, call me or text me or whatever and let me know how I can help."

"Why would you help me?" I ask.

He holds the phone back out. "Because Stella is one of my best friends—the kind who will have your back during your darkest days. I'd do anything to make sure she's happy. And I'm holding out hope that you're not completely beyond assistance, because for whatever reason, she seems to like being around you."

I take the phone back. "Thanks, Eli. I mean it."

"I'm not doing this for you," he says.

"I know. You're doing it for her. That's why I'm thanking you." I get to my feet and pick up my gym bag. "I'm glad she's got people in her life who love her enough to take care of her."

"Are you one of those people?" Eli asks.

"Yes," I admit. "But only if she'll let me."

CHAPTER TWENTY-FOUR

Stella

Two days after the fight with Anders, I'm wallowing on the couch in my sweatpants and pretending to watch old episodes of *The Bachelor*. This show is so scripted and shallow it makes me feel a little bit better about being single.

In reality, though, I'm focused on everything that's gone wrong lately. I don't know what to do about Anders. Maybe I should let it go, but part of me still wants to explain what really happened. But what's the point? If I could get him to listen long enough to talk sense into him, what would stop us from having another misunderstanding like this in the future? How can I ever trust him again to hold space for me? To communicate when the going gets tough?

How do I know that he's capable of *being* there for me?

Screw that. I'm not so desperate to have a boyfriend that I'm going to chase after him and apologize when I didn't do anything wrong. If anyone's owed the words 'I'm sorry' here, it's me.

And probably Marco.

I'm two episodes away from the final rose when my phone rings. I check the ID before I answer, both hoping and fearing that it will be *him*. Of course, it isn't, and my heart drops all over again.

"Hey, Eli," I say when I lift the phone to my ear. "What's going on?"

"Your two-thirty appointment is here," he says. "But you're

not."

I glance at the clock. It's twenty-five after, but that doesn't mean much given that I didn't know I *had* something at two-thirty.

"Who is it?" I ask.

"One of the models for your book," Eli says. "I showed him upstairs and told him you'd be here soon."

"Shit." I roll off the couch. "I've been such a mess lately it must not have gotten on my Google calendar. Did you get his name?"

"Am I your secretary now, too?" Eli teases. "The only thing I know is that dude has a major handicap. Look, if you're busy, I can send him away."

"No, no. Can you just ask him to wait for me, please? Tell him I'm running late." I brush some potato chip crumbs off the front of my oversized t-shirt. "Can you blame traffic or something?"

"I'll come up with something," Eli promises. "If you want, I can even show him the changing area and tell him to get comfortable. He'll be less likely to get bored and run away if he's not wearing his boxer briefs."

"You're brilliant," I tell him. "I could kiss you."

Eli snorts. "Ew. Save it. Just get down here before he changes his mind, okay? Models are so temperamental."

There's no time to shower, so I run the brush through my hair a couple of times before changing into a nice blouse and a pair of high-waisted linen slacks. When I bolt through the front door of the studio a mere twenty minutes later, Eli's messing around on his phone in the main gallery.

"Sorry, Stella, I just got an urgent phone call about a painting lost in transit," he says without preamble. "I'm closing the gallery up for the day. You've got your keys, right?"

"Yup. He's still here, I take it?" I pant, gesturing toward the ceiling.

"He surely is." Eli brushes an absentminded kiss across my cheek as he sweeps toward the door. "Good luck!"

I stop at the bottom of the stairs to take a few deep breaths before climbing to the second floor. I don't want to keep this guy waiting too long, but I also don't want to be red-faced and puffing when I finally get there. At the door, I stop to take a deep breath and straighten my hair. Since Eli said he has a major handicap, I prepare myself for what I might find. After all, I've invited models with prosthetics, cerebral palsy, epilepsy, polio, scoliosis, and ALS among other disabilities. Steeling my spine, I remind myself how grateful I am that these models have agreed to share themselves with me even while I'm behind the lens.

And then, when I step inside, I freeze.

Anders is sitting on a chair in the middle of my photoshoot setup, jiggling his foot as he waits for me. When he sees me, he looks up.

He's completely naked. No robe. No fedora. Nothing.

"What are you doing here?" I ask, eyes widening.

Dammit, why would Eli let him up here? He knows we're through. There's nothing to say, and I don't want to hear any of this man's excuses. Not after how he handled the billboard situation.

"I know that you're mad at me." Anders takes a deep breath, and I can't help but glance down at his chest. Why does he have to be so hot? So damn distracting? It isn't fair. "And you have every right to be."

"So you stripped down in the hopes of, what? Having make up sex? Doing things out of order?" I cross my arms and lean back against the door. "No way. Not happening. You're not forgiven."

"That's not why I'm here. I figured I should be... vulnerable, I guess. I feel raw and exposed emotionally, and I wanted my body to match." Anders shifts awkwardly in the chair. "I don't know what exactly happened the other day, and I'm hoping you'll tell me. But I have a couple of things that I want to say first."

"You have one minute. Maybe less." I have to turn away from him. My libido hasn't gotten the message that we're done with Anders, and his naked form is already softening me toward him. But after a few tortured seconds of silence, I slowly spin back around.

He scrubs a hand down his beard. "I love you, Stella."

I freeze, staring at the floor, wondering if I misheard him. Because all I've been doing since the last time I saw him was riding the crests of the waves of pain. "You what?"

"I love you," he repeats. "I've loved you ever since we met in Costa Rica. And then I found you again, and you didn't know who I was. You didn't recognize me at *all*. I'm not going to lie, that hurt like hell. Losing you now, after the last few months, would be even worse. I keep telling myself to keep my distance, to protect myself from rejection, but this sucks. I think it's even worse than letting myself love you with my whole heart but then letting you go." His voice wobbles.

I want to meet his eyes. I'm tempted to run to his side and comfort him. But I have to protect myself too as I fall into our long and vibrant history that stings and wounds even as it soars through the stolen moments of perfection.

"You said some pretty awful things the other day," I remind him. "You raised your voice at me. I can't have that. It doesn't belong in a true partnership."

"I was angry." The admission stirs up another storm behind

his eyes. "I thought you'd betrayed me. Not that it's any excuse—that's not what I'm saying. Every time I open up to you, I make myself more vulnerable. I make it that much easier for you to hurt me in the long term. But you're right about the raising my voice thing. If it helps, I promise I'll never do that again because I know I didn't handle my anger in a healthy way. I know I was wrong."

His apology comes with the threat of hot tears, stinging with emotion that refuses to be chased away.

I let my head roll back so that it knocks against the door. "I don't want to hurt you, Anders."

"You don't have to want to. Getting rejected by you would hurt plenty, even if you didn't mean it to." He clears his throat a couple of times. "Sorry, I'm not great at this. Talking about my feelings, I mean. *Thinking* about them, even. I've spent years squashing them down because I thought they made me weak, and then you came back here and turned me inside-out. It scares the shit out of me." He places one trembling hand over his mouth. "Stella, look at me. Please?"

It takes me a moment to build up the courage to lift my head, and when I finally do, the raw sorrow in his expression leaves me breathless. Our connection reignites and sparks like a livewire. It's crackling everywhere.

"It can't end like this," he whispers, his eyes reflecting that he feels it just like I do. "I'll do whatever it takes to make this work. If I only get to see you once every six months, I'll take it. I'll wait for you. If I have to fly to the Sahara or Machu Picchu or Indonesia in the off-season, I will. If you need a few more years to think about it, say the word. I won't see anyone else, whether you're here or on the far side of the globe. I can be patient, Stella. What we have is rare... it's special. For you, I can do anything."

I press my hand over my mouth and choke on a sob as tears I didn't know I was holding back spill over my cheeks. "What if you can't?" I whisper. "What if you change your mind? There are all those girls, Anders. Beautiful girls. They're everywhere and they want you."

"Well, I don't want them. I don't even see them. So I've got a past. This is about the present. The one I want with you." Anders smiles and emits a quiet laugh. "You don't believe me?"

The tangled knot of pain behind my ribs begins to unspool. "You said you should have known not to trust me—"

"I was wrong. And scared. And stupid." His laugh is a bit more relaxed this time. "I mean it, Stella. Your goals and dreams are equally as important as mine. We're a team. A partnership. I'm not going to change who I am for you, but I can compromise. Tell me what you need from me, and we'll figure out how to make this work." His smile fades. "Assuming that you want it to work."

I squeeze my eyes shut as the emotions I've been fighting for months swirl through my head. My throat aches with it, and I can't swallow them down no matter how hard I try.

I wait for him to say something else, but he doesn't. He just sits in his chair, watching me and waiting.

Just like he said he would. Taking a leap of faith starts right here.

For him.

For me.

"I'm terrified," I say at last.

He pulls his brows together. "Of what?"

Of losing you, I almost say, but it's more than that. I've been feeling awful about our breakup, but I could survive that. The real answer is deeper, and it takes me a moment to find the right words. When I do, they're almost too painful to say.

"That this isn't real," I breathe. "That it's too much, too soon. That it's going to crash and burn. God, I'd die if that happened."

Anders fidgets again, but he keeps his eyes on mine. "It's real for me. I've never been more sure of anything in my life."

I choke on my own breath as I stagger toward him and fall into his arms.

CHAPTER TWENTY-FIVE

Anders

I hold Stella for a long time, just stroking her hair and reveling in the comfort of being close. I can't believe I almost sabotaged the best thing that's ever happened to me. But now I know that I tried to do that because at that point, I still felt like I didn't deserve it.

Like I was constantly teetering on the edge of disaster.

Like I didn't deserve all the good things in this life.

But now I know that no matter what happened in the past—or how I got here—I'm worthy of love.

At some point, when her tears have dried, she stirs in my lap. "I accept your apology."

I chuckle against her neck. "Good. I feel wretched about what I did. That alone will make certain I never do it again. That tragic look that was on your face is still haunting me."

"I'm still not understanding why you had to be naked, though." She runs one hand over my chest. "Not that I'm complaining."

"I was thinking that you could take a picture of me. Uncensored." I indicate my exposed and slightly chilly body. "As a gesture of trust. It was important to you, so now it's important to me."

"Oh." She clings to my neck. "That's really sweet. Did Eli tell you what actually happened with the billboard?"

"Nope. He figured I should hear it from you." I kiss her forehead. "Your friend is very smart, by the way."

Her gaze searches mine. "Was this his idea?"

"No, but he agreed to go along with it." I shift her weight so that my legs don't go numb. "He was a little mean when we first talked but really helpful. I'm glad you have friends like that. Your happiness means the world to him."

Stella nods. "He's pretty much the best. As far as the billboard, Mom's actually the one who sent Dante the photos, just so you know. His assistant emailed me some story about how the photos needed to be reviewed to see if they passed the morality clause, and Mom thought she was helping me out when she replied. She does a lot of my digital correspondence when I'm traveling, and I guess she's just in the habit of checking my messages even when I'm stateside."

I nod. "So she fell for Dante's phishing scam, basically?"

She trails a finger down my forearm. "That's what it sounds like."

"What a dick." One of these days, somebody's going to have to deal with that guy. He can't go around treating people like this, and I'm going to have words with my agent to see if there's anything we can do about that friggin' billboard. In the meantime, Stella's pressed against me, and I'm inhaling her scent with every breath.

Her gaze is still filled with an uncertainty I can't wait to kiss away.

"Do you want to take the photos?" I ask. "Because if you don't take them soon, they're going to be more porno pics than art shots."

Stella raises her eyebrows and immediately twists around to examine my groin. "Oh, my. Did you really miss me that much?"

A chuckle rumbles up from my chest. "You have to ask?"

Stella's eyes sparkle. "We *did* just fight and make up. I

believe that sex is the traditional next phase of resolution, isn't it?"

"Way to turn this into an anthropological study," I deadpan. "Nothing screams romance like textbook vocabulary."

"Hold on." Stella gets up and hurries to one side of the room, where the fur rug that Marco was sprawled out on the other day lies in a heap.

Speaking of which, I *really* need to apologize to Marco. I should never have gone after the poor guy like that. Now that I know the lengths Dante's willing to go through to keep someone under his thumb, I feel a lot more sympathy for people who avoid crossing him. Is he holding something over Marco's head? Or is my friend just trying to avoid trouble? Either way, it's not fair of me to blame my teammate for my boss's shitty behavior. Marco's always there for everyone else, so we should return the favor.

"There." Stella lays the rug out at my feet. "It's a good thing Eli isn't downstairs."

"What, you don't want to keep our voices down like we did at the Abbott Christmas party?" The memory of that particular encounter makes my dick twitch.

"On the contrary, I'd like the opposite. I want to hear you." Stella winks at me. "But speaking of the party, I figure I owe you one."

"Owe me what, now?" I'm living in a state of suspended desire when it comes to her, but I like where this is going.

Stella settles down on her knees in front of me and lets her fingertips trail along my inner thigh. "Remember when I was on the ladder? When you had me *losing my goddamned mind,* while you were teasing me?"

I tamp down a shudder as I harden even more. "You think I could *forget* that?"

She kisses my knee. "Would you like me to go down on you, Anders?"

I groan as her words go right to my dick. "Hell to the yes."

She takes her time, kissing her way along my bare skin. By the time she reaches the crux of my thighs, I'm already aching for her. She wraps one arm around my thigh from below and blows cool air against me.

"You're a tease," I tell her.

Stella's eyes sparkle. "You said you could wait, remember?"

"I will. I can." I caress her cheek, running my thumb over her lips. She's so beautiful. I could fall in love with her a hundred times over.

"I liked it before, when you talked dirty to me." At last, her hand closes around me, and she drags her tongue across the tip of my cock.

"Yeah?" I groan. "You like that?"

"Mmmhmm." Her lips circle me. Even without the sensation, the sight of her alone is enough to send all the blood rushing out of my head. Like a detour, it's been rerouted to a more important destination.

"What if I have something else in mind?" I grip the edge of the seat with one hand and let the other rest on the back of her neck. "What if I want to talk *commitment* to you?"

Her abrupt laughter echoes through me. My balls are already aching. She pulls away long enough to say, "I'm not even sure what that means."

"It's the new kink," I tell her. "I'm just getting with the times. All the madly in love guys are doing it these days. Wanna give it a shot?"

She shrugs, like, *anything goes.*

My brain isn't working right, and my mouth is running on autopilot when I say, "Stella, baby, I can't wait to celebrate anniversaries with you."

She almost chokes with laughter and has to let go of me to catch her breath. "Excuse me?"

I brush a lock of hair away from her cheek. "You heard me. Is it working?"

"I don't know." Her eyes are full of laughter as she takes me in hand again. "Better experiment. Keep going."

"Stella, baby, I can't wait until we get to the point where we're buying furniture together," I pant as she swallows me deep. "Tables. Sofas. Chairs. *Beds.* I want to take you out for so many dinners that I know your favorite meals by heart. I want to celebrate holidays with you. I want you to be so comfortable around me that you let me hear you sing in the shower."

Stella swirls her tongue around the tip of my cock. "You're fucking weird, Anders," she tells me.

"I know. You *make* me fucking weird." I run my hands through her hair. "I want all kinds of stuff with you. I want inside jokes and that thing some couples do where they don't even have to talk to communicate. I want you to send me dumb memes just because they make you laugh. Is that crazy?"

"I'm not sure it's sexy," she argues. "I'm really not sure it's an okay subject for sexy time, you goof."

"No?" I slide off the chair and push her back until she's lying beneath me, sprawled on the rug. "How about this, then. I want to know your body so well I can make you come so many times that you beg for mercy. I want to spend so long in bed together that we lose track of time and miss appointments. I want to figure out your kinks and take full fucking advantage of them until they become mine." I unbutton her blouse and lick one nipple through the lace mesh of her bra. "I want to make love to you in totally inappropriate places. I want to get one of those remote control vibrators so that I can make you scream my name even when you're on the other side of the damn planet. How's that?"

"Warmer." Stella's voice is breathy and desperate now. "I'm on board."

Using two fingers beneath her chin, I tilt her mouth to mine in a sweet and gentle kiss that quickly turns strong and urgent.

She arches into my body, searching for my lips like she's dying of thirst and I'm her oasis. In this moment, I can't even consider a future that doesn't include her as my wife and the mother of my kids. I picture a little girl like Vivian, except with a camera around her neck instead of a tiara on her head.

And sons.

A fierce combination of me and Stella.

I capture her lips again, my tongue slipping into her mouth and tangling with hers. Her fingers slide through my hair and I groan.

We're on fire with love, anxious to revisit our shared past and ride it into the future. I suck on her full bottom lip and she moans, letting her legs fall open so I can settle between her thighs. My hands wind through her hair as my lips move to her jawline then her neck.

After we break apart, I say, "Good, because I'm just getting started."

I unbutton her slacks and slide them down while she takes off her bra. She lies back against the faux-fur rug with her honey-brown hair fanned out around her face. Her cheeks are blotchy and her eyes are bright.

"Keep going." Her confession is so soft, it almost isn't there.

Her words unravel the hurts of my past, and everything clicks into place in a rush of emotion.

"I want to have the conversations with you that people in *situationships* never have." I prop myself up on one elbow and kiss her neck while my free hand teases between her legs. "I want to have a plan for next year. For five years from now. For when I retire from hockey. I want one of those shared Google calendars so that we can see what each other have going on and work around it. I want you to have the code to my phone and all my passwords."

"Anders." Stella spreads her legs to make room for me as I slide two fingers into her.

"You're so wet for me," I say, and I kiss her other breast. "Maybe you could talk for a minute? Tell me what you want, Stella."

"I want—" She throws one arm over her head and clutches at the rug. "I want to know—"

"Tell me, Stella. Tell me what you want." I run my teeth lightly over her nipple, and she shudders.

"I want to know if you want kids," she blurts. "And how that would work if I'm traveling all the time. I want to figure out, *ah!* If we could ever move in together. And what happens if my Mom can't live on her own anymore. And—*oh, fuck, don't stop that, I don't know what you're doing, but don't stop.*"

I oblige, watching her face intently as her mouth falls open and her eyes roll back. I take note of what I'm doing, in the hopes of recreating her reaction in a few minutes, when it's not my fingers inside her. I'm still learning all her tells and committing them to memory.

She clenches suddenly, letting out a wordless scream of pleasure as her hips twist and her thighs clench.

"Look at you," I breathe.

"I think the commitment talk is, *hmm*, working." Stella shivers and goes limp. "Or something."

"Yeah?" I lower myself to kiss the tip of her nose. "I could use some more of it."

Stella smiles weakly as she wraps her legs around my waist. "Okay. Let me try some more." She traces my brow with her fingers, pushing my hair out of my eyes. "I want to be the person you come to when you have problems. I don't want you to ever feel like you have to go it alone. I want to be your soft place to fall."

"Is that so?" I position myself between her thighs, taking my time.

A tiny hiss of breath pushes past her lips. "Yup. And I want to be the first person you call when you win the Stanley Cup again. No, no. Scratch that. I want to be there. I want to be wearing your jersey and rush out onto the ice with the other wives. Then I want to jump into your arms and kiss you hard."

"Ooh, you know just what I like to hear." I'm joking, but the truth is that her words have me hard on the outside but with a soft and gooey center. She's melting me. Breaking down all of my walls. I've never felt like this with anyone—totally exposed, not just on the surface, but right down to my bones.

She whispers in my ear, "I want to feel you inside me, Anders."

Her wish is my command. I slide into her with no resistance. She's so wet, so ready for me, so welcoming. I can already tell that this is going to be a lightning round.

"Should I keep talking?" she asks.

"Mmm." I can't talk. If I don't focus, it'll all be over in a matter of seconds.

"I want a future with you." Stella exhales against my throat as I thrust, pressing her deeper into the rug. She's so sweet beneath me, giving where I'm solid. Soft where I'm hard. "I want to wake up and see you first thing. I want you to be the last person I text before I fall asleep in the jungle. When the signal's bad, I want to write you love letters and read them aloud to you when I come home."

She studies me and the air around us tightens, causing this moment to bleed electricity. I know there's no going back, and I don't want to. I want Stella forever and ever.

I press my face against her collarbone and whimper. I want her. I need her.

I love her.

She's mine.

I barely make a sound as I fall to pieces in her arms.

* * *

"Are you asleep?" Stella asks.

"No," I mumble, hugging her even more tightly.

She plays with my hair. "You sure about that? Because I'm pretty sure you were snoring just now."

"Slept like shit the last couple of nights," I murmur. "Missed you. Thought I ruined everything."

She kisses my forehead. "I haven't been sleeping well, either. How about we get up, get dressed, and head home? We can pick up some dinner on the way. I'll even tell you my favorite items on the menu so that you'll know for the future."

"That sounds perfect." I sit up and stretch. "I think you're going to need to get your bear dry-cleaned before anyone else uses it."

"It's not mine," she says. "Marco brought it from home. He thought it would look fierce if he were naked on a dead animal apparently."

I wince. "Looks like I owe him a new carpet *and* an apology."

A knowing smile plays over her lips. "Either that, or you owe him apology sex *on* the carpet."

"Oh, *gawd*." I shudder. "Don't joke about that. I know far too much about that man's genitals for that to be funny."

Stella squints at me. "Are we talking about the piercing?"

"You've *seen* it?" I screech.

"Well, yeah." She gestures to the carpet. "I've seen all of him. I have him on film." She chews on her lower lip. "Is it wrong that I wondered about how that feels, you know, inside? I wanted to ask him, but I didn't dare. His English isn't good enough. What if he took it the wrong way?"

"I think I'm traumatized now," I whimper. "But if you want to know that bad, we can Google it."

"Oh, please." Stella swats my shoulder and rolls her eyes. "You spend most of your days in the locker room with a bunch of sweaty naked dudes. Trust me, your junk is the only junk I care about."

"Fair enough." I'm about to get up when Stella places a hand on my arm.

"Anders?" She looks up at me from under her eyelashes. "Before, when you said I could take a picture. Did you mean it?"

I nod. "You still want one? As a trophy of your conquest?"

She exhales a little laugh. "If it's okay, I have an idea for the book. I won't do anything without your permission, but at the very least, I'd like to take the shot."

I don't have to think twice. "Okay."

She gets up and messes with the camera settings, radiant in the late afternoon light.

My tongue is heavy with questions, but I settle on the easiest. "Where do you want me?"

"There is fine," she says. "I'm going to set a time for thirty seconds. Aaaand... go." She hurries back over and crouches next to me, then wraps the rug around our shoulders like a blanket.

"It just occurred to me that Marco was naked on this

earlier," I say, eyeing the rug suspiciously.

"And we just had sex on it, which means that we're the dominant pair." Stella kisses my cheek. "Now smile for the camera."

I wrap one arm around her waist, and she leans against my shoulder. I don't know if she was serious about using this shot for the book, but I trust her to include me in the decision about what to do with this photo. We're going to be partners. No more surprises. No more secrets.

I turn my head to kiss her cheek just before the timer goes off.

EPILOGUE

Stella

"We shouldn't," I tell Eli.

"Really, Stella?" My friend crosses his arms. "We talked about this earlier. If you had complaints, you should have thought about them before signing the waiver!"

"I know. I just feel like doing this with another man isn't right." I stare down at the harness that I've spent the last ten minutes getting strapped into. "This is my first time. I wish Anders could be here."

This photoshoot was Eli's idea. Since the coffee table book is finally due to be released in a few months, he's been pestering me to get back on the horse and start photographing animals again. This is only my second international trip away from Anders since we started dating, but it feels different. Even though I haven't been here in years, Costa Rica is *ours*, in a way. Being here without him feels wrong, but that's one of the compromises we've made in our relationship. He has his needs, and I have mine. We don't have to be happy in the same place to be happy together in the long run. We've meshed our schedules together the best way we know how, and we've made it work for both of us.

And even though I'm not ready to admit it yet, my wanderlust has faded a bit underneath the weight of our love.

This, however, feels like the ultimate betrayal.

"Oh, for God's sake." Eli adjusts his helmet. "We're ziplining, not fucking, Stella. Get over it."

I stare out at the jungle, marveling at the untamed beauty of the wilderness. We aren't far from the resort where I stayed on my first visit, although it's not like we'll be close enough to see the places where Anders and I walked on that first day all those years ago. Our waterfall. The place where my future began even though I didn't know it at the time. Seeing that without the man I love would be too much.

"Well, I'm going." Eli nods to the zipline operator. Soon enough, he disappears into the dense canopy below us.

"Are you going too, Stella?" the guide asks.

"I guess so." I adjust my camera, which hangs around my neck.

The guide points. "There are three platforms between here and the forest floor. You remember how they showed you to brake?"

I nod.

She triple-checks my harness. "Then off you go. Whenever you're ready."

I take a deep breath, place my hands on the line, and take the plunge.

The feeling of stepping off the platform into thin air is both terrifying and exhilarating. In a way, it's like flying as if one were a bird. I was a little worried that my nerves would kick in when I saw my feet dangling above the trees, but it's liberating more than anything. I'm lighter than air.

When I reach the first platform, I scream in delight. "Oh my gosh." I take my weight off my harness and bounce on my toes. My adrenaline has never spiked like that before. "Where has this experience been all my life?"

The attendant laughs. "Glad you're enjoying it! We do have a minor problem, though."

"A problem?" I gulp, imagining Eli somewhere ahead of me

plummeting through the trees after an accident. "Is my friend okay?"

"Oh, yeah." The attendant chuckles and points a little way down the line. "We might be here a minute, though."

I follow the direction he's pointing until I spot the so-called problem. When I do, I scream again and lift my camera to my eye. The biggest sloth I've ever seen in my life is making its way through the canopy and has decided to make a pit stop on the zipline. I *knew* there was a reason I brought my camera.

With a sigh of happiness and a huge grin, I finger the necklace that Anders got me. Then I snap a few dozen photos of the sloth's perfect, smiling face. To me, they always seem a little bemused, like an old man who has wandered into a neighbor's party and can't tell if he's got dementia or he just needs a beer.

"I don't think I've ever seen someone so happy to be held up," the attendant says.

"It's a *sloth*," I say, as if that explains everything. "This is honestly the best part of the day. Maybe the whole *trip*."

He chuckles. "Have you been to the baby sloth sanctuary?"

I spin toward him. "To the *what!?*"

"There are pamphlets in the main building," the attendant tells me. "Ask for one before you leave. Judging from your reaction, you'll love it."

I hesitate for a moment, torn between the worry that visiting dozens of baby sloths without Anders might be unforgivable and knowing that I cannot possibly leave without surrounding myself with as many sloths as possible. "Thanks for the tip. I would never miss something like that."

At last, the sloth moves on, and the attendant radios the other platforms to tell them that all systems are go again. I wave to the sloth as I sail by.

At the bottom of the zipline, Eli is pacing a deer trail in the jungle. When I finally land, he lets out a huge sigh of relief. "I thought you actually changed your mind and went back."

"Nope." I wiggle out of my harness. "I'm good. There was a sloth up there. And did you know that there's a sloth *sanctuary?* We're going. Screw Anders, I require baby sloths. In fact, I may never go home."

"Screw Anders?" says a familiar voice behind me. "Rude."

I spin toward my boyfriend with my hands pressed to my mouth. "Anders! You're *here!* This is even better, I can have you and the baby sloths in the same place! *This is amazing!*" I launch myself into his arms. "Did you hear me say baby and sloths in the same sentence?"

Eli groans as his eyebrows about disappear into his hairline. "I told you this was a bad idea."

"I think it's great." Anders kisses my forehead.

"You're really here!" I pull him down for a better kiss. "How? When? *Why?*"

Anders flashes me a crooked smile and reaches into his pocket. When his hand emerges, it's clutching a small velvet box. "I had this whole speech prepared, but this isn't going exactly the way I'd planned."

I squeal and wrap my arms around him. "Anders! Are you *proposing?*"

He blushes a light shade of pink. This shy, vulnerable Anders might be the version I love most of all. "That was the idea."

"Lord have mercy." I turn to Eli, pointing to the box as I do. "Anders is proposing to me and I got to see a wild sloth on a zipline while I flew like a bird! *This is the best day ever.*"

Eli flaps one hand in my direction. "I hope you know that she's never going to change."

"I wouldn't want her to," Anders assures him. "In the meantime, since I *did* write the speech, let me give it a shot."

He sinks down to one knee and opens the box. "Stella, I love you. I loved you even before I knew your name. When I knew you as Bird Girl, I fell in love with your intensity. Then I got to know you better, and I fell in love with your passion. Your vision. The way that you put your whole heart into everything you do. I love your confidence. The way that the little things make you so happy. I used to think that the universe was trying to pull us apart, but now I'm pretty sure that it wants us to be together."

I sniffle and wipe a tear out of my eye. "I feel the same way."

"Which is why I hope you'll do me the honor of marrying me." Anders glances at Eli. "And, um, visiting a sloth sanctuary with me, too? Because baby and sloth always belong in the same sentence."

"Yes. Of course I will." I bend down to kiss him. He's right about one thing. We were never star-crossed lovers. We were scared kids running away from rejection, when we should have been running toward each other.

Anders slides the simple band onto my finger.

"Oh, wow." I pinch it. It appears to be metal, but it gives beneath the pressure of my touch. "What is this?"

"Silicone. Seemed a lot more your style than something flashy you could lose on a safari. But there's a flashy one at home for when you're there. With me, you get the best of both worlds."

The tears come in earnest now. His words promise so much because they represent forever. "You thought of everything."

"Which is why you like me almost as much as sloths," Anders teases.

"Maybe the adult sloths. Even you can't compete with the babies." I turn my back to him and lift my shirt. "I have a surprise for you, too."

"No!" Eli holds up his hands. "My eyes!"

"Settle down, you dork. I'm not doing anything scandalous."
I glance over my shoulder as Anders touches my back.

"You got a tattoo," my boyfriend says. No, not my boyfriend,
my *fiancé.* "Of a baby elephant with my name on its trunk."

"Do you like it?" I ask.

He tugs his lower lip between his teeth. "It's beautiful. But
I'm not sure I get the elephant part."

Eli smirks. "Seriously, Stella? You never told him why you
came back to Las Vegas?"

"To work on the book," Anders says.

"Sort of." I lower my shirt again so that Eli's eyeballs will be
spared the horrors of my sports bra. "Actually, I, uh. I *may*
have almost gotten trampled by an elephant. I got between a
momma and her baby."

Anders grips my arm. "What happened?"

"After such a close call, I decided to take a break from
animals for a while." I turn back to him. "But it was a good
thing, right? Because if I hadn't, I would never have met you
again, Blaze."

"Thank God for elephants," Anders agrees. He lowers his
voice so that Eli won't hear. "And I have another surprise for
you later."

All my breath catches in my throat. "Yeah?"

"I found our waterfall." His eyes sparkle as his arm snakes
around my waist. Then he lifts his fingers and traces the outline
of my sloth necklace. The one I haven't taken off since he gave
it to me for our first Christmas.

"Oh, is that so?"

The love of my life, my forever, clears his throat and utters
the same words he said the day we first met. "It sounds like you
want to save the world."

My eyes fire with recognition and then the fire that I could only ever feel for this incredible man that fate brought to me in a tropical paradise instead of the city where we both lived. "And that's a bad thing?"

He holds up a palm between us. "Hell, no. It's a *badass* thing. And my future wife's nothing if not a badass."

I kiss him once more for good measure. I thought that the impending expiration of our love affair was what gave it so much heat, but I was wrong. It was never an outside force. Anders Beck always was, and always will be, my destiny. We have so many adventures left to experience. And now we have a home to go to when they're over. When I think about doing life with him, I shiver with the intensity of my emotion. Happiness riots over every inch of my skin.

I want to hold his hand and jump in the tropical water that leads to our waterfall and slip back into the past that we both cling to because those memories will always hold a special place in our hearts.

It's where this all started. It was our beginning, and now we're stepping into our future together.

The one we never thought we'd have, but the one we both deserve.

The world is wild and full of possibility, and I can only begin to imagine where our journeys will take us.

ABOUT THE AUTHOR

"People are like stained-glass windows. They sparkle and shine when the sun is out, but when the darkness sets in, their true beauty is revealed only if there is a light from within."
— Elisabeth Kübler-Ross

Are you willing to discover the beauty within the flaws?

Then this is your tribe.

These are your books.

Colleen Charles is the USA Today Bestselling author of Perfectly Imperfect Romance for perfectly imperfect readers.

Take a chance and join her... you won't be sorry you did.

Colleen loves to hear from her readers and she answers all communications personally. You can find her at:

ColleenCharles.Com

Subscribe to my Newsletter online and receive email notices about new book releases, sales, and special promotions.

New subscribers receive an EXCLUSIVE FREE NOVEL as a special gift.

www.colleencharles.com/free

Printed in Great Britain
by Amazon

32454997R00148